The Judas Scroll

The Judas Scroll

by
Aramis Thorn

XULON PRESS

Xulon Press
2301 Lucien Way #415
Maitland, FL 32751
407.339.4217
www.xulonpress.com

© 2021 by Aramis Thorn

All rights reserved solely by the author. The author guarantees all contents are original and do not infringe upon the legal rights of any other person or work. No part of this book may be reproduced in any form without the permission of the author. The views expressed in this book are not necessarily those of the publisher.

Unless otherwise indicated, Scripture quotations taken from the New American Standard Bible (NASB). Copyright © 1960, 1962, 1963, 1968, 1971, 1972, 1973, 1975, 1977, 1995 by The Lockman Foundation. Used by permission. All rights reserved.

Scripture is taken from GOD'S WORD®. © 1995, 2003, 2013, 2014, 2019, 2020 by God's Word to the Nations Mission Society. Used by permission.

Printed in the United States of America.

Paperback ISBN-13: 978-1-6628-2777-8
eBook ISBN-13: 978-1-6628-2778-5

Epigraph

"I tell you the truth, whatever you did for one
of the least of these brothers of mine, you did for me."

Jesus of Nazareth

Books by Aramis Thorn

Fiction:

The Jesus Chronicles:

    The Foster Father of God

    The Praetor

    Magi: The Gift Bearers

    Sheet Rock on the Road

Sheet Rock on the Road – Leftover Panels (eBook)

The Twelve Tales of Christmas: A Collection of Short Stories for the Entire Year

Annals of the Four Horsemen:

    Chronicles of Thanatos the Reaper

Non-Fiction:

Thoughts and Questions on Ephesians (a Devotional)

Thoughts and Questions on Galatians (a Devotional)

Thoughts and Questions on Philippians (a Devotional)

Dedication

This writing must be dedicated to my beloved former spouse, Avalon, who first challenged me to examine the life of this much-maligned apostle without any presuppositions as to his standing and state. We judge people and cause so much damage. Thank you, Avalon, for the challenge.

It is also dedicated to all of those who have acted out of pure motive but in error. The end does not justify the means, but choosing to act in faith when you are wrong about your action, does not nullify your faith. As with all I do, this is also dedicated to my Heavenly Father, who knows the heart of Judas and will someday reveal it to the rest of us.

Acknowledgements

I wish to share my thanks with all those who endeavor to teach me to love God, to love my neighbor, and to love my enemies. As the years pass, I am learning it is impossible to do the first without endeavoring to always do the latter two. In the obverse, if I do all I can to love the Father, I find it much easier to love others. A special acknowledgement is due to my friend Dee for her efforts in applying this truth to her own life.

Further, I would acknowledge my Son, Bezel who really saw the darkness I was battling and chose to love me anyway. His choice showed me an aspect of the Father's love I would emulate every day. He is a good Son, a good man, and a good friend. I love you Son.

Table of Contents

Epigraph vii
Books by Aramis Thorn ix
Dedication xi
Acknowledgements xiii
Forward by Avalon xvii
Introduction xxi

Prologue–A Letter to Barabbas 1
Nightmare in Nazareth 3
Cobras in Baskets 7
Kicking the Basket 13
Galilee and Canna 45
Relationships and Recognition 77
Wine and Weddings 99
Wagons, Wines, and Weddings 119
The Funerals and The Pharisees 157
The Baptist in the River 179
The Carpenter King 191
Sheep Among Wolves 211
Son of Man 233
The Entry – Five Days until Passover 247
Fig Trees and Fear – Three days until Passover 251

Promises and Payoffs – Two days until Passover............253
Open Opposition – One Day until Passover................255

Epilogue – A Letter to Theophilus 257
After Word...259
Coming in the Future 263

Forward by Avalon

It's easy to strip someone of their humanity. When two countries go to war, it's natural to view the enemy as evil. You can downplay your own mistakes or failures by pointing the finger away from yourself and squarely at someone else. Let the 'other' be the scapegoat or the villain.

Judas has been the ultimate scapegoat for centuries, and for good reason. He betrayed the Son of God, the Messiah, the savior of the world. The Bible (Luke 22) even says Satan entered Judas. That's a big deal.

Here's what trips me up. If I'm honest, I can see myself doing the exact same thing. After all, I have been known to betray friends and family for much smaller stakes than blasphemy. True, no one was crucified... but I allowed my selfishness, fear, or anger to throw someone I love under the proverbial bus. Although there is difference in the severity of results, from a 'sin perspective', are my betrayals any better or worse than Judas'?

Judas is poetically called the Son of Perdition in John 17 (other translations say "the one doomed to destruction"). I grew up within conservative Christianity, and there was always a fear that perhaps God had doomed me to a predestined life of condemnation. After all, if God could damn Judas from the beginning of time, why couldn't He do the same to me or someone else I love? Was I "the Daughter of Perdition"?

I chose anger and cynicism in response to the hypocrisy that I saw in God. I did not want to serve a God that said He was loving and saved us by grace if He would also doom someone to destruction from the beginning of time. Where was the opportunity for free will or redemption? In my anger, I investigated Judas in an attempt to reconcile the double standard. I learned biblical Greek so I could understand the contextual nuances of words like 'sin' and 'remorse' and 'repent'. I studied the Hebraic law in the Old Testament to discover Judas' beliefs on what God required to atone for his betrayal.

I concluded that the church has historically vilified Judas beyond all practical context. I won't pretend to understand the reasons for this. Perhaps we need a scapegoat. Perhaps we want to distance ourselves from him so we can pretend that we could never be like him... he was different, set apart, chosen for condemnation. Interestingly, doesn't that sound a lot like Jesus, who came to become our sin and sacrifice on our behalf? Perhaps it's as simple as a good story always needs an equal nemesis to the hero. That's hard to do when your hero is the one and only God. Those are big shoes to ask either Satan or Judas to fill.

I relate to Judas a lot. I am not the disciple who believes easily. I have my own strong opinions of how things should be accomplished, and I know that they are often in conflict with God's ideas. I empathize with Judas when he points out that expensive perfume would be better used for the poor than poured over Jesus' feet (see John 12 or Mark 14). Perhaps there is more to a person than what they do. Indeed, what they do comes from a whole host of motivations, thoughts, and emotions. What makes a betrayer turn his back on those he loves? Likewise, what they do is judged differently by others. What decides what makes a betrayer a betrayer? What makes a sinner sin? Is it not the choices they make based on all the experiences they had up until the point of that choice? To make it personal to my own life: what makes a cynic cynical?

What Aramis has accomplished in this book is to give Judas back his humanity. He is a person simply living life. He is conflicted by ideologies of the time and culture. He struggles with his own insecurities. He runs the gamut of emotions from love to hate to indifference. Stripping away the caricature of Judas as the ultimate evil, we also strip away the caricature we have of what evil itself is and puts it in its proper perspective. Evil is not this big bad event that happens when we are overtaken by Satan. It is merely those places where we allow ourselves to be thieves and betrayers and where we open space in our thoughts for the devil to influence us. Evil, then, is every thought and action that does not fall within the will of God.

And that leads me to the most important conclusion from my studies on Judas and what Aramis shows in this book. God is a God of Love. He allows people to make their choices in hopes that some will return the love He extends. In a story that keeps Judas on the same playing field as every other human, it demonstrates that God is very God, and humans are not. He is Love and we are fallible. Yet, the two can work together because God knows we are fallible and if we accept His Love, He works in us, despite our consistent choices to put our own agendas ahead of God's.

Introduction

Welcome to my latest fictional offering of worship and entertainment. Before we go too far, you must ask yourself a question and answer it honestly. It is a binary question without qualifier or minced words. DO YOU LOVE JUDAS? From this question comes the story before you.

When was the last time you met a man named Judas? Often the popularity of names is associated with the fame or infamy of an individual in history. Sarah, one of the few names actually designed by God in the Bible, has been in the top-ten list of names for centuries. The names of stars, athletes, and political figures often appear in hospital nurseries across the country. We associate the name with the legacy.

We receive little in the way of background on Judas Iscariot. He first appears in the apostolic roll call and even there with a footnote. Each Gospel reports Judas as a "**traitor**". In the following excerpt from Matthew we see Judas is last and his future is foreshadowed in the introduction.

1 He called his twelve disciples to him and gave them authority to drive out evil spirits and to heal every disease and sickness. 2 These are the names of the twelve apostles: first, Simon (who is called Peter) and his brother Andrew; James son of Zebedee, and his brother John; 3 Philip and Bartholomew; Thomas and Matthew the tax collector;

James son of Alphaeus, and Thaddaeus; 4 Simon the Zealot and Judas Iscariot, who betrayed him. (Matthew 10:1-4)

It is important to note all four gospels introduce him in this manner. This makes the meaning of "betrayed" and "traitor" vital to our understanding of the role of Judas, the man of Iscariot, who handed Jesus over to the Pharisees. As we begin the journey in our tale, I wish to indulge in one lesson in language. Let us first agree on the meaning of this word to those who penned the gospels, and not necessarily on its meaning in the Medieval time or our current culture.

From the Greek text of the New Testament, the word used for "betray" is "*paradidomi*." The meaning of this word is primarily:

1) To give into the hands (of another), 2) to give over into (one's) power or use, 2a) to deliver to one something to keep, use, take care of, manage. (Thayer's Greek Definitions, G3860)

Freely acknowledging the truth; Judas did indeed hand Jesus over to the Pharisees, I do not accept the supposition that the intent was to harm or disavow him in any way. The word "betray," as translated here since the middle ages, has a far harsher implication, than does the translation "handed over." Motivation has been assigned by the definition of the word. Or perhaps, the word was translated to support a supposition. I propose the definition of the word may lead us to examine other motivations. This should be done in the light of all Judas was, and not just in view of his final days.

That Judas was interested in money is obvious. That he was prone to use the money belonging to the community of disciples for his own purposes is without argument save to say he most likely justified what he was doing as being what was best for all. That he was a Zealot, who was willing to do literally anything, to eject Rome from Israel, is also without question.

Remember what I offer is conjecture in the light of fiction. The story is told to entertain, but the primary intent is to ask you to

Introduction

think about Judas as he really was and not as history has painted him. Think about a man who experienced life with Jesus and who was zealously motivated to free his country from tyranny and oppression. Consider the fact of Zealots being devout and faithful to the Law of Moses in the extreme. Please recall as well, no matter how you judge Judas, you are required to love him like Jesus loves him.

Did Judas intend for his actions to harm Jesus? I think not. I submit Judas was overanxious and lacked a basic understanding of Jesus' overall vision, plan, and methodology. It takes a great deal of malice to organize and execute a scheme to have your leader, someone you have seen raise the dead, jailed and murdered. Until you can sit at the table with Judas, you may not be able to understand Jesus.

What I would ask is you see Judas for a moment as one of twelve men, chosen by the Father, to be a part of the earthly life of his Son. See him as a patriot filled with zeal to rid his nation, God's chosen people, of an oppressive and murderous invader, Rome. Ask yourself if his motivation is what you have always assumed it to be…Betrayal. If it is not, what can it be? If it is zeal to propel the anointed Messiah into the forefront and force him to act, then thereby hangs a tale worth telling.

A note on reading this is necessary. This is presented as a scroll written by Judas, presented to Barabbas in case something goes wrong with his plan. It is also written in first person present tense. I know this will bother my dear friend, Glenn but it is what I chose to tell this tale. As always, please share with me your thoughts and questions.

Wishing you joy in the journey,
Aramis Thorn

Prologue—A Letter to Barabbas

Greetings Jesus Barabbas,

Things are different now. My mind is clear and I can see what must be done. Ever since he wept, broken hearted over Jerusalem, he has not been the same. He has ceased speaking of establishing his kingdom and instead speaks of death. His followers continue to increase. You saw how they treated him when we entered the city. We expected to return to Jerusalem for the Passover and that is what has made it all clear to me. I know I must motivate him to add a spark to the tinder he has collected for the last three years. It is dry, oiled, and ready to burn.

Should my mission fail and the Sanhedrin discover my true purposes, I am sure my life will be forfeit. Who knows, they may find a way to kill me either way. I have not even told my father what I am planning. There are too many enemies I must trust to feel confident someone will not betray me or that my plans will not be revealed to him and thwarted.

I have not felt right about taking the money, but it has been necessary to buy the silence of my contacts within the Priesthood, the Zealots, and the Roman court. The corrupt leaders of our nation will find their failure to stand against the gentile oppression will cost them dearly when he overthrows Rome and sets things as they should be.

It is a surety he is the deliverer, the Messiah. I have seen his miracles and wonders. He has given the twelve of us power to heal the sick. I have seen him tempted and tested. He just needs a little push to get him moving in the right direction. Should my plan fail, or should I be wrong, give this scroll to the other disciples so they will know why I have acted in this manner.

I will meet with the High Priest tonight to arrange things. We will take him in Gethsemane, on Thursday night after the Passover meal, and away from the public eye. Keep this scroll safe until the Messiah destroys our enemies. I know that besides my father, the others would not see the necessity of my actions. I do not tell father so he cannot be implicated. When our enemies lay at our feet and Rome has crumbled, when we all see Jesus as our conquering King, crowned, and fully empowered, then history will acknowledge my choice was a necessary one.

Judas ben Simon of Kerioth

Nightmare in Nazareth

My father tells this story often when he is tired or angry. I do not ask him about mother even though I know he has beautiful stories he could tell because the only answer I will get is this story. I would like to know who she was, what she was like I put the only tale he tells down here for context. It is this beginning that leads to the real story. It is the first small pieces of tinder that will catch when the fire comes. Remember, not by water this time but, by fire.

I was only a few months old. Father sent my mother, Asta and I to Nazareth with my Uncle Jude.[1] Father remains in Kerioth for two days to conclude some business and bring the money so we may buy supplies on the journey home. My father is actually four days behind us and my family sets up trade in the Nazareth market area. With Uncle Jude are my cousins, his sons Josiah and Joash. They are working the market in Nazareth and waiting for my father to arrive with the additional funds. Father is unaware of their other purposes.

After collecting the money in Kerioth, my father makes the long journey to Jerusalem, rests for a day, arranges some business for the coming Passover there, and then stops in Sychar the same night.

---

[1] One may read the full account of this in the novel <u>Magi: The Gift Bearers by Aramis Thorn</u>

It is the halfway point of travel between Jerusalem and Nazareth. This is where the end begins. He met two young Roman officers there; Patrius and Longinus (Yes, it is the same Longinus who is Commander of the Jerusalem garrison). They pretended to be civil and even friendly. Father is convinced now they were hunting his family all along when they offered to escort him to Nazareth "for protection" on the road.

The ride to Nazareth was easy enough and father gets a tear in his eye when he speaks of his reunion with mother and I the first night. The following day those same Romans came into the market with two Legionnaires. They were taking advantage of and harassing the vendors as they approached us. Father told me for years one of them, Patrius made some lude comment to mother. They also threatened Josiah and Joash then took some of our best linen fabric and a measure of olives then turned to leave.

When my cousins went after them for payment the Romans attacked them. The soldiers murdered them right there in the market. Josiah and Joash each killed one of the Legionnaires. After the Romans killed my cousins, they advanced on my uncle. Patrius murdered Jude and Longinus used my cousin's own spear to kill my mother. They left father alive to warn others about the power of Roman soldiers and the danger of being anything less than totally subjugated. Father began telling me the story on the long painful journey home to Kerioth. He mostly did it to manage his own pain and loss. His voice kept me occupied.

After having me take goat's milk through a cloth in Sychar he sought a more natural solution to feeding me. In Jerusalem he found a woman, Shlomi, to nurse me for the remainder of the journey. Not having to share the money with his dead cousins and uncle made my father wealthy. He has never lacked for money since. He whispers to me over and over, "We will avenge them son. The Romans have killed your mother. They have darkened the light of God in my life. They have earned our hatred. We will have our hatred satiated Judas. We will find a way to destroy them."

Cobras in Baskets

When father returns to Kerioth he tells the dark tale of death caused at the hands of Roman soldiers. He takes in the wives of my cousins and raises their children as my brothers and sisters as the Law requires. It is these women who told me how loving and gentle my father used to be towards everyone. That man is gone. He died in Nazareth with my mother and the man who raised me hates Rome and all it is.

It was my family that showed me the clear path necessary for us to be proper Israelites. As I grew up, learning the laws of my people, the laws of God, I also learned of the ways in which our nation is polluted by the presence of gentiles who disrespect our ways. It seems from my first years of understanding; I have always been resentful of the extent to which our small nation has been the target of those who oppress and defile others for their own gain.

My father, Simon of Kerioth, began to study the Maccabean history of our people. He was one of the few who understood the reticence and tenacity of the Maccabees. Outwardly, it was his passion for our nation driving him. Inwardly, it was his hatred of two Roman soldiers and the empire they serve. I would see him in the evenings at home, constantly pouring over the scrolls containing the history of the Maccabee family. He paid a high price to have his own copy of them. His eyes would strain in the dim light of the olive oil lamp. It was from these scrolls I learned to read and write. The deeds of that noble family were the foundation of my skills. Purim sometimes felt more sacred in our home than Passover.

Father loves God deeply and believes it is disobedient to God to allow any foreign nation to have sway over the internal affairs of Israel. From the time I could understand him he spoke constantly of his hatred for the corruption in the political and religious leadership in Jerusalem. The Romans had learned from the Maccabees not to interfere with our religious freedom, but they still did not understand their gentile presence in our land was an affront to us both socially and religiously. I grew up hating Rome and all the trappings of its dictatorial power.

It is the Romans who set up the Idumean family of Herod to rule our land. The former Herod built great buildings and even rebuilt the Temple. No building can hide the ugliness of a man who is not a Jew squatting on the Throne of David. The priesthood is also filled with those who oppose and appease Rome. The Temple is a marketplace at Passover where buying and selling take precedence over sacrifice and worship.

The Legionnaires in Kerioth are docile enough. They collect taxes and buy from the local merchants, but they are still Romans. My father always says, "You can keep a cobra in a basket and he will sleep and sleep. You may forget he is a cobra and just a tiny bite is enough to kill you. The cobra, however, never forgets he is a cobra and when you awaken him, the first thing he considers is whether or not he can bite you today. The Romans are cobras and our Romans in Kerioth are just sleeping in their baskets. Whilst they slumber here the Romans in Jerusalem rape our women, defile our sacred customs, and kill our men on crosses."

The difficulty is too many of our people think the cobra has lost its bite and it will sleep as long as we do not jostle the basket. The inevitable truth is cobras get hungry and hunger awakens them no matter how quiet and careful you are. Father thinks we should jostle the basket more often so the cobra flares out its hood, shows its forked tongue, and spits a little. This way people will not forget it is deadly and should not be allowed to sleep in our house.

Father began to meet with some of the other men from our village just after returning from Nazareth. It was then he learned there was a growing contingency of men who saw the opportunity to rebel against Rome and make it too costly for them to rule us. At first, they met to discuss the ways to avoid becoming victims of the violence again.

The targets of my father's bitterness never extended to me. He was not hard on me, but even our simple conversations eventually turned to the Roman problem. He told me when I was old enough to understand there was a purpose to everything Rome did. An example he gave was the census, the taxing just before I was born.

Father told it this way; he and Juda were working in the linen barn preparing for a trip south to sell some fabric, olives, and olive oil in Egypt. A Roman Legionnaire rode up on a horse and nailed a document to the post of the town well just outside of our barn. The south end of the village uses this well for water. The notice was in Hebrew, Aramaic, Latin, and Greek. It had the seal of Caesar Augustus on it.

I, Augustus Caesar, Emperor of Rome and all of her States and Protectorates greet you. Notice is given to all of those who abide under the protection of Rome. Every man shall return to the city of his birth with his family. He shall there report to the magistrate of the Roman garrison or office to register for a census.

This census will be administered by our servant Publius Sulpicius Quirinius in all of Syria and Judea. All men must report between the ides of December and the end April. Documents will be issued to offer proof of registration once it is complete. So ordered by the seal of the hand of Augustus Caesar.

The census caused much upheaval in the entire region. We were four generations in Kerioth, so we did not have to go anywhere. Father set up part of the barn to help those who had to travel here. In those days his heart and mind were always focused on loving his neighbor and the stranger in the land. My aunt told me often of the kindness he showed to those traveling with nothing.

There was a Judas in Galilee during the census who led a band of people in revolt. He was killed and his movement came to noting. Father admired his politics and named me after him. He was glad of it once his admiration turned to hatred at Rome.

Once the fervor of the Census dies down, father and my uncle begin to travel again for business. The usual route was to Egypt and back, then to Jerusalem, Nazareth, and Antioch. Then they would trade all the way back to Kerioth. Father and mother were married a year after the census. I was born a respectable ten months later. I think father blames himself as much as he does the Romans because he suggested mother go on the road with him instead of remaining in Kerioth. Guilt over this may drive him as much as his hunger for vengeance does.

His resistance of our enemy was only passive before my mother's death. It could be marked by the way he charmed the cobras with kindness and graceful compliance. It could be seen in his obeying the Law of Moses regarding the stranger in the land. He would heap coals of fire on their heads by retuning good for evil. Things change.

Father still takes in those of our people needing shelter. He keeps a record of those who stay with us on their way either north or south. Years later we were looking through those records when reminiscing. Of note was the entry when I was a toddler of a carpenter, his wife, and son who stayed with us on their way to Egypt. He has an additional note they stopped again on their return journey almost two years later. They had a second son and the carpenter helped repair the doors on the shed.

By then father was deep into his meeting with other men in Kerioth regarding ways to thwart and eventually destroy the Romans in Judea. Now they meet to plan just how to exterminate the cobras have infested our home. When you must kill many cobras at once, someone will be bitten.

Kicking the Basket

Father spoke of his meeting with the others planning resistance at dinner again this evening. He said the puppet king Herod the Great has been replaced by his sons and the monarchy divided between them. Antipas will get our region including Kerioth, all of the Negev, Beersheba, and Jerusalem. Father says he is not as bad as the former Herod, but he is still a Roman puppet.

Father hates the Romans so much and he loathes the Herod family for the murder of the babies in Bethlehem. News of the atrocity has spread throughout the region. It has caused many men to take up the cause and there is even a sect growing who interpret the Law as demanding this is the only way to stay true to God.

When my father speaks of the slaughter, you can still see the rage in his eyes. He quotes the Law of Moses often and demands the eyes of those who kill the innocent. He reminds me often of the penalty under the Law for those who shed the blood of the innocent. The only penalty for shedding innocent blood is death and it is death of the Romans my father wants.

He thinks orders from God are permanent. God at one time ordered Joshua to kill all the gentiles in this land. I think Father has decided to finish Joshua's task for God. He will not be happy until the Romans and the Herod family pay for their crimes against the babes of Bethlehem. He may not even be happy were every Roman everywhere be killed. He has no peace. Father may never be happy again.

Some of the other merchants have begun to call father Simon the Zealot. He was not part of the assassination squad that ambushed the Romans but he would not hesitate to kill those who steal from us and defile our land, our customs, and our women. I learned only today he supplied them with the weapons through a merchant in Nazareth.

The Romans know the attack was instigated and planned in our village. That is enough for them to burn it down. Several families have moved to other villages based solely on the rumors. There is already a new epithet for us who have remained. In their Roman accent they call us Iscariots, people of Kerioth, but they say it as if they are swearing.

The Romans in the garrison here are no longer passive and quiet. They snarl instead of speaking now. In the market, they used to keep the peace for the merchants. Now they steal food for themselves and turn a blind eye to those who are dishonest in their dealings.

Today father had me deliver some funds to the local magistrate. Apparently, we were buying peace for the rest of the village until we could make arrangements to leave. It seems odd to pay those we hate to violate their own laws so we may buy time to arrange the keeping of ours. Father says I am old enough to begin working on my own to aid the cause.

Passover is coming and we are going to Jerusalem. Father plans to meet with some of those from other villages who share his views concerning Rome. Many tongues will wag over the attack near Bethany. Most of the soldiers there were killed. It is also rumored the Jews in Bethany aided the survivors. Father says this could be dangerous. Others may wish to harm those who aid Rome in any way.

Father and his friends have been kicking the basket and the Cobras are hooded and hissing. After that, to spare the village he loves, we are moving north to Cana in Galilee. It is close to Nazareth, to the southwest. This is both good and bad.

Nazareth is becoming the central area for activity for both the zealous resisters and some of the trade. It is also where mother was killed. I asked father if he thought being so close to the pain was a good idea. Father says he can process fine linens anywhere. He has taught my cousins the trade and counts on me to manage the olive pressing with our servants. We have been able to use our wealth to influence things here. It will not be the case in Jerusalem and remains to be seen in Cana. I only hope the reputation of Nazareth does not reach us in Cana.

The annual journey to Jerusalem grows sweeter to me each year. Even amidst the ruinous rule of corrupt priests and foreign barbarians the Passover celebration is observed by those who remember and anticipate a deliverer. We had a Moses and one day we knew we would have a Messiah.

Father has allowed me to take my own tithe of joy from the olive money this year. He says my understanding of quality oil and quality work are advanced for my years. I have six pieces of silver in my money bag and under the Law I may use it to purchase whatever my heart desires. Sometimes I enjoy just looking at the coins in the sunlight. It feels good to have money for whatever I wish. I must keep it safe or the Romans will find a way to make it taxable.

There are twelve of us all told traveling to Jerusalem and then to Cana after Passover. Father and my aunts travel in the main wagon with the young girls. My cousins and I travel in the three supply wagons. Two wagon loads of linens and a wagon of olives and oil will keep us busy trading at the market. This is the first year father did not have to hire someone to drive wagons for him. More money stays in the family and Elon, Calah, and I get to help.

I wish Father would wed again. He will not. I think about this almost every time I visit Jerusalem. My old nurse, Shlomi has a widowed niece name Zaphera. She is of good faith and reputation. She would ease father's heart, I think. We stay with Shlomi's family when we are in Jerusalem. They are grateful for our care of Shlomi after the scandal many years ago.

After mother's death, father took her in as nurse to me. She had just lost her own nursing child, born without benefit of a father. Nothing is ever mentioned about this by anyone. I once asked father about it when I was nine. He gave me the look says never forget what I am about to say and proceeded to require me to never ask about it again.

We love her as one of our own and she has been a mother to me and more. Both of my aunts, Sari and Puah are her age and the three of them provide a home for us rich with good food and fine care. Puah's daughters are all learning to be devout women. Father has mentioned he will begin looking for women of the same quality as betrothals for my cousins and I soon. I have no interest in this yet, but little of my destiny is in my hands.

The line of travelers to Jerusalem is long. As we pass each town the road grows ever crowded. The number going to Passover grows each year as well. Jerusalem will be busy and the business will be brisk. We will be able to go to Cana with enough wealth to establish a real home for us all and build our business quickly.

We will be able to pay all the taxes as well. The Romans will tax us for entering Jerusalem. There will be the Temple tax to bring our sacrifice, but must be paid in Temple coins which we can purchase with regular coins at a steep rate of exchange. I often wonder why the priests cannot use common coins for the Temple, accept them at the Temple, and spend them from the Temple coffers.

There will also be the tax on our market sales and the tax on our departure from Jerusalem. The market will provide enough for us to still make a nice profit. If we cannot purchase a suitable place in Cana then we will build one. The Spring weather is upon us and ideal for building a house. The summer rains will prove it before winter comes and we can get at least one crop harvested if there is arable land.

I begin to think of the olive pits, carefully dried and ready for planting. There are also the small saplings protected in father's covered cart. The three varieties of trees they will yield are offspring of our family planting, protecting, and pruning for over four generations. Father chose each of the young trees from the sprouting yard by our barn. He learned this from his father who learned it from his great-grandfather. In truth they have been harvesting and processing olives in Kerioth since his family migrated here from Jerusalem during the Maccabean time.

My thoughts on all this are interrupted by my younger cousin, Ehud. He is riding with me to review his Torah as we travel. Ehud will be presented at the Temple this year and the time will be set for him to read the Law in the Synagogue. He will be the first in our family in many decades not to do his first reading in Kerioth.

Ehud sits next to me on the wagon board. He has a dozen enormous black olives in a linen cloth with him. I smile at the young man, "You will eat our entire supply of black olives before we reach the Jerusalem market. I am pleased you love them but remember last year when you ate too many olives. You were stuck at Shlomi's recovering for almost the whole week. You can, however, share one with me."

The boy smiles back at me, handing me three of the rich ripe olives. "I knew you would share some with me cousin," he says. Then he asks, "Do you think we can get as suitable a grove from the soil in Cana as we do in Kerioth? Will the olives grow as large and plump?"

"I have been pondering as well cousin," I reassure him. "The soil will be good soil as it is all part of the land promised to Abraham. We will tend it when we should and rest it when we should. We will care for the trees and observe all the Law demands of us out of love for God. If we do these things, what does Joshua promise us?"

Ehud thought for a moment before answering with confident clarity, "Joshua wrote that the Book of the Law should never leave our tongues so we can see we are doing all that is written within it. We are to meditate on it from morning until evening. This is what will make us prosperous and successful."

"Very good," I reassure him. "You are ready to be presented at the Temple." I then reminded Ehud not to throw away the olive pits. He immediately fetched some water to wash the pits and cleaned them. He also put them in the course drying bag in the wagon. At dinner that night, a day outside Jerusalem, I told his mother Sari how well she has done in instructing her son in the Law. She was pleased to hear of my confidence in his readiness for the Temple.

Father sternly reminds us all we observe at the Temple because that is our tradition, but we cannot love a temple built by Herod the butcher. It should be torn down and rebuilt by only the people of God he reminds us. It was my place to guide the conversation back to more pleasant things. I inquired about the arrangements to manage our land and crops back in Kerioth.

Fortunately, father took the bait. He explains again how he convinced a distant cousin to oversee things weekly. He left our hired steward in charge of the daily work and we can journey back there when working the trade south to check on things. Father feels very proud of the way he made the necessary move north but still did so expanding our resources. We have all heard the story and were part the arrangements. It still is a good way to move the discussion away from Zealots and rebellion.

Still ,my thoughts turn toward the future for my younger cousins and the changes happening in our land. I drift off to sleep wondering when we would get the promised deliverer of our people. The truth is, Rome is strong and a little basket kicking may be what is needed to remind people. I got up that night and lit a small oil lamp. Using some scraps from my father's books I inked some notes about these thoughts. Those have been lost but I used some of my own money in Jerusalem that year to buy this scroll and began to write the story in earnest.

Ah, but I am getting ahead of myself. We are not in Jerusalem for Passover yet, are we? We will not get there until there is a little more dry tinder for Rome to light. Whilst we are journeying north, the new Governor of the region is on his way south from Antioch. He too is headed to Jerusalem in time for Passover. Please remember I heard this part of the story from that Greek physician who traveled with us in Galilee and Jerusalem. It has been verified. I was not there.

Valerius Gratus was appointed Prefect of Judea when I was fifteen. His primary assignment was to bring the political unrest in Judea under control. His thought was the priests were to blame for the failure of the Jews to submit fully to Rome. One of his first acts was to depose Annas as High Priest. That Rome gave him to the power to do it was without question. That he did not understand how dangerous it was becomes evident.

Outsiders do not understand the power the priests hold over our people. They wield life and death over us. They can pardon us from sin or seal it to our souls. They know the Law forward and backward. They have centuries of practice in using it to their advantage. They have years of practice corrupting the Law to their own ends.

Those of us who believe God is all he claims to be in the Torah see the emptiness of the Temple when it comes to those who are supposed to serve it. That they are corrupt is without question. I do not believe anyone grasps the depths of the corruption and its damage to the people of God. It is yet another reason we are so hungry for a Messiah.

Gratus arrives in Jerusalem the day before we do that year. He set up immediate laws regarding the ability of the priesthood to carry out the Law. If there were going to be a death as a result of infractions of the law the Prefect had to approve. The process was the priests had to submit each case to the Prefect and it would either be set aside or Rome would "wash their hands of it."

The Prefect did not care if the Jews killed each other under their own laws. He did want the power to frustrate them in the attempt if it went against his purposes. He did also wish to preserve the excellent tax source this trade route from Egypt to Rome possesses. He deduced if he controlled the High Priest, he would control the rest. Much blood is required to cover the error of this assumption.

As this unfolds, bear in mind I hold to my belief. I am a faithful and devout Jew. I do not possess the righteousness of Job, but I do have the tenacity of Jacob. I think I have wished to be like him my whole life.

Gratus appoints Ishmael ben Fabus as High Priest first. He is presiding over the Passover. His first act is to double all exchange fees at the Temple and raise the Temple tax. We hear rumors of the changes, but they do not impact us until father sends me to the

Temple to exchange our coin and register the lambs we have brought for our offerings.

The rest of the family sets up work in the market our first full day there. Shlomi's family has secured our usual spot in the market. As soon as all was ready, I set out to the Temple with my string of lambs and enough coin to exchange for the Temple fees. This is the first year I have my own lamb as well. I had raised it carefully after picking if from father's flock and paying him for it. He was reluctant to take my coin but proud of my integrity.

I can hear the crier on Solomon's Porch at the Temple long before I got to the Temple. We always allow an extra day before Passover week to be sure are ready to focus on business and avoid the crowds at the exchange. Still there is enough of a throng that the crier stands on the short dais reserved for his work.

"Sacrificial animals to the left," he cries. "The coin exchange line is to the right. We will divide the sacrifice lines by animal type and condition. You may use any money changer you wish."

I think it wiser to turn over the lambs first. Then I can move more easily through the crowd. I stand for perhaps half an hour in the line for "unblemished" lambs. When I am near the front it becomes obvious very few of the animals are acceptable to the young priests doing the judging. Faithful Jews are directed to another line where they can exchange their unacceptable animals for acceptable ones, already approved by the priests. It took little observation to see the priests were reselling the lambs they have just taken as acceptable from other faithful men.

There is also a "miracle" or two to be witnessed as well. A priest declares an ox or lamb unacceptable. Then, the man wishing to present the offering creates a flash of silver light with a coin or three. The dazzle of the beauty of the silver mesmerizes the priest and he suddenly sees the animal is acceptable. Once he touches the coin it all seems to be as it should be and the man can go on his way assured his sacrifice will be made in his name. I love the flash and feel of silver as much if not more than anyone but I had no idea of its healing properties over eyes and livestock.

When I came to the head of the line the priest barely looks at my very clean lambs. He intones judgment, "these are not acceptable for Temple use. You may exchange them by the pool on the porch."

Stepping closer to the priest I whisper gruffly. "My next sentence will be to proclaim loudly that you are stealing money and reselling these animals by the pool should mine not be suddenly and miraculously found spotless and pure."

The priest thinks for a moment he will argue with me. He sees the anger in me and knows it is a sleeping fire he would not unleash. It is a fire that would consume him and he is just wise enough to see it and quell it. Taking a half step back he responds "Your lambs are acceptable please hand them over to the men to my left."

Without another word I turn and give the lambs to the handler the priest points out. I notice the man in front of me pays a fee to hand over his oxen. When the handler stretches out his hand for the same fee, I say just loud enough for the priest to hear me, "The priest said because my lambs are so very exemplary there will be no fee."

The priest realizes just how well my voice carries over a crowd and his pasty complexion grows a little gray. He locks eyes with the handler and nods his agreement lest I say more. Placing the lead in the outstretched palm of the handler, I turn to go. Something is rising in me I do not recognize. I shove it away and move toward the money exchange. I already feel something within me is stirring. I already know the money changers steal from our people. I do not know in this moment what Gratus has done.

People who will accept injustice like lambs to the slaughter over livestock will rise like furies when you steal their money. As I approach the money changing line, I see the priests well understand this. There are six Temple guards and four Roman Legionnaires posted behind the changing tables. Among them also is a Centurion Commander. He is dressed in battle armor; not the ornamental shiny armor preferred by most officers. He carries a gladius and a spear unlike any I have ever seen. The wood of the shaft is so dark it appears to be black. The spearhead shaped like a broad leaf has silver sharp sides. It is longer than a pilum but shorter than a long spear.

His look of command distracts me just enough I do not realize until I am at the table, he is also wearing the tunic of the Garrison Commander. We have heard of the military commander of Jerusalem. He is reputed to be hard as iron and a fair judge of men. My assessment of the Commander is interrupted by the man at the table.

"How much do you wish to exchange?" he asks without looking up.

Giving him my full attention, "There are twelve of us with offerings; three men, one boy, six women and girls. Two of the women are widows under the care of my father."

The man at the table checks his scroll. He still does not look up at me. He still does not acknowledge his own countryman as he taxes him to worship our shared God. He quotes the price. It is half again as much as last year. It will take almost all of our extra coin to meet the price. The anger and fire ignited by the animal exchangers catch full at this robbery attempt.

Without thinking I slam a hand on the table and bark at the man, "You would devour our silver with laws not written by Moses. Would that the ground would open and swallow you as it did Korah."

Now the man looks up. "That is the price. The new High Priest, Ishmael has increased the tax based on his perception of the Temple's needs. If you wish to present your offering it must be done with pure Temple coin. There is a cost associated with purifying and producing this coin."

His response serves as oil to my fire and I grow louder. "You create a tax that is not needed. You use it to devour the resource of the people you are required to serve. There is no coin offering that can redeem your sin against your people. I will not...'

I am interrupted by the very sharp point of a spear touching my chest. The Centurion has descended from his watch post giving me the honor of his full attention. He speaks to me in my own language barely accented, "If you have a problem with the money changer perhaps you should handle it in a more quiet manner. No amount of coin will bring you back from the place where your anger leads you."

Fury still grips me but I can also feel the point of his spear has pricked my chest. One thrust from this Roman and I will be able to discuss my views on Temple taxes with the LORD directly. Looking down I take a step back but am stopped by a strong hand on my shoulder. Out of the corner of my eye I can see it is not another Roman but a Jew who has his grip on me.

Before I can react, he speaks, but to the Centurion and not to me, "It is good to see you again Longinus. We have had a prosperous year and I will gladly pay the way for this young man's family. You should have supper with us this evening friend. We are set up in the market by the spice vendor you like from Joppa. Bring Syrah and your sons."

Longinus pulls back his spear. As he does my focus is on it and I catch the word *Fatum* engraved on it and filled in with silver. "Joseph," he sighs, "you turn up at the strangest times. For the sake of our friendship this man may go as long as he causes no further disturbance in the courtyard today. You and your son may tell Mary we will gladly dine with you tonight. I presume the children have all grown more in the last year than we wish."

I turn to the man who still has a firm grip on my shoulder. Had I not felt the power in his hand I would think him meek and nothing more. His son next to him fishes some coins from a very heavy purse and passes them to the money changer. In turn the money changer gives me twelve Temple coins. He also hands over nine of them to the young man who paid him.

Turning to thank Joseph his son speaks first, "You are right. These men rob God. They also are worthy of our patience and kindness in any case. The Law is for everyone and no one is without the very sin we pay to have pardoned. When God knows how they will tax us, he provides to care for us in response. We must do as our forefathers did and hold our peace whilst God fights for us."

His words sound so rich and true I cannot respond. I mutter a hasty reply of gratitude and make my retreat. As I walk away, I hear Longinus speak again, "Your son is still confounding people at the Temple, Joseph. We will see you tonight at dinner. Portimus has left for Rome, but Patrius is here and will wish to see you. He will not admit it, but he will wish it."

They converse further but I am too far from them to hear it. As I walk back to the market, everything about the words of Joseph's son ring clear in my mind. It is also not lost on me that these kind men consider the Garrison Commander a friend. I ponder perhaps they are just Roman sympathizers with smooth words.

Then, I realize I have the temple coin and the amount of father's coin I expected to pay for the Temple tax. Putting the Temple coin in my father's bag I add the amount I would have paid last year from his coin to my own purse. Rome did not get it. The corrupt priests did not get it. Father will not miss it and will not rant about the higher Temple taxes.

The day is a busy one. The devout of Judea all have money to spend on whatsoever their hearts desire. Moses included the instructions for those of us who have to travel far to Jerusalem.

> *Every year be sure to save a tenth of the crops harvested from whatever you plant in your fields. Eat the tenth of your grain, new wine, and olive oil, and eat the firstborn of your cattle, sheep, and goats in the presence of the LORD your God in the place he will choose to put his name. Then you will learn to fear the LORD your God as long as you live.*

> *But the place the LORD your God will choose to put his name may be too far away. He may bless you with so much that you can't carry a tenth of your income that far. If so, exchange the tenth part of your income for silver. Take the silver with you, and go to the place the LORD your God will choose. Use the silver to buy whatever you want: cattle, sheep, goats, wine, liquor; whatever you choose. Then you and your family will eat and enjoy yourselves there in the presence of the LORD your God.*

Since the time of the Maccabees there has been a vast market here during Passover week. This is always a large marketplace in Jerusalem. During Passover week, however, it is easily ten times the size. People pay for the best spots. Families have had their stalls in the same location for many generations. The buying and selling goes on all day and into the night from the day after Sabbath before Passover until sunset before the Passover meal. Those who are not Jews come here for the market as well. The Law makes it clear; they are to be respected and treated well. This does not mean they respect our ways. The merchants who are not Jews will buy and sell through

Passover and the following Sabbath. We are still bound by the Law to care for the priests and the strangers in our land.

> *Never forget to take care of the Levites who live in your cities. They have no land of their own as you have.*

> *At the end of every third year bring a tenth of that year's crop, and store it in your cities. Foreigners, orphans, and widows who live in your cities may come to eat all they want. The Levites may also come because they have no land of their own as you have. Then the LORD your God will bless you in whatever work you do.*

It is in this passage the Passover bazaar is born. It is also how the Priests attached their Temple taxes to it at first. Now, the Temple taxes stand on their own as an obligation for the people to care for the Levites. It has grown into a business of its own to rob the faithful who wish access to God. When Messiah comes, I am sure he will have something to say about it.

The other part is our care for strangers in our land. So many merchants come for Passover week who have nothing to do with the Holy Day and our deliverance from Egypt. I truly wish we could be delivered from them all. We do, however, obey the law and feed those in need with our third-year tithes. That will not be until next year. We will manage the year anticipating this. It may be less though since we are all moving to Cana.

If this first day of business is an indicator, we will be well provided for when we leave for Cana. As merchants and customers come and go father tells everyone to look for us in Cana after Passover. We have enough linens and olives for five days of trade. We sell enough the first day to cover almost two days.

As trading slows down for the day father instructs us to raise our prices. If sales are hindered tomorrow, we can lower them again and make it up on the third day. Father always knows how to regulate prices so we trade with honor and make as much profit as possible. In celebrating the lucrative day, he sends me to the food vendors to get some baked sweets for us to have with supper. He says he has already acquired some wine from one of the vendors from Joppa. He claims the sea air makes the grapes sweeter. I think he likes it because the wine is stronger.

The food stalls are all very busy this near to dinner time. I follow the scent of warm honey, nuts, and spices to a wagon made into a booth on the far edge of the food vendors. The woman behind the bench is striking and customers are three-deep ahead of me. The wagon is laden with spices and herbs but the woman does a brisk trade in a baked cakes; the source of the alluring aroma.

I am sure the taste of the cakes will be as sweet as the aroma. I am unsure if they will be allowed under our dietary laws. Many devout Jews are buying her cakes, but that will not be enough explanation for father. My thoughts are interrupted by a voice behind me.

"It seems we are destined to spend at least part of our lives waiting in lines together. It would be more enjoyable if we exchanged names," he says.

I turn and it is Joseph's son from the temple earlier. He is smiling at me as if we have been friends for life. I do not usually offer my name first. My father's caution because of his secret activities infects me even when I wish for it not to. Still I am compelled to do it. "I am Judas ben Simon from Kerioth. I would express my gratitude again for your father's generosity at the Temple today. I am also thankful for his intervention on my behalf."

"It is my father's nature to act for the good of others even when he is not required to do so. It is one of the many things I hope to emulate", he responds. "I am Jesus ben Joseph, from Nazareth. Are you here to buy some of Veena's placenta cakes?[2] She makes it without the cheese during Passover so we can buy it without concern for the Law being violated."

Something about him compels me to talk. "Father asked me to find something for a sweet finish to our day. Business has been good and we are going to celebrate as God wishes us to do according to Moses. Knowing another good family speaks for the purity of her food will ease my father's ever ready concerns."

"It is good you think of the Law in your dealings," he responds. "In speaking and living the Law are our people prosperous and successful. God provides for us so we are not tempted to steal, but moreover so we see how he demonstrates his love for us."

The extra coins, my father's coins feel very heavy in my bag as I pay Veena for enough placenta cakes, made with layered dough, nuts, spices, and honey for my family. Whilst Veena wraps the cakes, Longinus and another Centurion find Jesus in the crowd. Again, the greeting between this Jew and the Roman is warmer than any I have ever witnessed. The second Centurion is not as friendly, but he greets Jesus with a civility one does not expect from Romans toward Jews. It was neither forced nor faked.

Jesus purchases his cakes and turns again to me. "You have met my long-time friend Longinus. This is his and my friend Patrius. They are both good to my family and always have been." Turning to the Romans he continues, "This is Judas ben Simon of Kerioth. He is about to experience Veena's skill in baking sweets for the first time."

A look passes between Patrius and Longinus chilling me with raw fear. It is one of recognition not acknowledgment. As I stand here confronted with the villains of all my father's stories, I feel

---

[2] A Placenta Cake is one of the earliest forms of what we know as Baklava. The recipe dates back to the third century BC.

neither anger nor hatred. I do fear they have already made the connection and I have put my family in danger.

Longinus' words make it clear the look had another meaning, "This is the man who objected to the new High Priest robbing his own people." Turning to me he continues. "You have secured my victory in a wager with my friend Patrius. He bet me a day's wages no one would dare object to the new Temple taxes. If what I hear is true, you not only objected but forced them to accept your offering animals without the new fees. Be careful Judas of Kerioth. They will think you are stirring up rebellion."

As he says this, Patrius hands Longinus some coins and gives me a look causing a rivulet to run down my spine. I decide it is time to leave before I do endanger my family. Clutching the linen-wrapped cakes I bid them a good evening and turn to leave.

I have only taken a step when Patrius speaks, "Stop, Judas of Kerioth." I turn to face him as he advances to me. Placing a broad strong hand on the bundle of cakes, he instructs, "Remember to bring the linen back when you come for more cakes. Veena will give you a better price. You will come back for more."

I sputter some thanks as the Centurion turns back to his friend leaving me to make my retreat to our wagons. Before dinner I slip coins from my bag and return them to my father explaining I forgot to give them back after a kind stranger had paid our tax for us. Father seemed more concerned it was a devout Jew who aided me over anything else. I mentioned neither of the Romans' names in the story.

Our dinner of roasted goat and rich vegetables is accompanied by good conversation surrounding the day's business and events. The linen and olive goods were all selling as richly as if next year were a Year of Jubilee. Father attempts to engage me on my interaction with the Romans at the Temple. I deflect by mentioning how proud I am of Elon and his help with our olive oil customers.

I point out he more than once was able to sell much more than the buyer wanted. I punctuate my praise by giving him one of my silver coins for the celebration. I also realize he missed some things in his count at the end of the day. I will remind him later how important it is to account for everything so we remain good stewards of what we have.

His awe at having his own silver at age twelve years distracts everyone from my encounter with Longinus. Dinner is finished with the strong wine and the placenta cakes. They are as good and better than I had been told. As I enjoy a second one, I fold the linen they had been wrapped in to take back to Veena. I notice the quality of thread in the linen is poor and wonder how many cakes are ruined because of the poor wrapping. As I go to my rest a plan forms to do more business and perhaps get free cakes. That would have to wait until morning.

***

When Puah and Sari are preparing breakfast the next morning, I bring the linen wrapping from the cakes with me. My aunts weave the linen we sell and know its lack of quality in an instant. After they serve breakfast, proffering it to them, I ask, "What do you think of this piece of fabric?"

Puah almost laughs, "I will not even touch such poorly woven cloth. Someone thought to save money making it. It is not even worthy to be used as sitting rags."

Sari, always gentler than Puah adds, "This would be useful for straining cheese or boiled fruit if it would hold up. Why do you ask, Judas?"

I can see both are interested in my question. It is just as I wish. "We always have odd pieces after you cut fabric for custom requests.

You are both skilled at using every scrap well. It does, however, take time and I have heard you both say you wished there were a way just to sell it." Both are nodding, listening. "Suppose," I continue, "we barter the leftover bits to the cake vendor. I can convince her why she needs better linen. You simply need to tell me how much we need to make from the scraps to account for their not being used for other things."

Puah cannot resist teasing me, "And is this baker of cakes also pleasing to the eye? Do you perhaps hope to acquire more than another trade agreement?"

Sari blushes on my behalf and defends me, "Any good woman would be blessed to have Judas as her husband. Look how well he does with the olives and the oil. He will be a great provider. He is also honest and generous. Elon fell asleep clutching his silver coin. I am sure he dreamt all night about what he will buy with it."

I feel the sting of my own conscience as she speaks. I am not honorable but I am devout. I do not think of marriage or family. I do find Veena very attractive but I know even if she is a Jew, she is not devout. We do not have many single women who are in business without a father or brother to protect them.

I need to steer the conversation back to the linen. I know threatening to withdraw the opportunity will push Puah in the direction I wish. "Perhaps my idea does not possess the merit I thought it held. Thank you for breakfast. I will eat and go back to my olives."

Puah is easily nudged in the direction I desire, she insists, "No Judas, we are only having some fun at your expense. We could use the time to much better advantage than accounting for scraps. What are you thinking?"

She continues, "I will invite Veena to dine with us. Another family has assured me she is a reputable woman. I think she will like the idea, but I would like for you two to explain the problem with the quality of her wrapping cloths. I am quite sure she does not weave them, so she should not be offended. You two should , on what you wish in trade before she arrives."

The women agree with me and the easy part of my plan is in place. As the remainder of the family gathers for breakfast, I my desire for us to keep this to ourselves until I speak to Veena. The family meal is a hasty one. Today most of those traveling from around the area will arrive in Jerusalem. The market will be busy. The trade will be brisk.

When leaving our tent for the olive cart, Sari hands me a folded piece of linen, "Have your friend compare this to the one you have," she whispers. "We could supply her with enough of this to last a year. I have been saving it in hope I can make something new from it. It is the right weight and strength for wrapping delicate cakes. She will find other uses for it as well."

Tucking the two pieces of linen into my robe, I depart for the wagon. The morning is cool and the sun is bright. It will be a good day for business. Elon runs to the wagon ahead of me. He is thrilled to show me my reward has not spoiled his desire to work hard. There are already people waiting at the wagon to buy oil and olives. One of them is Joseph.

"Good morning," he says. "I have recalled something you may not have."

"Oh," I answer, "what might it be?"

"I have met your father before, and perhaps you," he replies. "We stayed overnight with a family in Kerioth on our return journey to Nazareth about fourteen years ago. My oldest was just a boy. Your father had a building where he stored supplies obviously arranged to welcome guests and travelers in need. My parents had only three children then. Now there are seven children and the two of us. We are blessed that the carpentry trade is a fulfilling one."

I want to avoid learning anything further about this family. Still, this man is just being friendly. "I know my father takes in many travelers. It is part of his way of honoring the Law. You should know he may not remember you. Such is the way with those who host many for a short time. They are memorable but remember little."

"It may be so," offers Joseph, "I would still like to see him again and know you all better. You were of service to my family in time of need. I would feel good if I could offer something to all of you."

"It is not necessary, Joseph," I counter. "I will pass along to father your request, but for now I must attend to my cart and customers."

"Of course," he responds, "I will leave you to it. I would like two measures of olives for our dinner this evening. I remember the ones served to us in Kerioth. I am sure they are dear due to their quality, but Mary will enjoy them greatly."

I pass him on to Elon who measures out the olives into the basket Joseph has brought. He charges Joseph the new price and I think for a moment to intervene. Caution gets the upper hand in my thoughts, however. Any favoritism might further the danger of an encounter between my father and the Romans he hates so deeply. There are plenty of customers and I must attend them.

I say a brief goodbye to Joseph and work on the line forming at the gate of the wagon. Joseph quickly disappears into the crowd. The day is busy and profitable. We will be out of olives by mid-day tomorrow at the pace we are working. The oil will last longer. There is much more of it. The higher prices are not a deterrent. Near mid-day Sari and Puah bring us some meat and vegetables wrapped in bread. There is also a portion of the placenta from last night. Puah has also brought Calah to assist us and his hands are welcome. Puah returns to the linen wagon where sales are also high. Sari stays suggesting I go invite Veena to dine with us.

I am still hesitant. It feels too close to the Romans. It is crawling with the real danger of my father and Longinus finding each other and my father seeking his vengeance. I still cannot understand my lack of hatred for the man who killed my mother. Sari, however, is insisting we extend friendship and hopefully a business arrangement with Veena. She is right, and her heart is for friendship with her, business or no. I check I have both linen samples and make my way across the crowded cacophonous market.

Veena is there working as busy a trade as we are. I wait for a lull, which takes half of an hour. When it happens, I approach her booth. "Greetings, Veena," I begin. "Joseph introduced us yesterday. The placenta cakes were delicious."

"I saw you standing there," she counters. "If you wanted more cakes, you would have just purchased them. Do you wish something further?"

There is an edge in her voice. She does not know me and I am sure many men have sought more from her. I am reminded again how difficult it is to be a woman alone in this world. My gratitude for my father caring for my aunts is renewed. I am aware of the struggle it is to be alone in this time and this place. I know the dangers all of our women face.

I look her in the eyes, "My aunts would like for you to dine with us tonight. They would like to discuss some business with you, but also want to meet the woman responsible for our delicious desert last night."

"What type of business could two respectable women wish to discuss with me?" she asks me without hiding any of her animosity.

"I can actually answer your question," I reply holding out the two pieces of creamy white linen. "Can you see or feel the difference in the quality? We all think you can enhance your cakes by trading for our linen which is better quality and will keep your cakes fresh longer."

"I will come but I am dubious this will work in my favor," she frowns, "I will bring more placenta cakes to share."

I had not thought her so angry and jaded. Still she agreed to come. Leaving the linen samples for her to consider I turn to make my way back to the olives and oil. Just a few feet away are Patrius and another Centurion. I lower my head hoping he does not see me. It seems to work. I make my way past them keeping people between us. I am just past him when I overhear Patrius command the other Centurion.

"We will make an example of some of the vendors tonight," says Patrius. "The order from Prefect Gratus is to make it known the higher tax will apply to everyone not just the locals. You will have five Legionnaires to help enforce the new law. Do not kill anyone, but see to it the message is delivered clear."

The Centurion answers, "Has anyone been exempt as a target? I know some merchants pay the priests and the palace for special protection."

Patrius nods, "I have a list for you. The carpenter from Nazareth is not on it, but he is our friend and will be left alone. Both Maxim and Portimus would be enraged were Joseph and his family given any trouble. See to the list and warn them Amulius. I will speak with Joseph. Get it done before the dinner hour. We will strike after nightfall."

Hearing this I cannot get to my family quickly enough. I know father will be hard to manage but he will also know how to protect our interests. Father is at the larger linen wagon. Everything is as it should be; the crowds buy bolts of linen and robes made from the same fabric. The dyed linen sells at a cost significantly higher.

Between their trade with the Egyptians and the Ethiopians our family is able to acquire the best and rarest dyes.

Approaching my father quietly, I ask to speak with him privately. He motions toward our tent in the midst of the wagons. I nod indicating this will do and follow him to the tent. He asks Puah to take his spot at the linen cart.

"What is it, son?" he begins. "We are very busy."

"We are also in danger," I retort. "I overheard the Romans are planning some trouble tonight to drive home the seriousness of the new taxes."

"So, the cobras have grown restless," he growls.

"Father," I begin with compassion and hesitation, "there is more you need to know but you must remain calm."

He gives me the look demanding information and promises no patience will follow. I have begun so I must continue. "The Centurion giving the order is Patrius. He is following orders from the new Prefect. No one is to be killed but there is danger. We must move everything before dinner."

The anger flaring in my father's eyes could set fire to water. He speaks with no hint of understanding we must be restrained. "I knew Longinus was here. He is Commander of the garrison. That Patrius is as well is opportunity. There are enough of those here who hold my views on Rome to end these two miserable men. Let them come. They will die."

I must try to stop him because it is more likely he will be the one to die. "Father this is not the way. It is Passover. We are to be focused on God and the Law. We are supposed to offer peace and kindness to foreigners. We are obligated to hospitality."

His anger at full boil will scald any who try to simmer it, "We are obligated to protect God's land. We are required to defend his Law. These two men took what was most precious to me and they will pay. Rome will pay. Anyone who violates our family will pay. I will not serve anyone but God and will serve him by severing the lives of these two like I would a poison limb from an olive tree."

"Father," I protest, "we are in a city with a large garrison. Even if we succeed, we will not escape."

"There is no 'we' in this," insists father, "I will act and will include some friends who would die to see these men get justice. You son, you will care for the family and get them safely to Cana." Turning fiercely, he leaves without another word.

I let business continue until there is an afternoon lull. Then I instruct the family to pack everything and move it to the home of Shlomi's family. Everyone protests but my statement father has ordered it is enough. We move everything amidst questions from the seed vendor on our left and the man with charms and talismans on our right. The only answer I give them is my father has said to pack up for the night since our business has been so fruitful.

The talisman vendor presses me and I simply tell him I honor my father's wishes and it should be enough. He is not a Jew so does not understand this thinking. When I finish packing the wagon and he is still questioning me I give him a measure of our best olives and a flask of oil to shut him up. It works and I pull the cart out of the market. After the night is over, when I return to the market in the morning to assess the damage, I realize my gift contributed to his death.

Father returns just before midnight. He is dirty and bloodied, though none of the blood is his. As he enters the house, he cautions Sari and I to be quiet. We have waited up for his safe return or whatever else unfolded. Sari silently brings water to wash him. As she cleans her cousin, he reviews what has happened.

"The Romans entered the market from the far end from our place there," he begins. "They were armed with cudgels but had on full armor and carried both gladius and pilum. We had clubs and sica but no armor. There were twenty Legionnaires and the two Centurions, Patrius and some other I do not know. There were six of us in hiding behind one of the houses ringing the market area."

Father's expression shows he knows the mob was outnumbered and outmatched. "The Romans began to overturn carts and stalls immediately. Anyone who resisted was cudgeled." He pauses, takes a breath and a drink of water, then continues, "I urged the others to hold back. I knew we could not stop the soldiers. There were just not enough of us."

He pauses again. It is easy to see how difficult it all is for him. The pain in his eyes moves me to stop him but I let him continue. "Silas of Bethel moved first. He is always, or was always mindless of the danger. He was all action and no thought. One of the Legionnaires cudgeled him cold when he ran at the group of them screaming epithets. He was not dead then. When the real violence began the same soldier returned to where Silas lay unconscious and put his gladius through him without a thought. When Silas first fell the other men advanced on the market. I did not."

Father pauses again in his telling. The death of Silas has him near tears. The rest seems too much for him to tell. He still does. "When the men attacked the soldiers, they immediately closed ranks to repel us. Trained soldiers who follow their training outmatch Zealots with no plan every time. It was true in this case. I knew we would all die and so I stayed in the shadows. They all did."

He takes another long drink of water and a few sobs escape him. "I watched them all get cut down. The Romans switched to swords.

Everyone one else was running from the market. The soldiers killed a few of them as well. Then they set on their original task. They began turning over and burning carts and stalls."

My father goes on to explain they chose vendors at random and destroyed all they could. If money fell from a cart or booth the Romans took it. Once they made a complete circle around the market, Patrius gave the order to stop. The soldiers did so immediately. Father said he withdrew and checked on the place where our carts had been. It was there he found the talisman vendor. He was already dead but still burning. The smell of burnt olive oil was obvious.

Father observed it looked like the fire was the result of the broken flask of olive oil spilling on the man and his being set on fire. He could not tell if it were an accident or intentional. He offered that either way the Romans were guilty of the man's death. I had to agree.

We convince father to go to sleep and the rest of us try to do the same. I lay awake for some time pondering the implications of the night. Who would react to the attacks and how? The resistance would surely be emboldened. The priests would have to publicly condemn the act but I wondered how they really viewed it. I drifted into a restless sleep and in the early morning wakened with alarm. My thoughts were on Veena, the spice merchant. I quickly dress and make my way to the market.

Nothing seems to have been cleaned up yet. Some vendors are tentatively returning to the market area. Legionnaires are posted all around it but ignoring everyone. Their presence is to drive home the message of the previous night and deter any response others might dare levy against the normal compliment of sentries in the market. I can see none of the Centurions I know. In fact, there are no officers present. This also seems curious.

The lovely wretched aroma of burnt spices draw me toward Veena's booth. She was supposed to come for dinner. The assault by the Roman's prevented it. The wood of the booth is still smoking. Bubbling oils put forth a sickly-sweet pungency repeatedly assaulting the senses. Veena is nowhere in the rubble. This both sooths and alarms me. At least I will not find her like the talisman monger. She, at least is not a burned corpse among her own wares. This does not mean she is unharmed so I continue to search.

Since her wagon is back further than her booth, I search there next. I find it damaged and empty. A quick check of the wagon rubble also reveals it has been searched and looted. Perhaps the Romans set the booth ablaze and went around it. Still, I need to find Veena. Emerging from behind the smoldering booth I find her standing there with the carpenter.

"I suppose I am late for dinner," she quips. Her casual words do not sufficiently mask her pain at the loss.

I try to match her timbre but my heart is not in it, "I am pleased you are not harmed. I came to see if you needed help. We were going to invite you to do business with us. My sisters thought of the idea. If you do need assistance, you are welcome to come to our home. If we can help you recover, we will."

Her smile softens and is genuine. "Joseph and his family cared for me over the night. I was able to escape with my coin. I was just coming to see if my wagon was usable."

I nod at Joseph then reassure Veena, "Your wagon is lost as well. I am pleased to see you are well. I can help you move what is left to you. You are welcome to join us for the remainder of the week."

Joseph remarks, "You are welcome with us as well Veena, though you may find the company of the olive and linen merchants more entertaining than my constant creation of wood shavings."

A ripple of genuine laughter passes between us and Veena looks at me for reassurance. I nod. Turning to Joseph, she speaks, "Thank Mary for the meal and the comfort. When I replenish my stocks, I will send the oils your daughters were going to purchase. I will get them to you in Nazareth."

"Nazareth," I respond involuntarily. "I did not know you lived in Nazareth, Joseph."

"I do," confirms the carpenter, "I have lived there for some years. I have a small carpentry shop. It does well enough because the city is on a trade route."

"We are moving to Cana after Passover." I offer. "We will be practically neighbors. If you come with us Veena, we can help you establish a place. The land we have will make it easy for us."

Joseph nods his understanding and Veena gestures toward the wagon. "Let us recover what we can and join your family. Perhaps I can be of some help with their remaining trade efforts."

We easily gather her few remaining belongings and return to Shlomi's family home where ours are. Puah and Sari come out immediately to see to Veena. She obviously does not need their care but allows it out of kindness and humility. It gives me a glimpse into her character. She is strong and kind. Those two things are not often seen in balance as they are in Veena.

The women retreat back into the house. Father tells us to get our carts back out to the market but to cut our prices to cost for anyone who is a fellow merchant. His thought is they have suffered enough. The day before Passover is a somber one when the air should be filled with mirth and anticipation. The dead are prepared for burial with the rush of caring for them before the Sabbath. Some from far away must buy or borrow tombs. The somber nature of this Passover will be remembered for many years.

We choose not to stay for the market after the celebration. We take the meal with Shlomi's family. Veena helps as if she has prepared the meal with my family her entire life. We pack up the day after the Sabbath and begin our journey to Cana.

We invite the carpenter and his family to travel with us. He explains his eldest son is meeting with some old friends from the Temple and they will not depart until he is ready. Joseph introduces me to his nephew, John, who makes a joke about them leaving their son behind one year. Joseph laughs but there is something in his eyes.

As we part ways the carpenter offers, "I have a house in Nazareth. Please stay there overnight on your way to Cana. I will give you a note for the garrison commander there. He is a good man and a friend of many years."

Father turns red at the mention of another Roman. He also accepts graciously. Joseph gives him a hastily written note explaining Maxim will know his writing and accept them there. We say our farewells then make our way out of town.

Father's anger is renewed as he has to pay the exit tax imposed by Rome. He wonders if he will ever be shed of Rome. He considers never coming to Jerusalem again. We both know when he counts the profits from the market he will relent. His conversation on the road turns to Cana and the possibilities ahead of us.

Galilee and Canna

We spend most of the first day's travel paying attention to our wagons. The flow of people north is less than the flow south. We are used to the heavy exodus south of those from the more populace lower two-thirds of the nation. Still the road is crowded and movement is slow. The hope is to arrive at Sychar for the night.

Father had left word at the inn there on a trade trip we would require lodging after the Passover. He has stayed there several times over the years. It is where I was cared for on the way back from Nazareth after mother was murdered. The innkeeper there is good to my father.

We stop mid-morning for water. When we do, Veena chooses to ride with me for the remainder of the mooring. As we make our way up the road all is quiet at first. The day is cool but the collective heat and dust of the many animals, carts, and people on the road make it unpleasant. There is also the smell. Still we only have to endure it a few times of year.

After about an hour Veena breaks the silence, "I wanted to ask you about your family's expectations. You seem to be good people but I wanted to be sure there were no surprises. What will be expected of me what we arrive at your new home?"

It takes a moment for me to understand what she means. When I do, I feel a rush of embarrassment. "We will give you a place with the other women and you will be treated with all respect and purity. We observe the Law of Moses in our home in all things."

Veena laughs at my formality. I can hear in her laughter relief as well. As a single merchant, I am sure she has been put in threatening positions often. Looking her in the eye, I promise, "You will be safe with us. You will be treated like family or better. We will help you establish your business and work together to benefit each other."

Her eyes soften for a moment, "Thank you for indulging my fear. I was uncertain I had made the right choice and I meant no disrespect."

We grow silent again and enjoy the morning ride. When stopping for lunch, Veena moves back to the wagon with the other women. Father gives me a look asking if he needs to know what was going on between us. I wave it away with a pointed look and put the thought from my mind. I want a family eventually but the unrest in the world and our current lack of settlement makes those ideas hold a lesser priority.

Still, I consider Veena. She is smart, strong, and hard working. She would surely fit in with our family. Perhaps she will find someone in Cana. It occurs to me in the moment Veena is beautiful and would make a good wife. If father gets it into his head to make a match for us, I will have little choice. I will not consider this now, however, we have a village to reach and a home to establish.

We reach Sychar just before the sun sets. The innkeeper confirms the space father reserved is available. He comments it was wise of father to plan so far ahead of the time. He has rented out all his rooms, the quarters reserved for Romans, the cattle shed, and the stable. He has even set up several booths in the garden to allow for people to at least have shelter for the night.

Galilee And Canna

The Samaritan may not be welcome at the Passover in Jerusalem, but he is smart enough to profit from it. He seems a good man and is attentive to every guest. The meal he offers us fits our dietary laws and is also rich and plentiful. Tables are set in the large common room and in the court area around the well. His son and servants see we are all fed and our needs are heard.

As the meal is ending some men form the town come by to inquire if any repairs are needed before travel continues in the morning. Throughout the evening other travelers arrive and none are turned away. The area around the well is cleared and people are allowed to set up their area of rest for the night there. Again, the innkeeper collects only a modest fee to cover the evening meal and another one in the morning.

Even though our room is spacious, we are a large group and it is slightly crowded. Father erects a curtain to separate the women and the men. We all lay down to rest for the night. The sounds of the inn grow quieter. I lay awake pondering the last week as sleep claims the others one-by-one.

It is in this still darkness, surrounded by resting family I feel the pressure of the times in which we live. The cobras are stirring and will not remain in their baskets. Even strong people are not safe alone. I drift off pondering we need someone, something to set the course for our freedom, our future. I wonder how we will rid our nation of the cobras and protect women like Veena. It is in this thought in this night I decide my father is right and my heart becomes that of a Zealot.

In the morning we rise early. The great flood north of people traveling from Jerusalem will begin today. As new guests arrive from

Jerusalem here, we will arrive in Nazareth. I am concerned as we break our fast and begin the journey my father will feel his heart-wound freshly opened. Were it up to me, we would move east and take the longer road to Galilee. The risks of being on the greater road are worth it in my mind compared to the pain my father still feels over my mother's death.

Father is determined to go to Nazareth, so north we head. We are the first to leave Sychar and have the road to ourselves for most of the morning. The road to Nazareth is both well-traveled and well made. We can travel at a leisurely pace and still make the city before nightfall. Father suggests at mid-morning we allow Ehud and Elon to drive our respective wagons so they can learn whilst it is safe.

He suggests we walk behind the wagons so we can talk and still observe the young boys as they drive. The beasts pulling the wagons know this part of the journey and will follow the wagons driven by Judah and Caleb. Father waits until the wagons and walkers fall into a steady pace before he begins to speak.

"Judas," he starts, "we have business to discuss you should know. Whether you take part in it or not, I have a reason for going to Nazareth."

I presume the moment I have wanted is here at last. Father is about to tell me what he really does and involve me in it. I am not disappointed as he continues, "We are meeting some men in Nazareth to receive some weapons. We will store them in our new home so they are available to our supporters when needed."

I am clearly puzzled as I inquire, "Our supporters?" I ask, "Who is supporting us in what, and why?"

He pauses, takes a breath, and answers, "Since before your uncles were killed, our family has been one of the lead families of the rebellion. We have been Sicarii since your Grandfather was alive. Your uncles were delivering weapons when they were attacked by the

Romans and killed. Had the soldiers searched their wagon I would be dead as well. At that time, I had not made the decision that you have to make on this day. I was not yet a Zealot."

There it was. The admission was laid at my feet by father. He and his brothers were Zealots. He and his brothers were part of the rebellion against Rome. I had often wondered when his trips for the merchant shop were business and when they were for other purposes.

Twice I had secretly followed him out of Kerioth to learn what he was doing. Both times he had met with other men. They talked long and money changed hands. I had been able to pick out specific words and knew that these discussions would lead to great danger for our people; for my family.

I can do nothing but listen. Anger and awe coursed through me. I had just chosen to become what my father is. I was certain of it. Now God was opening the door for my chosen path in the simplest way possible. Still, I do not wish to hate but I am filled with anger. I do not want to be violent but we are in a silent war. There must be a way to follow the path of a Zealot without taking up the Sica; without becoming a Sicarii. Now, father has stopped speaking. He looks at me, waiting for my response.

Looking at him in a new light with great determination I answer, "I want to join you. We must free our nation. We have to defend our homeland. It is our duty to cleanse the corruption of the palace and the temple. We must build our forces and become organized."

"Slowly son, slowly," he responds. "We will get there soon enough. The move to Cana is to put them off our trail. It is also to bring us closer to people who will fight with us. In Kerioth we could not reach our political foes easily enough. We can build our forces and draw less attention to who it is troubling Rome. For today we go to Cana in Galilee to establish ourselves as good honest merchants."

I can hear the confidence and surety under the resentment. He is angry. He is filled with hatred for Rome. He is also cunning and shrewd. Eventually I will ask him how long he has been playing his patient waiting game. For now, I can tell he has said all he wishes.

"Father," I begin, "I will do as you ask. We will build our business in Cana. I will learn what you need me to know. Then, together, we will rid our land of cobras."

Father smiles as he moves forward at a trot. For a moment he seems younger and I see what it means for his son to join him in the fight against the darkness in our land. He swings up into the head cart and takes the leads.

It has been a decade since I heard what happened next. Ten years ago father took me to Egypt with him for the first time to begin teaching me the trade and the trade routes. It was just the two of us for the first time since father brought me home from Nazareth after mother's death. When we set out from Kerioth, he told me this time was for us to build what we would become as father and son who were also men.

We discussed the Law of Moses. We pondered the great questions surrounding God and his ways together. Father was pleased at my depth of memory and understanding of the Law and the Prophets. We allowed our cart to move at a slow pace because the conversation made it all seem to be slipping by too quickly.

As we stopped in each town where father had trade business, he proudly introduced me as his son. He announced to the merchants and local authorities he was teaching me his trade so I could represent him in the years to come. There were jokes and jibes at my expense because I was young. I could tell it was all done in a light-hearted spirit.

In a couple of towns, I noticed men passing father packages or scrolls but no coin exchanges hands. Father puts these items in the cart underneath the bags and bedding sitting closest to the front of the cart with our personal belongings; not our trade goods. When we bed down in the cart on some nights, after he thinks I have fallen asleep, he moves these to a compartment under the cart seat. I was tempted to peek when he was away but my value in the trust we are building is too great.

When we crossed into Egypt father explained there were some customs we needed to observe carefully here. He cautioned me not to speak to anyone he had not already spoken to unless they spoke to me first. He explained most merchants here would hand me what they wished me to examine and we would have to do the same. Egyptian merchants did not barter in the same way either. It is a more graceful dance but items still get bought and sold at a price fair to both parties.

The long journey through Egypt is going well. Father says I am learning quickly. He lets me handle a few trades on my own to see if I understood the balance between haggling over a price and winning. He observes I have done well but I push too soon. He advises I need to wait until the merchant is ready to act or I risk losing the entire effort.

I know father is right. I am anxious about disappointing him or that the merchant will not buy. I listen to father but there is something deep inside me needing to push the event; needs to demand the merchant act. Still I learn and force my efforts to comply to father's wishes. Then the moment comes.

We are making our way north again from Egypt during this journey; stopping in a small town where father says he we will rest for the Sabbath. The slow pace requires it, but I do not mind. There is an inn in the town. We are the only guests. The innkeeper asks if we will join them for dinner. Father explains we cannot because we must observe our traditions. The innkeeper shows us to a room leaving us to settle.

As we put things away, the innkeeper returns with unleavened bread and sweet wine for us. He explains, "My wife always makes a few loaves of Sabbath bread each week in case we get travelers from Judea. The wine is from a Jewish merchant as well. Please enjoy it with my blessing."

Father thinks I do not see him sneak the piece of paper from under the bread basket. He slips it into his tunic adroitly but not unseen. We pray the Sabbath prayers and dine. We enjoy the wine and discuss the final leg or our journey. Father suggests I head off to sleep so we can enjoy the day together well rested. I conclude he is anxious to read the message and do not let on.

I drink the last of my wine and retire to our room. I awaken when father comes in later. I pretend to be asleep and listen as he settles for the night. Father is quickly asleep. I know he will sleep late. He always does on the Sabbath. He takes the day of rest quiet seriously. I drift back to sleep wanting to awaken early.

Father is snoring deeply when I awaken to the first tendrils of dawn. I slip quietly out of the room and go to the wagon. Carefully reaching over the supplies in the wagon, I open the compartment. The note is there on top of the other things father has sequestered away. Noting its place and position I take it out. I carefully unfold the thick paper. The note s brief and cryptic.

> We have acquired the weapons needed for the meeting in Jerusalem. We will adopt the clever knives provided by Alexander in Asia Minor. His metal work produced a short fast blade he calls a Sicar. We requested enough of them to arm us all. We will use them to identify each other. The weapons will drain the lives of our enemies

through deft strokes, deep and quiet. Meritus, my son will meet you at the market to make the exchange.

Putting the note back carefully and closing the compartment, I hurry back to our room Father is still asleep when I return. It occurs to me I am unsettled by the idea of a weapon designed only for killing. I am also troubled that so soon after joining my father in learning his business I am already deceiving him.

I wonder in which city father will make the exchange. Pondering the danger of being caught by Roman soldiers with even one sword let alone a cache of weapons unnerves me. Further, these weapons will be instantly recognized for their purpose.

Considering how all of this fits within the Law, I wonder how father plans on living out the command Joshua, David, and even Solomon failed to obey. The nation is not what it was then. I think only Messiah could overthrow Rome. I pray he will come. Then, father stirs form his rest.

We pass the Sabbath Day at rest. We talk and eat and pray. The innkeeper provides us with fresh water and breads. Father will not work on the Sabbath but sees no harm in honoring a host who does by enjoying his warm flatbread. In the evening we are given roasted lamb and root vegetables In the late evening we rest again intending to get an early start.

Whilst drifting off to sleep, again I ask God to send our deliverer with urgency. I do not want father to be in danger. I do desire for our nation to have its proper place in the world. I do want all things made right again. In the night I dream of a nation where Messiah rules and our enemies are our servants. In the morning, what I remember clearly is the white horse he rides and the power of his voice to turn men to his will.

Father and I begin the return journey north as soon as it is light enough to see. The day is not uncomfortable and we are able to travel well. We visit two small towns where father picks up raw supplies needed to dye the linens we make. He is pleased to get a good buy on the ingredients for our dark red dye. We sell the red linen and wool for much higher prices than the other colors. The only thing more valuable is the blue rendered from oysters collected on the Great Sea. We do not, however, trade in the blue dye even though we could make a higher profit. The law forbids consumption of oysters, but father goes further. He will not even use them.

There are others sources of blue dye. They are more costly and less beautiful. Father is satisfied with the law and keeping it. I ponder often if God really wishes us to be poorer by taking the law further than it is written. When I asked him about this once he explained the idea of the letter and the spirit of the law. His interpretation of their relationship seems to always make things harder or more restrictive.

The contrast is his thinking hatred for things defying the Law or defiling our culture is somehow a permissible interpretation. The command to love our neighbor gets a narrow assessment of who our neighbor is from him.

The fervor of hatred for our enemies widens and grows. Still, I am determined to support him. I will hate Rome with him and find a way to make a profit. I will do whatever is necessary to advance our freedom but I will not kill; at least at this moment I believe I will not. I am again getting ahead of the sequence. We will get back to this.

Galilee And Canna

Arriving in Nazareth is unimpressive. Father leads us far around the Roman Garrison. We can see Legionnaires moving in front of the gate at the low garrison wall. The guards at the city gate barely slow us down. The traffic will be heavy on the primary roads and little worry is given a few Jews who are obviously returning from the Passover.

Father sees a woman selling honey, wax, and candles from the porch of her home. He inquires politely as to the location of the home of Joseph the carpenter. She directs us to an open area toward the northern gate of the city. We find it easily enough. The rustic house is simple but well-kept and clean. The goat pen behind the house has upwards of twenty goats and there is a small shed with chickens in it. The building beyond is obviously the carpentry shop.

Out of respect for Joseph, we enter only the house. Father quickly asks the younger men and the women to see to the feeding of the goats and fowl. Veena brings back eight eggs and mentions it is obvious someone has been caring for the animals. If the carpenter's family has been gone for over a week, there should be more disarray and less care. Father and I agree and I take up sitting in front of the house to receive whoever comes to check on Joseph's home.

Our own supplies are added to the eggs and soon the smell of dinner reaches me sitting on a well-made stool in the front yard. I stay my post but poke my head into the house to see what is being made. Veena sees me and smiles. She holds up a plate of flatbread frosh from the stone oven. Checking to see she is unnoticed; she throws one to me with a playful smile. I take a quick bite of the warm nutty loaf and think to return to the stool in the yard. A strong, stern voice behind me freezes my motion.

A deep rich commanding voice asks, "May I enjoy one of those? They smell wonderful. I have had a great variety of myrrh here but none that smelled like that."

An older Roman officer stands there armed and armored; carrying a gladius and a pilum. He is smiling as if we are old friends. I do not know what to say, so I tear my bread in half and hand the unbitten part to him. "I suppose you are wondering why we are at Joseph's home."

The Roman officer smiles broadly. "I am used to Joseph saving people a few coins by letting them stay in his home. I am here to care for the goats and chickens. It must make me look out of place to say so, but Joseph is a friend; a long-time friend."

I sputter, then I recover enough to respond, "I am Judas. Our family is on the way to Cana to live. Joseph offered us his home for the night."

"That is understandable," he begins. "I am Maxim, I command the garrison in Nazareth. Where is your family moving from?"

It was at this moment father emerges from the back of the yard to check on me. He finds me in the midst of conversation and breaking bread with a Roman. It is not just any Roman or Centurion. It is General Maxim of Rome. He is legend and he is rumor. He is deadly and dangerous but also reputed to be kind to Jews. He is standing in front of me and father is right behind me.

"Father," I begin, sure there is actual terror in my voice, "this is General Maxim, leader of the Garrison. He is here to check on the chickens."

My fumbling introduction is a gift from God. Maxim laughs. Father almost laughs. I feel embarrassed and foolish. Still the moment prevents something unpleasant from emerging. My pride matters little if father does not act out in anger. The laughter fades and my father further surprises me.

Simon of Kerioth greets the General with Ernest warmth, "We are guests in Joseph's home. I am sure he would not mind if we offered you dinner. Please dine with us and we may know each other better."

Maxim returns the genuine kindness, "I would like that. The bread is delightful and I would avoid the garrison food tonight. Gallus is cooking and he can make water taste overcooked."

Leading the General to the doorway, father calls to the house, "We have a guest for dinner, make some more flatbread."

Dinner is soon set; we all gather at Joseph's table. It amuses me how quickly we feel at home in a relative stranger's house. I am further intrigued by the dinner conversation between father and the General. Maxim reveals that even though he retains his rank, he is retired officially. He has chosen to remain in Nazareth because of his proximity to Jerusalem and his relationship with Joseph's family.

Father relates tales of the trade routes and the two discover they have been to many of the same cities. Even though the garrison at Cana is small, Maxim offers to send an introduction to the Centurion there. He also mentions there are two different tax structures and he will ask our family be given the lesser one.

Veena has made many extra rounds of flatbread. Maxim eats two more entire rounds whilst the men talk around the table. He dips the torn pieces in olive oil flavored with herbs from a small basket Veena shares with no one. He also explains he is officially retired but retains his connections to Rome.

Maxim continues to explain he remains in Nazareth primarily due to his relationship with his younger officers. As he says this, he also mentions none of them are so young any more. Maxim is friendly. He and father talk long discussing the politics, travel, and trade of Galilee. When the evening finally ends, Maxim takes his leave and a bundle of fresh flatbreads with him. As he departs, he mentions, "My key officers, my adopted son, Portimus, Patrius, and Longinus in Jerusalem will know of you all and be advised to assist you whenever possible. Joseph invited you to his home. It is enough for me to think of you as friends."

I feel father bristle at the mention of Longinus and Patrius. I hear him take in a breath to speak words will harm us all. Stepping in front of father, I speak, "We are honored by your friendship and will send word of our progress once we reach Cana. Thank you for your kindness and respect General Maxim."

The flicker in his eyes is brief and barely perceptible. He senses something is not right but leaves it lying there unspoken. We will leave in the morning and we will continue to build toward real rebellion. We will also remember this man and his treatment of strangers. For now, however, I cannot close the door quickly enough and attempt to comfort father.

The women have cleaned everything to perfection. The children have aided the other men in loading the wagons and moving them to the road in front of the house. It is newly daylight when we depart. Father has left a note for Joseph and requesting he be able to return the hospitality should they ever come to Cana.

We put Nazareth behind us but father is still vexed. He speaks of robbing the man of his son in the way he was robbed of his wife. He talks of hatred and vengeance all the way to Cana. I know he is right about Rome but still cannot resolve the hatred with the Law. I find I am again praying silently for Messiah to come to destroy our enemies and make the rule of God a reality on earth. This is what occupies me all the way to Cana.

Cana perches on the high point before one begins the downward journey to the Sea of Galilee. It off the main trade road but not even a whole day's journey from Nazareth. Maxim had not been

Galilee And Canna

wrong about the garrison being small. The town was also quite small. It was not until we viewed our house and olive grove, we realized it was the largest thing about Cana. Wishing to arrive quietly did not unfold as we had hoped.

Another aspect of Cana is the rapid spread of rumors. Everyone is aware of what everyone is doing. The kinsmen who deeded the house and property to father had mentioned to the soldiers we would be coming after Passover. When our carts crests the ridge, a call goes out from the lone sentry at what passes for a gate to the town. It becomes immediately obvious we are expected and eagerly anticipated.

The entire village rushes out to meet us. Stopping outside the gate, we wait to see what will happen. A young Centurion and an older Rabbi stand at the head of the throng. He is taller than most Romans and his complexion is darker. He wears the typical armor and uniform of a Centurion who is always ready for and anticipating unrest. He even wears the shiny crested helm. The handle of his gladius reflects it has spent much time in hand. It is worn from use.

The badges on his leather depict him as having served for only five years. He must have someone's favor to reach the rank of Centurion so early in his service. Further observation reveals he has been to other places.

One of the markings on his vestment is the chevron with the eye of the pyramid at its center indicating he has served in Parthia. It is likely Maxim has requested him personally for this area. Next to him is an older Rabbi. He is in worn robes revealing little pomp or plumage like those in Jerusalem.

The Centurion steps forward in greeting, "I am Amulius Aratus, the commander of what passes for a Garrison here. At General Maxim's request, we have anticipated your coming and seen to it

The Judas Scroll

your home is prepared. This is Rabbi Esau, who serves as our town's Jewish and spiritual leader."

Father introduces us all to the two men but does so loudly enough that the rest of the gathering can hear him. Rabbi Esau steps forward and points down the path outside of the gate. "Your home is just past the end of the wall down there. The people have cleaned and provisioned the house in anticipation of your coming. We are all anxious to get back to what we are used to around here."

Father looks perplexed but no one questions the obvious implication. At his movement we follow father toward our new home. So does the Centurion, the Rabbi, and half the town. The crowd escorts our family to the house and insists on helping us settle. They set to unloading the carts and tending to the animals pulling them.

I am the only one who notices father's alarm as people begin unloading his cart. I know there is contraband in the compartment. I quickly ask young Keren to sit on the bench of the cart so she may watch the activity without being under foot. She is happy to do so as she never gets to sit in the front of the cart. The little girl will sit there and no one will disturb her.

They were serious when telling us they had cared for and provisioned the house. The food and other household needs are plentiful. The rooms are clean and free of any sign of neglect. Women from the village show Sari, Puah, and Veena the functional parts of the house. It is much more spacious than father led us to believe. Rabbi Esau shows father and I the rooms. When we reach what appears to be a large empty room the Rabbi pauses. "This," he begins, "is where the wedding feasts are hosted."

The room is paneled in fine cedar. It smells like a well-crafted chest. One can easily seat a hundred people here in addition to banquet tables. Even with people seated it has room for dancing. The outside wall has large sliding panels allowing the room to be opened to the yard. Celebrations can flow from inside to outside easily in good weather. The space is designed for celebrations.

"Wedding feasts?" inquires father with a hint of alarm.

"Yes," confirms Rabbi Esau, "all of our wedding feasts are hosted here. It is the only place in the village large enough. There are over one hundred and fifty years of tradition hosting weddings in this room. It would be a shame to abandon this legacy. Many young women already look forward to their own wedding feast here."

Father actually sputters. I am not sure which is more alarming. He would not want his home invaded whenever there was a marriage but he also is wary of the secrecy required in order to pursue Rome and her destruction. Adding to this, Rabbi Esau sees his shock as hesitance.

"Do not be concerned," reassures Esau, "the families take care of most of the expenses. The former owner, however, was known for his wine and its quality. I am sure you will settle in and provide great wedding feasts and fine wine for years to come."

Father, still speechless. nods in understanding. The Rabbi interprets this as agreement. He smiles and speaks his first blessing over our new home.

After all of our belongings are settled and the animals cared for, the villagers depart. Amulius lingers and makes sure he knows every family member's name. Father explains Veena is from Joppa but came under our care in Jerusalem. He tries to avoid mentioning the trouble during Passover but chooses to tell the tale to Amulius. He includes the part where her cart and all her wares were burned.

The Centurion nods as he listens. When father is finished, Amulius responds, "I will enter a note in the town census and advise my men she is part of your family. No one here will harass her and I may be able to arrange for her to meet some oil and spice purveyors in the area." He smiles broadly as he continues, "I know the wedding conversation surprised you. It is not as much of a burden as it sounds. You have enough wine in your stores for years to come. One of my men comes from a family of growers outside of Rome. He would gladly share his knowledge and lend a hand."

Father regards the man for a moment. From where I stand, Amulius is genuine. He tries to keep the peace in Cana by being good to the people. We must watch to be sure but the first steps in Cana seem peaceful enough. Even if Cana is all it presents itself to be, father will not long stay from his activities with the resistance. Would we could stop encountering the few Romans seem to be men of character. It blurs the line I have so recently crossed.

Realizing Amulius' comment requires a response, father acquiesces, "Please, send your man around. My knowledge of vineyard work could use some expert guidance. I am sure I can compensate him for his time."

Amulius holds up a large callused hand, "I will not hear of it. The success of the village keeps the peace. That is my primary concern. It also helps me understand the people under my care." The Roman rises, "I will leave you to settle your home, Simon. Welcome to Cana. If you are up early you will be able to smell the wind from the sea. It is quite lovely."

Father smiles again. It is genuine. He walks to the gate with the Roman and stands there watching as the soldier walks the short road back toward the garrison. I wait in the doorway for him. He turns and waves me over to him at the gate. He gestures toward the bench that is part of the low wall around our yard. It is the first time we sit on the stone bench in the late evening. It is not the last. It will become my favorite place for communication and connection with others.

We talk of the Roman and his apparent kindness. Father is skeptical. He expresses disappointment that I am impressed. I struggle with the disapproval and with the idea of a Roman living out the command to love your neighbor and father is not. Moses made it clear. We are not to *"seek revenge or bear a grudge against anyone among your people, but love your neighbor as yourself. I am the Lord."*

It is the "I am the Lord" part that concerns me. It is very clear God wants us to love each other and not be vengeful. Father would counter that the Romans are not "your people." He has before. The prophet Malachi reminds us God says, *"So I will come to put you on trial. I will be quick to testify against sorcerers, adulterers and sojourners, against those who defraud laborers of their wages, who oppress the widows and the fatherless, and deprive the foreigners among you of justice, but do not fear me," says the Lord Almighty."*

Again, there is the reminder it is God who commands us to love the strangers in our land. I listen to father with growing wonder at how I will balance obedience to him and adherence to all of the law. I love the Law of Moses. I love my father. The two seem to be strained in their relationship. I will pray before I sleep. Perhaps the morning will bring answers.

Morning comes. It is a clear day and after morning prayers I go to care for the animals. After breakfast I go out to inspect the vineyards with father. The soil here is rich and dark. It is clear the former owners cared for the land well. Father is carrying a scroll written on sheepskin. As he approaches, he holds it up.

"This is wonderful," he begins. "There is an entire set of instructions for planting, caring for, pruning, and harvesting the vineyard. There is another in the jug room for proofing and storing the wine. We will be successful here, I think."

I am as elated as he is. Then my mind dares to hope he will abandon his quest for vengeance and my joy flees. I know he will not. I know it will take something much more than good land and sweet grapes to ease the bitter pain in my father's soul. I shake off the pain of the moment and try to see the hope he feels and make it my own.

That first week we spend getting to know the land, the buildings, and the village. Ample grain and fodder have been left for planting and feeding. The instructions include a rotation cycle for leaving one seventh of the fields fallow each year. There are complete records going back six generations. The owners have observed a Year of Jubilee every seventh year as the law requires. The records confirm God has been faithful in his provision. Father assures me we will do the same.

We celebrate our first Sabbath at the new home. The food is rich. The time is both devout and joyful. After the meal I retire out into the yard to sit on the stone bench along the wall. The stars fill the night sky with their brilliant song of the Creator's glory. The moonless night allows me to watch and think through the events unfolding before me.

After about an hour a figure exits the house, moving toward me in the darkness. The only light is behind the person so I cannot tell who it is. The mild breeze reveals her identity before she reaches me. The scent of oil from lemons reveals it to be Veena. She carries a small jug and a cup.

"I have brought you some of the sweet wine we enjoyed at the end of the meal," says the woman. "The air will chill soon and if you are going to sit outside to rest, you had best keep warm."

Veena has also brought a cloak. My first thought is she is being very forward. Immediately, however, I recall her experience is not like a proper family of the chosen people. She does not know her actions are only used to express subtle interest in a man who is unrelated to her. The simple understanding is a woman who does things for a man who is not family one would do for family is seeking to be family.

The bench is wide enough for her to join me without us sitting more closely than protocol allows. Though the Pharisees would likely still frown upon it, I invite her to sit with me. It is not the first or last time I violate the practices reaching beyond the Law. God wants us to obey those who lead us. He does not, however, require us to live in the bondage they use to make our lives more burdensome.

Veena accepts my offer to sit. She pours some wine into the cup and passes it to me. It is sweet and she has warmed it on the cooking stones. "Thank you," I offer, "it is kind of you to be so thoughtful, or is it thoughtful of you to be so kind?"

Her laughter at my attempted humor is almost as sweet as the wine. Further ignoring protocol, I offer her some of the wine. She accepts it without hesitation. She drinks lightly but surely. I had seen her as independent and solitary. As we talk late into the spring evening, I begin to see her as complementary and strong. We talk of the future of the land and the potential of the vineyard. We discuss the patterns of growth and harvest, work and festivals, or our people. She is clear she is not virtuous or devout enough for a good family like mine. I am equally as clear my family is devout but we do not weight our loyalty like the Pharisees. Father has promised her safety with our family. I reassure her we all feel the same way.

I see the desire to trust this in her eyes but she is still unsure. We talk about the plans to begin work in town to establish relationships and learn the culture of the market. Long after the Ram has risen in the eastern sky, we choose to turn in for the night. I ask her to proceed to the house ahead of me at a respectable distance. When I do, I also see in her dancing eyes we both feel the undercurrent of what is there, but that rivulet is too unknown to navigate and too tenuous to name.

The morning after the Sabbath, I breakfast and go to look over the young leaves on the vines and check on the condition of the arbors. Clearly the arbors have been made with care and patience. Constructed of older, well cured grape vines, the supports are twisted from green wood, allowed to dry, and then bound together with smaller vines. The process consumes much time but yields long-lasting support for the growing vines.

As I inspect the planting of both the arbor and the vines a shadow falls across me. Unmistakable is the human form and the silhouette of the Roman helmet tops it. When I turn to meet the owner of the shadow, I am stunned by size of its owner and the darkness of the man. He is obviously Ethiopian. He is also the largest Roman soldier I have ever encountered. He carries a gladius and pugio but not a pilum. Instead of the common Roman spear he carries an oddly shaped pruning hook.

"Forgive me for giving you a start," begins the man. "Amulius sent me to help with the vineyards. I am Darrius. Well, that is my Roman name, given me by my benefactor."

I rise from the vines. "Welcome Darrius. I am Judas ben Simon. I will recover from the startle. We are already grateful for your help and counsel. "

We continue to exchange pleasantries. Then Darrius reveals he has long wished to inspect this vineyard. He explains the wine from here is almost legendary. He recounts how often it is the keystone to starting off parties and feasts, especially wedding feasts. Darrius admits he and the others at the garrison enjoy the feasts and almost always get invited.

As I listen, he transitions from history to the present. He explains he has been caring for the vines whilst awaiting our arrival. We walk through the vineyard and I can see yet another Roman who has character and desires to be neighborly. We agree to work the vineyard together. I insist I be able to pay. He counters he is forbidden and asks instead I supply the garrison with wine for the soldiers.

I realize there is a greater story to this man. I also understand it is not my place to know it yet. I also consider it valuable he cares to honor the men with whom he works. I take Darrius back to the wine house where we review the notes left by the previous owner. As he thumbs through the pages, he murmurs that the process used is excellent and offers there are possible adjustments to improve production volume and the fermentation process. It is clear this man is more at home in a vineyard than I will ever be.

We talk over plans for improvement until mid-day. Darrius agrees to dine with us. The day is cool enough out of the sun. Veena suggests we all eat outside. She collects the necessary things in a basket and we take our bread and cheese out to the olive grove closest to the house. Puah and Sari bring the children. Father joins us with a jug of wine from the stores. He pronounces a long blessing over the impromptu feast including Darrius by name in the blessing.

Darius greets each adult politely and allows the younger children to warm up to him. He learns each of their names and uses them to interact with their comments. Keren is the most resistant. She is always shy but also sees soldiers in uniform as something to fear. No one has told her to fear them. It reminds me most lessons for children are caught and not taught.

We linger for an hour over lunch discussing how we will begin to incorporate Darrius' ideas. Father is amenable to it all. After a time, Darrius excuses himself explaining he has duty at the gate in the afternoon. Sari and Puah herd the children away to their chores and afternoon lessons. Father, Veena, and I remain.

Father looks at us both, "We seem to be getting a handle on running the vineyard. We know how to attend the groves," he says gesturing to the budding trees. "We should use the afternoon to set up a grafting table so we can prepare new growth and take out some of the weaker trees. I will plant the saplings I brought from Kerioth. This soil is ideal for using branches to spawn suckers and those will be vibrant and well rooted. We can build prosperity here, but we must not forget our mission."

There it is again. Father feigns peace and friendliness. There is also always a river of venom lingering just below the surface. I wonder for the first time if we might be the cobras in baskets. I consider the people here have been kind and supportive. They have welcomed us. I will continue to wrestle with this. There must be a way to be faithful and not hate all Romans. For now, however, I have a table to build. I wonder if there is a carpenter in town.

Father rises. I choose to ask about my thoughts, "Father, we have plenty of funds, perhaps I should find a carpenter to build a table for us. Veena could accompany me into Cana and we can look for sources for her spice trade. Do you think it worth the effort?"

He nods, "Yes, we must get to know our neighbors and what benefits we can offer and receive from our new community. Veena should go with you. We would all profit from her trade. It is she, not just the spices creating her success. When you return, we should mark off a plot for her to grow what she needs to re-provision a spice wagon. If you find a carpenter, have him give you an estimate on a wagon to match the one she lost in Jerusalem. She is family now and we will support her."

Veena blushes and burns all at once. I can tell she is at war with her gratitude and independence. She looks at both of us, "I am grateful," she stammers. "I also insist I contribute to all of this."

Galilee And Canna

We both rise as father responds, "I see the way Judas looks at you. I see the fire in your eyes. The other women do not need help in the house. Grow your herbs and spices. Build your business and your trust in us. We will let God work guide in how to handle the rest." Turning to me he continues, "We may have found a hard-working virtuous woman, son. Best for you to start gather your rubies. See to it she is treated like family with every bit of respect that entails."

It is my turn to burn a little. I think I am keeping my reactions free of those Veena evokes. Then again, father is an astute observer of people. I choose the evasive path. "We will find out about a carpenter. If there is not one it may be worth it to visit Joseph in Nazareth for a wagon."

"Do as you think best," responds father. "Veena will choose where to invest in what she needs. It will be a good measure of her head for business. If you go to Nazareth, take one of the boys with you. They should begin to learn about trade and negotiation. It will suffice to please propriety in less loving strangers as well. Be sure to let the garrison know of your travel."

Again, there it is; father intentionally including the Romans. His motives confuse me but his reason is sound. Putting together a chain of safe encounters with them will build our security and has the impact of complying with the Law of Moses. No one is stranger in our land than the Romans.

After putting away the luncheon items, Veena joins me at the gate. We walk the path to the village in short time. Cana is small as towns go. Including houses there are less than fifty buildings. The market serves as the town center with a well and pens for sheep and goats. Clustered around the well are semi-permanent stalls for merchants. It is a market day and the stalls host sellers of cheese, beans, fresh vegetables, honey, olives, dates, figs, and chickens.

Veena suggests we visit each of the merchants. This takes a couple of hours as we must relate the story of our arrival here and our plans for the vineyard. It is clear there is already a general knowledge of our presence and we come from Kerioth. No one seems to know Veena joined us in Jerusalem and we do not choose to point it out.

We learn from Eli, one of the dairymen, that there is no carpenter in Cana. That settles the thought we must go elsewhere. He suggests the carpenter in Nazareth is an excellent one. We also choose not to reveal our knowledge or Joseph and his family. The thing I learn that is the most valuable is Veena takes my cues and follows them. She is savvy and wise when it comes to dealing with people.

She immediately makes friends with the one vendor selling spices. Tessa is the woman. She only offers basic spices like thyme, sesame, and dill. She states her business only flourishes because of the need. Were someone else to offer to sell what is needed in the village, she would gladly remain home and tend her husband's flocks with him. He sells goats for Sabbath and Festival meals. They also are the other vendors of goat's milk, cheese, and butter to the small town.

It is late afternoon before we complete our tour of the market. Veena agrees we should journey to Nazareth in the morning. She says she will have a sketch of the wagon she wishes built to take with us. We discuss what spices, herbs, and aromatics she thinks will flourish in the vineyard. Having walked the land a couple of times now, I think I know just the right area to make her garden. After dinner I will show her what I propose and let her decide. I do see the need and think we should gather seeds and cuttings whilst in Nazareth as well.

Supper is simple and excellent. Gathered around the table, we discuss plans for tomorrow. Father asks about our visit to the village. "Did you find a carpenter? Will you be able to get what you need?"

I shake my head as I answer, "No, father. We will need to travel to Nazareth tomorrow. If Veena and Calah can be spared for the day, I would like to take them with me."

Puah and Sari exchange glances briefly. Puah answers first, "We were thinking there is not enough to do in the house for all of us. Simon mentioned Veena might better serve the family by gardening and building spice trade. We agree. If Simon approves, we can care for the home and Veena can help when needed."

Sari adds, "It would be good for Calah to begin to learn how to trade with other men. He may go as long as he stays close by your side Judas. You know how we feel about Nazareth. We have lost enough there."

Her bitterness almost shocks me. Sari is kind and gentle. For this to rise in her must mean it is long seated and deeply rooted. It occurs to me I have never considered how Puah and Sari feel about the losses they carry because of the Romans in Nazareth. It has been twenty years, but it is not time that heals wounds like this. It is forgiveness and grace. It seems Sari has not forgiven.

"I will care for both Veena and Calah. We will only journey to Nazareth and back. It will only be for the day. Calah will stay close by me at all times. I assure you of this Sari." After I answer I search her face for a reaction. I see only sadness. Father has brought us here for his purposes with the Zealots. I do not think he considered the impact on the proximity to Nazareth for Puah and Sari.

After too many moments, Sari nods her agreement then leaves the table to refill the bread plate. She does it to mask her tears and give herself time to push the flood back down into the well.

Elon and Ehud both want to come to Nazareth with us. I save their mother the decision by denying them. "We will be going for business," I explain. "If we find what we need, perhaps we can all go when it is time to collect it. Perhaps you two can come up with a list of things we need from Nazareth to make our home more comfortable. Father and your cousins can help."

The speculation is enough to divert the attention of the boys. They immediately begin to inventory all the things they want and none of it sounds practical. Sari and Puah both shoot me glances of gratitude. To distract herself, Sari joins in the speculation with them.

Turning to Father, I suggest, "I will take one of the donkeys in case we find supplies for the garden we may purchase at once. We do not need to wait for the wagon to be ready to begin our venture."

"Yes," agrees father. "Take the oil wagon and enough coin to pay for the wagon and buy what supplies you can bring back. Remember to inform the Romans you are going there. Check in with the garrison on your every arrival and departure both here and in Nazareth."

Father continues to baffle me but the plans he has are his own counsel. I will do as he requests because I respect him and it is a wise course given the Romans involved. I turn to Veena and suggest, "Perhaps we can look at the plots in the vineyard I think will be suitable for you before the daylight fades. The knowledge of the area may help determine what you wish to purchase."

Grunting his agreement, father gets up from the meal and joins the younger boys in their speculation about our needs in the house. When Tabetha says to father she wishes a comb for her long hair, he ceases the opportunity to distract them all with a story. "Oh, that reminds me of a tale," he proclaims in his most whimsical tone. "Grow very silent children and I will tell you the marvelous tale of the Princess of Punt and the Tortoise Shell Combs."

This is one of the tales he told me when I was very young. It is one of my favorites. He has many stories of the Land of Punt and the mystical adventures had by traders to that ancient land. Veena's eyes dance with mirth and she sees the children gather around my father. We step quietly toward the door, taking advantage of the distraction.

Galilee And Canna

As we exit the door, I can hear the beginning of the story I know so well, "Long ago there was a breathtakingly beautiful Princess of Egypt. This was many years before Joseph was Prince in Egypt and he brought Israel and his children there to protect them from the famine. It was longer still before the Law of Moses and even long before Abraham left the Chaldeans to live in the land of promise..."

After we are out the door Veena asks me about the tale of Punt. I explain there are many of them. Each one teaches a lesson concerning good character and how to live with integrity. The sun is not quite down and the golden glow of its descent create the same feelings of wonder held in father's story.

Together we walk up a slight rise to the northeast corner of the vineyard, just on the edge of the olive grove. It is the highest point of the land we have. In the place where the grape vines and olive trees stop there is a large area of fallow ground. According to the records of the former owners, this land was left fallow last year to renew the soil. It was used previously as a vegetable garden. The current location of the vegetable patch, tended by Sari and Shlomi is closer to the house on the southern side of the vineyard.

In the evening glow one can still see the dark richness of the soil. Without hesitation, Veena strides ahead of me to the fallow field and immediately stoops down to put her hands in the well-rested earth. Turning with delight in her eyes, she speaks her heart, "This is excellent. I can grow almost anything I need in soil this good. We will need ash from the fires for some of the plots. It makes the soil right for some herbs and berries. We may be able to grow some very rare spices in such fine dirt."

"I am glad you are pleased," I reply reveling in her genuine excitement. "May I assume you would like to do your herb gardening here?"

She stands and moves to me quickly, "Yes, you may assume the same. You may also assume I begin to believe your family is sincere in caring for me. I begin to feel like there is a home for me after all I have seen and endured."

The feelings flood me so quickly I barely have time to notice them. Veena is not being vulnerable. She is expressing hope from her pain and strength. She is taking a risk. I find I am drawn to her, long to protect and support her. I want her to feel safe but do not want to hinder her spirit in the slightest. I want to build with her. Foolishly I say, "You are welcome in our family. You are safe here and we will treat you well always."

I will learn soon enough to see the spark in her eyes that ignites anger in her heart. I see the spark tonight as honeyed sunlight plays across her face. It is not anger I see because I am blinded by the beauty. In a movement I will grow to know too well, she turns, glides back to the soil, and pours the love of her craft into thoughts of the potential before her.

It is the way she deals with her fiery fury. She will not lash out. She will not argue. She directs the fire into a crucible of thought and action serves to refine her into doing excellent things. I admire her devotion to the potential in my ignorance. I am too foolish to realize she was showing devotion to me and not just our care.

As the sun sinks lower, I take in the beauty of the moment and relish the feelings I hold rather than thinking of hers. I see her, the sunset, the vineyard, and the field in the ending day and realize we can build something here if we hold to our faith and values. After the sun slips below the horizon, I dare to interrupt her reverie to speak to her.

"Will this be enough room for your needs? We can find more space if necessary." I watch as the ruddy glow of evening frames her. An almost silhouette approaches me as she realizes she has used the last of the light to inspect her field.

"I can grow all I need and more," she says softly. "We can go to some of the further markets and get what we need to plant rare spices and herbs. I am sure we can get what we need to grow thyme, sesame, cardamom, turmeric, coriander, dill, onions, garlic, and leeks now. Tomorrow we will get what we require and we can have seeds in the ground before the Sabbath." Veena leads me to a large olive tree where the roots form a V perfect for sitting in to rest against the trunk.

Urging me to sit, I do so. She sits near me but not in a way appearing improper to father. That last light of day is in her eyes. It shows me hope has kindled there and I can see something more. She breaks the gaze we share and whispers, "Tell me one of the Tales of Punt, Judas. My father never told them to me and I want to hear one from you."

I still do not understand this woman is offering more than friendship with her gentle mirth. I lean into the olive tree and she reclines along the raised root. As the first stars wink into the night I begin, "Long ago there was a breathtakingly beautiful Princess of Lavana. This was many years before Joseph was Prince in Egypt and he brought Israel there to protect them from the famine. It was longer still before the Law of Moses and even long before Abraham left the Chaldeans to live in the land of promise…"

Relationships and Recognition

I value an early start in all journeys. Veena, Calah and I depart for Nazareth just as the sun spreads across our easternmost groves. We take the small wagon and it is pulled by our best donkey. The morning is cool and the day promises to be bright and warm. Veena and Calah, sit in the back of the wagon. Calah can sing and blesses our journey with one of the Songs of David.

The road leads past the Garrison. We stop as requested to inform Amulius of our destination and when we expect to return. It is clear he appreciates the cooperation and respect. The man prefers to gain loyalty rather than demand it.

He brings out some figs that have just come the previous day from Jerusalem. Offering them to us he asks, "Would you enjoy these for me on your way to Nazareth? I am asking because I need your assistance and would not ask it without pay."

I smile, "We both know Roman law allows you to demand almost anything of me, but I am grateful for you asking. How may I serve the Garrison Commander?"

Amulius admires my threading the needle between subservience and rebellion. I did not offer to serve the Empire but, rather the Commander. His smile tells me he is not offended and he understands. "I have some dispatches to send to Maxim in Nazareth. If you could deliver them for me, it would be helpful. I can even pay you as a courier."

I like the idea of money not related to the family and further that I can perhaps keep us in good stead with the Romans. "I would do this, but I would like a letter recognizing me as serving the Garrison so that in the event anyone questions me, I am not in trouble. You do understand I think."

Amulius departs into the small garrison building to retrieve the dispatches. Whilst he does, I ponder what this will mean to father. We can gather fresher and better information about troop movement and where the Romans are weak. We may be able to get further news concerning what they plan concerning further control of our lands and what they know about us.

My thoughts then wrestle with me about trust and honor. This man has been kind to me and made our family welcome. He has offered help with our vineyard and allowed Darrius to work the land with us. Guilt and the desire to please my father war inside my mind. Amulius returns with a dispatch bag and a quickly written note with his seal on it.

"Present this if you need to but keep it if you do not. It will get you safe passage anywhere you need to go in the empire. I have also added a note to General Maxim informing him you will be serving as a courier for us when you are available. I was clear this is assistance not conscription. You will be free to refuse trips if it interferes with work at your home."

I thank him and take the bag and letter. The red wax seal on the letter can be seen through the loosely-woven protective linen. As we ride away, I burn to know what lays under the seal. I also realize the wax, intact and stuck to the linen could save all of our lives depending on the situation.

Once we set a steady pace toward Nazareth, I fall into conversation with Veena and Calah. We plan to meet with Joseph as soon as we deliver the dispatches. Veena expresses her desire to visit the market. Calah immediately agrees with her. There is no genuine reason to avoid it. Still I wish to avoid the place still ringing of death to me.

Calah only knows the story of my mother's death as a family history. Veena has not been told about it. It would be only for my own sake we would skip the market. Were father with us, we would avoid it at any cost. I was there but only as an infant. I only know what father has told me. I realize it is time to tell Veena. I excuse Calah to the back of the wagon and move over so Veena can sit beside me.

"I remember none of this," I begin. "It all happened when I was an infant. Father, mother, and I were in Nazareth with Sarah and Puah's husbands. They are my deceased uncles. They and my mother died in Nazareth." She listens intently as I relate father's version of our history with Nazareth and the Romans.

Further to her credit, Veena's response is genuine and kind, "You do not have to recall an event for the pain to be real. It shows courage that you are willing to face this place to help me. It is one of the things I grow to admire about you, Judas."

The last part takes me aback. I am uncertain I ever think of myself as someone to be admired. I think if she knew the war in my heart, she would not be so endeared. The other war in me is I admire her as well. Almost imperceptibly she slides a little closer to me on the cart bench.

She continues, "Whatever the challenges in Nazareth, we will face them together. Your family has stood by me and I will return the loyalty. I begin to think standing by your side is a good place for me altogether."

Her boldness is captivating. "I like it when you are beside me as well, Veena. If you are in agreement, I will speak to my father. We can perhaps turn all of the changes visited upon us into something good"

For the first time Veena seems more demure than confident. "I am willing. You should know; however, I am not worthy to be a bride. Against my will, I have become impure."

I have thought more than once she knew too much of the world to be innocent. Father may have trouble with this but I will find a way around it. My response, intended to be reassuring is not well worded. "I will not be deterred by your past. Perhaps father can overlook it because he will not have to pay a bride price."

Her cheeks flare into crimson. I will grow to know this anger when I summon it in her. This second summoning, however, takes me unprepared. "Yes," she whispers, "it is good that you will get a woman at a bargain. She comes with skills, strength, and good childbearing hips. Sure, she is a little used but there are no visible marks or scars. How nice for your family the Romans burned my spice cart."

Before I realize she is angry, she has moved to the back of the cart and engaged Calah in conversation. Her back is to me but she is as rigid as a stone. I turn my attention to guiding the cart and ponder my foolish response.

Not for the first time it occurs to me money matters more to me than it should. It is practical and good that we will save money. It is also foolish and evil to have put this ahead of a woman confessing to me she has been raped. I did not put love and compassion over practicality. Not for the first or last time, I have been a fool.

We travel on in relative silence for another hour. I can hear Veena and Calah have ceased talking. I glance back and notice Calah has fallen asleep. He is still a boy and the excitement has exhausted him. Arriving in Nazareth rested will do him good. Veena notices my glance and does not look away.

If I am to not fully fail this first test of our friendship, I must say something. I do. "I was wrong to consider anything but kind words in responding to you. My father has already pointed out your price is far above rubies."

She knows the Book of Wisdom and understands I am not repeating the offense. Moving to the cart seat again, she whispers differently, "I step away when I am angry to avoid saying things that are unseemly and unkind. We can suspend our talk of a union if my condition is unacceptable to you or your father."

It breaks upon my understanding like a wind driven wave just how much Veena risks by being honest about all of this. Her integrity far outpaces mine in the run of things. In that same wave or realization, I consider I am the one who is unworthy of her. I choose to be honest as well, "I am the one who is not pure enough. My heart does not obey the command to love as it should. I am the one who is not suitable for a woman as priceless as you. If, however, you will overlook that flaw, I will make sure everyone accepts you as family and as my betrothed. Perhaps the first wedding in the new home should be ours."

Veena only nods. Then her smile returns through tears and she tentatively leans into me. For the moment, I care not for propriety or decorum. I hold her close and focus only on her and making sure she feels accepted. We remain close until cresting the ridge showing Nazareth. Veena moves to awaken Calah as we prepare to enter the city.

Our first stop at the Garrison should be brief. The door warden, a Legionnaire regards us as the cart pulls up outside the gate. I know better than to get out of the cart. He reluctantly steps out of the shade of his post and comes to the gate.

"Merchants need not check in at the Garrison," he barks with the impatience born of hating the people surrounding him. "The guards at the gate or in the market will see to your registration as traders here."

He reaches the gate as he says the last bit. I nod my understanding, "I am sure that is the best way to do things and I will remember it. Today, though, I have dispatches for General Maxim from Amulius in Cana. My instruction are to give them to him personally."

It is clear the Legionnaire does not wish to be bothered with me. The truth is he is only a Legionnaire and Amulius is a Centurion. No matter how high his rank, every Legionnaire must obey the orders of a Centurion. He is also aware my life is forfeit if I am lying. Wishing to be in his shade, standing his post, he orders me to wait where I am.

Turning he retreats to the Garrison to alert the General. I can hear him cursing me under his breath. He is only gone briefly and returns with two Centurions. Both are known to me, though I do not think they realize I have met them both. Still the situation is dangerous. There is the remote chance the Roman Lieutenant may remember just who I am and decide my family is a loose end to his crime.

He speaks first, "Who thinks to summon General Maxim to the yard like a common servant? Your errand had best be one of value or this will become unpleasant for you and satisfying for me."

The General raises a hand to still the younger officer. "This man is known to me Patrius. He is a friend of Joseph's. His family hosted

Relationships And Recognition

me to a meal when they passed through a few weeks ago. It is like I keep telling you, we must be civil with the locals. It makes for a better peace."

Patrius learned long ago the ill wisdom of arguing with the General in the presence of the locals. He nods affirmation but not agreement. There is something dark and foreboding in Patrius. He is loyal to the General but also has a law of his own and it may not always subscribe to his orders.

I carefully pass the satchel to Maxim, "Amulius has included a letter to you of introduction. I chose not to tell him I already met you. He wishes for me to serve Cana as a courier when I travel between there and other cities for trade."

"This is good, Judas," he responds as he retrieves and reads the letter from the Centurion. "You are welcome to aid in our deliveries as well as have free travel in Judea as needed. I will draft a bill of passage for you. What brings you here today though?"

"I am going to visit Joseph. We need a cart built for Veena. She trades spices and her wagon was recently lost. There is no carpenter in Cana. We would commission it today and return for it when it is ready."

Grinning broadly the General offers, "You will get a better cart than you could hope for. I know the entire family is here. Perhaps we can accompany you to Joseph's home. Mary makes seed cakes during the week with honey and sesame. They are best when they are warm."

"Please do," I offer. "We have only met Joseph briefly in Jerusalem. Since you know the family well, your presence will be of value. Also, knowing there are good seed cakes will help remind Calah of his manners."

Veena, ever bold, adds, "I have known the family for some years. We have shared space at the market during Passover since the sons of Joseph were young. Back then my father and mother were the spice vendors and I was the young girl who packed the orders and counted the supplies."

"Then we shall have a reunion of sorts," announces Maxim. "A prime reason to have seed cakes if one is needed. Come Patrius, we should not keep the seed cakes and Joseph waiting."

I guide the wagon at a walking pace behind the Romans and we make our way through town. It becomes evident we will not return to Cana today. I am sure we can find suitable lodging since we seem to be in the favor of the military commander of all Judea. I also consider father will either laud or loath this situation.

On further speculation, I ponder how nothing prevents father from doing both. He could easily loath our favor from Roman leaders and be thrilled at the opportunities it presents for his rebellion. Close enemies are easier to kill. Enemies who think you are friends are convenient for betrayal. Is that not the purpose of the Sicarii, the small swift blade? Yes, father will seek an opportunity to betray all of these men who think we are building a friendship with them. He will seek the opportunity to strike the cobras whilst they are still in their baskets sleeping. I begin to ponder the facets of betrayal and how it can be used as an advantage.

As we move through town, Veena asks Maxim about the market and local spice merchants. He expresses there are a few but the best thing to do is inquire of the caravans passing through Nazareth. He adds that the best thing is to visit the great bazaar at the port of Joppa.

Veena looks kindly at the General. "I have been to the great bazaar of Joppa. It will have what I would wish to rekindle my business. I would rather wait and get through trade what I need. Other merchants going there will gladly get what I want for a fee. I can use that to spread the word Veena is now doing business in Cana of Galilee and with your permission, in Nazareth on occasion. I can arrange to set up a day or two a month here and collect deliveries on the trade route."

Maxim turns to me grinning with a friendly mischief I have never seen in a Roman. He laughs out the first sounds, "You must keep watch on this one, Judas. She has a keen mind for business. She may be running things in your household sooner than we think."

Having learned my lesson about Veena and assumptions, I choose support over whit. "I am sure she will accomplish anything to which her mind is set. I am just as certain if she chose it, she would be running the empire before long."

From behind me a voice I do not know speaks, "Ah you speak of a woman of noble character, *'She considers a field and buys it; out of her earnings she plants a vineyard. She sets about her work vigorously; her arms are strong for her tasks. She sees that her trading is profitable, and her lamp does not go out at night.'"*

Maxim's eyes twinkle, "Ah Rabbi Samuel, how kind of you to happen upon us as we make our way." He turns to me, "Judas, this is Rabbi Samuel ben Jonas. He oversees the Synagogue in our small town. He also has a keen sense of when there may be food in the near future."

I am uncomfortable with this Roman even though everything about him is friendly and kind. He has a sternness about him I would not provoke. He commands the men who killed my mother. He is the symbol of Roman power in the region. Why then, I wonder is he in Nazareth? Why is he good to those who should fear and revere him? Perhaps he is a cobra and Nazareth is a humble unnoticed basket.

My pondering is interrupted by Veena saying my name. "I am sure Judas will want to help with the education of our young ones in any way possible, though their mothers, both widows see to their learning the Law and the Prophets. His father is so learned in the scrolls one would think him a Scribe."

That last would make father both proud and embarrassed. I support her, "Yes, father loves the Torah and pours over it for understanding. He orders and directs our teaching and gives great cause to love and fear the LORD."

Rabbi Samuel smiles warmly, "I would journey to Cana to meet your father should time allow. Except for Joseph's oldest boy, I find little to challenge my ponderings. What is your father's name?"

I am off my guard and answer too plainly, "He is Simon ben Ezra. We are from Kerioth, recently moved to Cana."

Patrius does not react but there is a flicker of recognition in his eyes. That he is searching his memory for something is obvious if you already know what that something is. I do. Patrius looks at me as if to draw the knowledge from my brain since he cannot find it in his.

We lock eyes for a moment and I can see the soldier in him working it out. I can see the killer in him wondering if he has forgotten old prey or found new prey. He is not there yet and my mind screams for a way to distract him. God has already worked that out and the distraction presents itself.

"Here we are," states Maxim. "I suppose the men will be in the carpentry shop. We should begin there."

Patrius and I both turn to see we are outside the gate to Joseph's home. The talk and tension have distracted us. We turn to walk toward the carpentry shop. Two men emerge. It is Joseph and one of his sons. The young son rushes up to Maxim and Patrius. The boy, almost a man is strong and well-suited to the work of carpentry. He is not the son we met briefly in Jerusalem. Maxim embraces the boy like family and even the hard Patrius becomes more amicable for the moment. Since the encounter with Patrius, I can only see basking cobras.

"Good day, Maxim," begins Joseph. "We were not expecting the General of Judea today, but perhaps I should have. When you and Rabbi Samuel arrive together it must be Tuesday. I think Mary's seed cakes are cooling, but they should be ready soon."

This may have been the only time I saw genuine laughter in Patrius. It was at the expense of his General so it was a product of his love for the man he followed. The palest of blushes spreads across the General's cheeks. The tension that had burned in the air dissipates.

Maxim turns to me, "Joseph, you should remember Judas from Jerusalem."

Turning to me, Joseph's face offers immediate recognition. He claps a strong hand on his son's shoulder pulling him from Maxim. "Simon, go tell your mother to prepare seats for our guests in the garden. Then fetch some water for them. While you speak with your mother ask one of your sisters to bring Jesus and John to join us."

The reluctance to leave the Romans shows on the boy's face. His determination to obey his father is there as well. He moves to the house whilst Joseph leads us around it to the garden. It is a small but well-maintained garden. My previous visit to it preceded its summer care. The flowers from spring now reveal they will all bear fruit or herbs of some kind. Bees drift among the remaining flowers and the table we enjoyed shows the dapple patterns of summer sun on it. In only a few weeks the world has transitioned to promise provision and speaks that someone in this family understands a proper garden. I look forward to seeing these same movements of the season in our garden with Veena.

Joseph gestures for us to sit. Soon three of Joseph's sons and two of his daughters join us. Mary arrives with some fruit and bread on a smooth skillfully-organized platter. One of the other daughters follows with a large, ornately carved pitcher of water. James, the second oldest son, rises to help her.

Wooden cups are passed around and the water is served. Linen napkins are filled with fruit and bread. Joseph offers a simple prayer of thanks and we begin to enjoy the berries, dried figs, and dates. Joseph and Maxim share a side conversation over an order placed for new chairs for the garrison terrace. Maxim smiles when he is told Judas and Simon, Joseph's younger sons will have them ready by month's end.

During a lull in the conversation, Joseph turns to me, "I am sure you know we are pleased you pay a visit to us. I am equally as certain you have a reason other than a social one. How may my family be of service?"

Father would like how Joseph gets to business so politely. "Veena joined our family after losing her spice wagon during Passover. The activity in the market claimed it along with other stalls. We would like to commission a new one. We have drawn out what we wish and believe your family has the skill to craft it."

Patrius hides from others the scowl on his face as I mention the Passover trouble. He may not have known of the burning of Veena's wagon. Still, he knew of the plan and even though he said there were to be no deaths, there were.

I pass him her drawings and his sons gather around him to examine them. They are muttering approval and one can tell they like what they see. Joseph looks up at me then to Veena. "Have you considered," he asks, "making the storage cupboards so they can be removed. We could make two or three sets fitting the frame so you could load and unload different families of spices as needed. We can even fashion covers for the cabinets so they can preserve their contents if left behind."

I look over at Veena waiting for her to respond. "Well," she hesitates, "I have never considered that but depending on the additional cost, it would be an ideal situation."

One of the daughters walks around refilling the water cups. Joseph nods his approval. "This is good. Let us consider a moment before giving you a price."

Joseph leads James and Jesus aside to a thicket of bushes near the table. Their voices are audible but unintelligible. Rabbi Samuel seeks to fill the silence. "How is Rabbi Esau in Cana? I am sure he is relieved to have the wedding house occupied again."

"We have met him," I offer. "I am unsure of his feelings about the wedding house, but we intend to be generous in keeping the with house history. Father and I are planning how to best manage the vineyard. Amulius has offered his man Darius to help us and seems to have vast knowledge of the growing of grapes and fermenting of wine. We are thankful for the welcome we received."

Rabbi Samuel shares a look with Maxim. The General speaks, "I am pleased you have been welcomed and included. You will be able to sell all of the wine and grapes you wish at the market here in Nazareth. Since moving my standard to the garrison here, we have had little trouble. It has been some years since there was trouble causing anyone harm."

The harm of which he speaks summons my father's voice in my mind. His tales of violence and my mother's murder seethe inside me. Thoughts of cobras in baskets take on reality as we sit in the cool shade of the garden dining with our enemies.

Joseph announces his return by commenting, "Unless you mean the trouble of Patrius buying up all the best wine for himself and his fellows. Still, even with the Roman discount, the wines from your vineyard will fetch a fair price and you will have it in plenty."

"That news will please father," I reply. "I am sure we can produce from the olive groves on the land there as well. In Kerioth this was our primary work."

"Yes," replies Patrius, "You were selling olive oil and olives in Jerusalem."

Something in his tone is ominous and warns me to be more guarded. It is this family that has me off my guard. Veena is saying something but I am chasing the tone used by Patrius. Again, I am startled out of my reverie.

The strong carpenter's hand on my shoulder gives me enough of a start that I jump. I turn to a face with bright eyes and instant mirth at my surprise. "Whatever has your thoughts so distracted, I considered you would like to hear what Father, James, and I propose." Jesus continues, "We want to welcome you to the region and show kindness to Veena. Our year has been quite a bountiful one. If you would not be insulted, we will build Veena's wagon as discussed for the promise of a small barrel of olive oil and quarterly deliveries of Sabbath wine for a year."

The price, beyond fair, carries with it further encounters with his family. They are offering friendship along with commerce. There is trust in the offer and hope for our prosperity. I accept as humbly as I can.

We spend about another half hour discussing the details, going over the measurements, and talking materials. I spend that time conflicted over my hatred for the Romans and this good family's obvious love for Maxim and his men.

For now, I will choose to follow the lead of Joseph and his family. They offer to take us in as friends and neighbors. I will accept it because of the laws of hospitality. I will keep my hatred of the Romans in the background until I have obvious cause to unleash it.

Relationships And Recognition

I read over the terms of the purchase of the wagon one more time. The agreement is they will deliver the wagon to Cana in four weeks. I offer to arrange a small celebration so we can dedicate the wagon to use for the Lord and his blessings.

Rabbi Samuel prays a blessing over our agreement to end the formal part of our business. We conclude our time together and stand to walk back toward our wagon.

Jesus offers, "Surely you do not intend to travel back to Cana now. There will be no moon tonight and darkness will settle before you arrive home."

His father picks up the thread of conversation, "Jesus is correct. You three must be our guests for the night. It will also give you time to visit the bazaar tomorrow and journey back to Cana safely. I hope you will stay."

Looking to see if Veena has any objection, I see nothing on her face to betray that. I feel the hesitancy to be in this city overnight again. I choose to avoid the obvious danger of traveling the road at night. "We gratefully accept your hospitality. Having stayed here once before, it feels only right we should enjoy your home with you in it."

Veena, Jesus, and James all laugh at my clumsy attempt at formality. Mary comes to my defense. "Thank you for your respect and for staying with us." She turns to Maxim, Samuel, and Patrius, "You three must stay for dinner as well."

Samuel nods excitedly. Maxim responds for himself and his subordinate, "I can return at dinner time if I am welcome. Patrius must ride to Jerusalem and must leave soon to be there by tomorrow evening. There are dispatches that cannot wait. Longinus awaits my answer on some matters important to Harrod."

Mary makes it clear Maxim must return, "You will come back for dinner. Patrius, before you leave, we will put together some food for you to carry with you. I recall you do not like the inn at Sychar as much as others. You will not have to stop if you do not wish it."

Patrius, always uncomfortable with kindness, nods his agreement. The General and his aid depart. Samuel says he will also attend to some other business and departs as well, promising to return in time for dinner.

James sees to our cart and guides the donkey to his stable. Returning with the bundle we packed in the event we were to remain the night in Nazareth, he asks his sister, Salome to show Veena where she will sleep.

Joseph suggests Simon and Juda find something for Calah to do together. He excuses them from work for the remainder of the day. The three run off already lost in the potential of the day's freedom.

Only Joseph, Jesus, and I remain under the shade of the garden trees. I express concern we are interrupting their work. Joseph reassures me, "We are ahead of our commitments. It is just as much a service to God to be good to traveling friends as it is to mend joints and fasten legs. Carpentry we can do anytime save for the Sabbath. You are only here for a short while."

The kindness of this man flows from him like a river. I ponder how unkind I was to Veena earlier. I want to be like this carpenter is to his wife. I feel I can never be as long as my family goes unavenged.

Both men see the trouble in my heart flicker through my eyes. Jesus rises, "I will see t my brothers have cleaned the shop well enough to stop work. I think they had started the curing fire and we cannot let it burn unattended." Looking at me he continues, "Whatever troubles you, I have always found my father is a good man to talk to about difficulties."

As Jesus walks away, Joseph leans in and speaks softly, "We both see something bothers you. My son is much wiser than he lets on, but I will listen if you wish to unburden your heart."

Relationships And Recognition

I can feel the desire to talk about everything rise up in me. All that is conflicted inside me tries to come out at once but I settle on speaking about Veena. I explain our situation and my beginning love for her.

After I recount her situation and my concerns, Joseph remains silent for a moment. He straightens up and looks directly into my eyes. "Without going into too many details," he begins, "I had to make a similar choice when Mary and I were betrothed. If you remain in Nazareth for any length of time you will be treated to the gossip version of the tale."

I nod, listening and he continues. "I had to choose whether to proceed with our plan to wed or to put her away privately. I was unwilling to leave her in the hands of the Law and the Pharisees. Someone took the time to open my eyes and show me things were unfolding as they should. I have learned over the years it is not a person's past that matters. It is who they are now that is vital."

"I can see that," I begin, "I suppose I am concerned about my father's thoughts and if Veena will be happy with me."

As I say this, Jesus returns and sits beside his father. Joseph continues, "In my situation, Mary was already carrying Jesus. It was up to me if I was going to allow the situation to deny me the potential joy of being with her even though I was saddened by the situation."

I see he is sincere. I can also tell he respects Veena. Jesus offers his opinion, "We have known Veena for three years now. In that time, we have never seen her act in a dishonorable way. Even if we had, we all need to forgive others and provide a way of restoration for them. We have encountered her at Passover and other festivals. She has no living family to represent her honor. I am sure if she would accept it, father and I will take on the role if needed."

When Jesus says "honor" I feel every guilty thought that has ever risen in me. Instantly, instead of feeling superior and righteous,

I am filled with guilt and unworthiness. Joseph cuts through my mounting tension, "Do not fear to accept Veena as a bride. All that is in the past will be forgotten as the two of you build a life together. After all, she could have hidden her past from you had she desired."

The truth of his words squeezes my heart. I am judging someone who risked her future to be honest with me. I can see that in a few weeks I have been given a treasure demands I love it as I love God. Any doubts I have disappear in the warmth of the carpenter and his son. I nod my understanding. The desire is still there to tell them everything; the Zealots, the murder of my family, and my desire for money all clamor to be spilled out in the garden on a lovely Spring afternoon.

Jesus leans in and touches my shoulder. "Enough troublesome talk for now. I am sure we will have other opportunities to speak. Let us instead speak of how we plan a wedding and resurrect the old celebrations at the new home of Simon of Galilee. Cana must become known for its wedding feasts again."

We spend the afternoon planning who will attend and when we will proceed. We agree Joseph will stand for Veena's family in the planning. When the women return to the garden with dinner, Veena and Mary agree Joseph is the proper adult male to represent her in these dealings.

By the end of the meal, Veena has agreed to terms and our feelings are free to grow because save telling father, we have a formal betrothal. Something about this family pleases me. We talk long after the stars blaze and a chill grips the night air. When we finally turn to sleep, my thoughts are filled with rehearsals of how I will tell father of my desire and hopefully our plans.

The three of us are up early, ready to return to Cana. We eat breakfast with Joseph and Mary whilst his sons prepare our wagon and some provisions for our short journey. As we stand by the wagon saying our goodbyes, we agree Joseph will deliver the wagon when it is ready. Maxim and a Legionnaire I do not know arrive and Maxim bids us farewell too.

I notice Mary passes a linen bundle to Maxim. The smell of honey, sesame, and cardamom waft from the bundle to betray the contents. She hands a similar bundle to Veena and I hear her mention my nephew. Maxim gives me three scrolls bound for Cana. All are for Amulius.

We mount the wagon and begin the journey home. So much has changed in a day. We sought a wagon and came away with a family. Veena sits up front with me, just far enough away to be proper. Calah sits in the back, already eating his third seed cake. When I rest my hand on the bench between us, she rests her little finger on mine. I want to reassure her in the morning sunlight.

Struggling for words I begin, "I will speak to my father as soon as we return. He may object or question but will not refuse."

Veena nods her agreement, "I know he will not but he is so devout he might struggle over a questionable Jew with an impure history and no real family to speak for her."

"Yes," I concur, "he may struggle but he will not be cruel about this. He was concerned enough about the possibility I would not marry at all. He likes you and values how hard you are willing to work. All will be well."

Her finger glides along mine again and I feel the stirring inside me that is love for her. I sense the longing I have rarely considered to have a fellow traveler; a companion. In the longing I can now only picture Veena.

Turning the conversation to her spice cart, I ask how she will use it. She becomes excited as she tells me all her plans for what she will grow, how she will use the market in Nazareth, and the benefit it will be to our family. She has already created a list of herbs and flowers she wishes to grow for their value as food and medicine.

She even has seen something in Joppa allowing one to have bees, harvest the honey, and have them remain. I laugh a little at this not realizing she is quite serious. I see the fire begin to smolder in her and realize I must not forget how quickly tinder catches.

Veena tails off into a reverie of her thoughts and I can hear Calah snoring in the back of the wagon. I reach back and find a seedcake in the bundle and nibble on it as we ride. Amidst the joy of this day, there is still the undercurrent of my father's other activities to consider. How will I remain loyal to Veena and the Zealot cause of my father all at once? I also ponder the feelings I had when talking to Joseph and Jesus. I want to be like them but I do not know how.

I come out of my own thoughts as we start up the hill to Cana. The Legionnaire on duty sees us. He steps away from the garrison gate offering a greeting. Being recognized and greeted by Romans is still uncomfortable. Knowing some of the ones with whom I become familiar killed my mother is troublesome as well. I still have no way to balance my pain and hatred with love and peace. It is not in me.

Shoving these thoughts aside, I greet the Legionnaire politely. I pass him the scrolls meant for Amulius and we ride on to the house. I want to speak with father quickly. I need the hope of my future with Veena to steer away from the other things cloying for my attention. Both hope and horror vie for my attention. The path ahead is filled with hope and potential. The way is also lined with baskets like a narrow ally though a merchant quarter. I worry about the baskets when what I wish is to dwell on love and life. I must find a way to thread the path without kicking the baskets.

I recognize the truth; if I am to hold on to my hatred, I am going to have to lie to myself about some other things. I ponder how I can wall off my love for Veena so it is not infected by my hatred. For a moment I consider discussing it with Veena; telling her about my loathsome secret. I choose instead to lay the first stone in a wall that will eventually become a prison.

Wine and Weddings

Father is pleased we have secured favor in Nazareth as well as a spice wagon for Veena. The evening meal is filled with discussion of further plans for the vineyard, the olives, and trips to Nazareth and even Jerusalem to sell our produce. Veena expresses her excitement and gratitude for the care, a home, and the potential of a future in Cana.

When Veena joins the others to clear the dishes, I follow father outside to sit in the garden in the cool of the evening. No one joins us and I see this is the time. I understand I am risking everything in a conversation. Father begins to talk about his hopes for the fortunes of our family, "I am pleased we are establishing trade connections so quickly. We can add the ones we already have in the northern half of the nation. Perhaps in a year or two we can even recover the ones in the south."

"Yes," I concur, "All things seem to be running as we wish them to run. I would like to ask you about something more personal if I may, father."

"I know you are concerned about the seeming lack of activity in our cause," he assumes. "I think we can safely make contact with our allies when you have made a few 'unburdened' trips throughout the region. I am as anxious as you are to be rid of Rome but we must play the long game. As much as Maxim and his Lieutenants seem to be good men, at least two of them are the cobras who struck your mother."

"I understand, father," I respond, "but I wish to speak of something more pleasant; more easily attained."

Squaring to look me in the eye, he asks curiously, "What could be more joyful than freeing our nation?"

I realize he has given me an opening and he has revealed a way to ask that he cannot deny. Still my throat tightens as I try to ask. "I would like to make our family more secure. I would like to honor mother by taking a wife and solidifying our prospects for the family in the same turn. I wish to marry Veena. I think if mother is all you said she was, she would be delighted at this."

Father sees my tactic but I think he is prouder of it than offended by it. Ever looking for ways to move against Rome, he sees my manipulative move as one he can use in future endeavors. He is also touched beyond his desire to be moved by me speaking of my mother and her memory. He eyes me with the edge he uses when he is going to correct me. I can see him turning it all over in his mind.

"You should not try to manipulate the one who taught you how to take advantage of circumstances," he chides. "I see, however, the way in which you have gone after a good thing using the opportunity in front of you. I agree you should wed Veena. We should see to it immediately if we can find her family."

In his eyes I see a hint of love and joy I have not seen. It sparks hope for me that he can be turned from the path of the Zealots. In the same moment I realize I walk that path willingly now, just with less fervor than him. We will both need something greater than ourselves to find our way.

"Father, I know it was out of turn but Joseph's family offered to stand for Veena. They have known her for a few years and she has no family to turn to that is blood. We know Joseph is a good man. Will you allow this to be enough?"

His face softens further, "It is enough. Come, let us go tell the family and we can all face the coming months with joy and hope."

True to the moment, father gathers everyone and with a mischievous grin at Veena announces the betrothal. He explains the support of Joseph's family and marks the date so the betrothal year can begin. Ever the one to surprise me, he suggests I will have to sleep in the wine shed for the year. If we are going to do things properly it will not do for me to sleep under the same roof as Veena.

I had not thought of this but it is true. Veena laughs, father smirks, and my aunts hand me bedding. It is clear my fate regarding where I sleep for the coming year is decided. Calah offers to join me in the shed and I can see being there alone would garner much more rest for me. I ask him to help me set up a bed but prefer he join me after I get things settled.

We have the bedding set in the corner of the shed where we transfer new wine to sealed jugs. It is clear and will not be used until fall. Calah reluctantly takes his leave and I choose to go to sleep early. The hidden corner is dark and quiet. It is easy to focus on my evening prayer so filled with joy. Sleep finds me easily and I contemplate the possibilities as my final thoughts of the day.

I awaken to the sound of items being moved in the outer room of the shed. Sitting cautiously, quietly, I spy to see who is out there. All I can see in the dim morning light is a man in a tunic. I suppose I am not sufficiently quiet. The man rounds on me with a pruning hook in one hand, ready to fight and obviously able.

Realizing who it is, I sputter out, "Darrius, it is Judas. Why are you here so early?"

Letting out a rich chuckle, he answers, "Then I will avoid pruning you. Why are you sleeping in the vintage shed?"

I am about to tell someone who is not family my great joy. It is a Roman soldier even though he is a Nubian. He is also our vintner. My recent shock allows for my nervousness as I answer, "I have taken Veena as my betrothed. It is not proper for us to sleep under the same roof."

Darrius laughs fully now, "This is cause for great joy. We shall have to have a celebration and see to it Amulius celebrates with us. He is fond of your family. We shall also have to find better sleeping arrangements for you. We cannot have you arrive at your wedding day unrested."

As he says this there is a noise at the doorway. It is Sari and Veena. Veena will not come to me alone until we are wed. They announce the morning meal is ready. I ask Darrius to join us. He says he must get to the vine work he wishes before the sun is up. He also asks if Calah can work with him for the day. I promise to send the lad along after breakfast.

The women walk back to the house with me and as promised, I ask Calah to join Darrius in the vineyard after our meal. He agrees. Father mentions he needs me to check the olive and fruit trees. He thinks he wishes to put water jugs throughout the trees to collect rain and store water for the dry season.

I assure him I will. We eat, planning the rest of the day and tomorrow. Father mentions he would like me to get an early start in the morning and travel to Nazareth for some supplies needed for the vegetable garden and there are some other supplies he wishes me to gather. He suggests I take journey with ease and return in time for Sabbath dinner the following day.

We work through the day and I sleep well in the shed that night. At breakfast Thursday morning father tells me he has the large wagon ready to travel. He has included provisions for my trip, a list of things he wishes for the garden and groves, and list of lumber

Wine And Weddings

supplies for Joseph. I am to bring back what he has available and say I will return the following week for the rest.

Father explains he would like us to make weekly trips to Nazareth on Thursdays and most of the time return the same day. Since I will need to seek the vendors best for our needs, he has allowed the extra day this time.

We fall to talk of the vineyard and the work Darrius is doing to improve things. He has thinned many of the vines and is planning to graft in some cuttings from other vines to make grapes that will produce more robust vintages. Father is pleased and also irritated because he is pleased.

After the morning meal I take my leave. Veena stands by the wagon to wish me on my way. Now that we are betrothed, we can verbalize our love whenever we wish. She gives me a letter for Joseph to verify the arrangements and confirm the date for our wedding. It will be held here on the day after Sabbath one year from this week.

I stop by the garrison and Amulius has letters for Maxim and reports that will go through Maxim to Rome. If the Empire does anything, it collects its reports. I assure the Centurion that Darrius is serving us well. Amulius is delighted and expresses it will allow his servant to be fully discharged from the legion but still feel useful. The Nubian will enjoy his relative retirement without losing pay or his pride. The Garrison Commander explains this will aid Maxim as well.

The day is warm but will not become overbearing. The donkey pulling the wagon has pulled wagons for our family for eight years. He knows what roads are and that when whoever is in the wagon stops for the day he will be well fed and watered. I spend the quiet ride to Nazareth pondering the Law and the Prophets, the Zealot cause, and the potential future between Veena and I. It seems there will be some narrow threading if I am to bind it all together successfully. I ponder as I ride and pray the way through it all will become clear to me.

◉◉◉◉◉◉◉

As will be my custom, I report to the garrison upon arrival in Nazareth. Maxim, Patrius, and Portimus all come out to join me. Portimus and Maxim greet me as a friend. Patrius keeps back and greets me with something between formality and familiarity. I do not know the story from his perspective and he does not know it from mine. We both are ignorant of things that would create a whole truth for us.

I pass the dispatches to Maxim and explain I am headed to the market then to see Joseph. I include father intends to establish weekly visits on Thursdays but it will be uncommon that I stay the night as I will this week.

Maxim takes all this in and then gets to what truly interests him. "I need to know about the girl," he starts. "Did your father approve? Are we going to see another family turn a bad situation into a good one?"

The General realizes he sounds more like a doting parent than a Roman Commander. He looks at Portimus and Patrius. The former chuckles and dismisses the social gaff with an observation, "We have been ensnared in the goings on of Nazareth and this region for twenty years. Joseph's family has long been a friend to our fellowship. Maxim has kept the peace most of the time for twenty years. He is allowed a little levity. Do you not agree Patrius?"

The other Centurion nods his agreement but does not smile. Instead he offers, "All of our fates seem to be tied to Joseph and more specifically to Jesus. It will not come to a good end but we must find the joy where we can. I am pleased for the betrothal Judas. I hope is does your family good."

After some further light conversation, I leave the wagon and walk to the Nazareth market. Veena's letter is not a letter as much as it is a list. She seems to want seeds to every herb known to man. I find the herb vendors easily enough and the two there to today laugh as I try to pronounce some of the obscure names.

When they realize I want quantities and seeds they try to instruct me on growing certain things in this region. It is clear it is all lost on me and they laugh again. I assure them the one who made the list knows the herbs and spices well. She will plant, dry, and harvest them.

As I receive the many herbs, spices, and small seeds on the list, the older of the two women pauses. "Who is the person buying these seeds?" she asks. "Some of these requests would only be made by someone with great knowledge."

"It is my betrothed," I reply. "She has many years' experience but lost all of her supplies in the early spring. Since we are betrothed, I am helping her rebuild her stores so she can pursue her business."

The women look at each other for a moment and the elder woman speaks again, "May I enquire as to the name of the woman you will wed? We know almost everyone who deals in the spice and herb trade in the region."

I feel the suspicion of all strangers I have learned from father rise in me. I also ponder these two women who sell plants could not be a danger to Veena. I reply, "She is Veena of Joppa. She came under our care after her spice cart was destroyed in Jerusalem. Do you know her?"

Both women smile with recognition. The younger one almost squeals with delight. "Veena has been our friend for many years. We have wondered why we have not seen her in any of the markets these past weeks. Is she well?"

I nod in the affirmative and tell them of here losses during Passover. I add we are acquiring a new cart for her. "She will be able to grow her own herbs on our land. We hope to have her back in the market by the end of summer."

The two women confer for a moment and then turn back to me. "We want to help," states the older of the two. "We will prepare a parcel of cuttings and seeds for Veena. If you return to us this evening, we will have it ready for you. It will contain all she needs to grow enough to fill a new cart."

"I have another obligation tonight, but I can come in the morning before I return home." I respond.

They look at each other again and then nod in response. "That will be fine," the younger woman assures me.

I bid them farewell with much gratitude. Veena will be pleased. It occurs to me I do not know their names. Turning back to them I ask.

"I am Esther," says the older one, "and this is Susa."

"I am Judas ben Simon of Kerioth, but now I suppose of Cana. I will return in the morning." I turn again and return to the cart. As I ready it for the short ride to Joseph's home, I ponder the fortune of my visit to the market and offer a prayer of gratitude.

Patrius comes out of the garrison whilst I am climbing into the wagon. Dismissing the Legionnaires on the gate, he waits until they are out of earshot before addressing me. "I am not going to cause you any difficulty Judas. I do think that what is between us must be spoken of so it can be dismissed."

I feel tension, both anger and fear rise in me. I know I have not done anything wrong but this is Patrius. He is the connection to the past. He does not know how much I know.

The strong rugged Roman continues, "Your family died when you were a babe because of their actions. Your uncles were Zealots. You and I have a history but it can remain in the past if you allow it. Your family and the carpenter family do not cause trouble. I would even call you useful."

I realize he is trying to explain his refusal to allow the past to color the present. I stammer out a simple, "Thank you, Patrius."

There is opportunity here. There is also danger. What would this man do if he knew father and I had taken up my fallen uncles' mantle? He among all the Romans we know would see to our deaths and likely by his own hand.

I break the awkward silence, "I will be at Joseph's home and hopefully spend the night there. I need to collect some wood for one of my father's projects. I will be making the trip to Nazareth weekly for the foreseen time."

Patrius already regrets being personal. He imagines I will try to pursue friendship with him. He nods in acknowledgement and dismissal. I tap the mule indicating he should begin walking. What I do not know at this time is events have already unfolded putting this Centurion and I on a collision course that can only end in blood.

──────────

The short distance to Joseph's home does not give me enough time to consider how perilous closeness to Patrius could be. Salome, Joseph's youngest daughter is in the front yard spreading wood shavings in the pen that holds their chickens. The shavings, a waste product from the carpentry shop, are used for many purposes around the home.

The young girl waves at me and darts around the house to the carpentry shop. By the time I have dismounted the wagon and tied the mule to the fence, Joseph and all of his sons come around from the shop to greet me. The smiles on their faces would make one think I had been gone for years not a day.

Joseph takes me in a strong embrace as soon as he reaches me. "It is good you return so soon. Please tell me others are with you."

I shake my head, "I am alone and all business today. Father wants me to purchase wood from you for one of his large projects. I do not want to talk business until I greet all of you, however."

Joseph, Jesus, and James chuckle at my adherence to formal business dealings. James offers, "We like being greeted but you do not have to be formal. Besides, we need to know about the betrothal."

I smile, feeling the tension drain from me after the conversation with Patrius. "We are betrothed and the date is set for one year from Sunday. Father has me sleeping in the wine shed to observe proper practices. It has not been too bad but it has only been two days."

"Where are you sleeping tonight?" asks Joseph. You cannot be planning to drive back with a full wagon this late. It would be well after dark when you arrive home."

"I had intended to stay," I assure them. "Some herb vendors who know Veena will have supplies for me to take to her in the morning."

"Then you must stay with us," insists Joseph. "Mary will be cross with me if I let you stay anywhere else. We can discuss the wedding plans and your needs for lumber."

I nod, having known they would offer me hospitality. I cannot imagine this family doing anything less. I fish the lumber request from my pouch and pass it to Joseph. He studies it for a moment before looking up at me. "We have some of this but will need to acquire the rest. Your father mentions he does not need it all right away. We can bring it to you or you can come for it in a couple of weeks."

Wine And Weddings

"I will come for it," I answer. "Since I will be coming weekly it will be easy enough to travel here. It is clear you are busy. How may I assist you for the remainder of the day?"

"Keep us company and tell us about Cana," answers Jesus. "We all have our tasks and teaching you what to do will only take more time. Your stories of our neighboring town, however, will pass the time and allow us to work."

Joseph nods his approval of this arrangement and dispatches Simon to get me some water. He also asks Jude to tend to the donkey. We agree the cart can remain here for the night and be loaded in the morning. The troop of Joseph and his sons lead me around to the carpentry shop. It is larger than I thought and is right next to the small stable housing their donkey and a pair of oxen.

Jude leads my donkey into the shed and the two animals exchange brays for greeting. One of the oxen lows as if giving his opinion on their guest. The men and boys set back to work. They are constructing doors that look like they are a quality intended for the house of a wealthy man. I notice Salome comes in with her basket to gather more shavings.

I ponder the harmony of effort here is what Veena and I discuss when we dream of the future of the Cana property. Joseph checks his list from father again and turns to me, "Do you know what your father intends for this much wood? He has ordered a good quantity of quality lumber. I have no objection; I simply wish to choose what is best for his intent."

I shake my head in the negative. "Father did not include me in these plans." What comes out next comes from the confusion in me and it is darker than I realize. "He seems to only be thinking of his own agenda these days."

Joseph and Jesus are the only ones who react. They both meet my gaze. It is the Son who holds it. He seems to be looking deeply inside of me in a way both disquieting and comforting all at once. There is nothing but kindness in his eyes. The moment passes and neither of the men says anything.

As if to dispel the tension, Mary, Joseph's younger daughter arrives with a jug of water almost as large as she is. She loudly proclaims, "Mother says you are all being rude hosts. Guests must be offered water when they arrive."

Joseph laughs deeply with a richness I envy, "You are quite right little one, and so is your mother. I will see to our guest getting his water if you will let your mother know he is staying the night."

Little Mary places her hands on her hips, looks up at her father, and says, "WE already know. Mother also says not to talk about the wedding without her."

Jesus picks up his little sister whilst Joseph pours water from the jug for all of us. I can hear the eldest son talking softly to her, "Thank you for delivering the water and the message. Just so you know, father already instructed our guest be given water. Please tell mother we will save any further wedding talk for dinner."

Setting her down, Joseph's eldest son looks to see all the others have water before pouring a cup for himself. I notice each of them has a beautiful olive-wood cup with his name carved into the side. The one I am handed matches the others but is nameless. The skill of the carpenters of Nazareth shows even in common drinking vessels.

Since the wedding talk must wait for dinner, I tell the carpenters about our farm, vineyard, and the herb garden we will grow. I mention Esther and Susa from the market. And James smiles broadly when I mention Susa. No one seems to notice this but me.

Joseph comments that the women used to sometimes travel with Veena but they also ranged further south and east than she did. He found it good they are willing to help her. "Veena has always been willing to give to others in need. It is why people like to work

Wine And Weddings

with her. She seems rough at first but has a generous heart. I am pleased you saw past the roughness. You have found a good thing in finding her for a wife."

The afternoon slips to evening and Salome comes to call us for dinner. We line up at the outside water tank and Jude fills the washing trough so we can wash our hands before going in. Joseph has devised the trough so that after wash up he lifts a gate at the end and the water flows to the drinking trough in the stable. We wash up and move to the house.

Dinner is a giant bowl of stewed chicken with vegetables and there is a generous pile of flatbread. Joseph offers a hearty prayer of thanks and includes me in the gratitude he expresses to the Father. The meal is lively and Mary requires me to tell her all the information concerning the betrothal. I can see she would have been bothered had the men already discussed the arrangements and events without her.

I ask about their betrothal out of politeness more than curiosity. They exchange a look communicating there is a story there not often told. I want to give them an out but am unsure how.

Joseph clears his throat, "Mary and I faced some challenges in our betrothal year. The hard part was hers but I was not helpful at first. You will learn the story but not today, friend. You asked an innocent question but it has a complex answer."

I nod my understanding indicating his answer is enough. I also notice Mary looks at Jesus instead of Joseph as he speaks. I surmise they are not the only couple to not make it through the betrothal year without giving in to the temptation I feel for Veena. I quickly change the subject by asking what I think is a simpler question.

"Joseph," I begin, "have you always lived in Nazareth?"

He smiles, thankful for my understanding. "No," he answers, "Mary and I both grew up here. We lived in Bethlehem for a bit during the census because I had to go there to register my lineage. Afterward I found work in Memphis for a time and then we returned here. We passed through Kerioth on our way to Memphis and on our return, enjoying your father's kind hospitality both times."

I had forgotten Joseph knew my father briefly when we lived there. When we met again in Jerusalem, he mentioned it. "Yes, the taxing and the census inflicted so many. I do not recall your visit when I was small. I am thankful we have become friends now. We need each other if we are ever going to be free of the yoke of Rome."

Joseph measures his response, "We are blessed that the Romans here are good to us. Maxim, Portimus, Longinus, and Patrius have always been good to us. Even though Patrius acts like a sanding stone on pink skin, he listens to Maxim and will not act against us."

For the first time I feel the stories of my family pushing me to anger towards another other than Romans. "You may have seen their docile side. They are still cobras we allow in our house. Patrius is the one who killed my mother right here in Nazareth when I was an infant."

Mary gasps. Joseph exchanges a look with Jesus and James. He takes a sip of water before responding, "Your loss grieves us. For this we hold great sorrow for you. We will not discuss it with anyone not at this table unless you give your leave. It may be possible for there to be forgiveness and restoration in the plans of God bringing you back into the same vicinity. We will pray for all of you."

I realize the anger I have shown is out of proportion for the atmosphere at this table. There is a portion of love here greater than I have known at my own family table. "I apologize for the harsh words in your home. If you like I can spend the night elsewhere."

Mary speaks with a firmness telling me never to cross her, "You will do no such thing. You are our friend and our guest. You will stay here whenever you spend the night in Nazareth. If I hear differently then I will also hear the reason."

I open my mouth to further apologize and Joseph holds up his hand. "My wife has spoken on the matter of hospitality. I have learned over twenty years this is enough. You do not want her to think you are resisting or objecting. It will go harder for us all should you."

Jesus and James laugh at this, nodding their agreement. James is closer to Mary and gets a gentle swat for his mischievous grin. He seeks to save himself from her light-hearted disapproval, "Mother always says it is not enough to believe the Law. We must live it out with others for it to be real to those who do not believe."

Mary smiles deeply and approvingly when her son quotes her tutelage. It brings to mind the many hours my father has spent teaching me the Law and the Prophets. I too smile as I see the love shared in this family. The dinner descends into less troublesome chatter. Mary brings out some yellow sweet smelling bread. She explains it was made with a rare spice Veena had gifted them just before her wagon burned during Passover. The bread is filled with figs sweetened with honey.

The after-dinner prayer includes Joseph asking a blessing on my rest and the gratitude he feels that I am staying with them. Joseph invites me to join him on the bench in the front yard by the chickens. He brings a jug of water and two plain olive wood cups.

Pouring the water into the deep cups, he passes one to me. Setting the jug aside and easing back on the bench, Joseph looks at me and speaks, "Things sound like they are unfolding well for your family. I hope the blessings of God fall richly on all of you."

I knew this blessing was not given as a conversation starter. He meant it. "I wish the same for your family," I respond. "The times are peaceful enough but I hope we can manage all of the work that needs doing."

"If you find you are behind, I will send a couple of my sons to aid you," the carpenter offered. "I know little about growing olives or grapes. What I know about growing vegetables and herbs would be easily surpassed by Veena. My sons are strong and know how to work hard. Most days, Jesus and I can get all the work done here. We keep the others busy so they learn the trade."

I thank him again and drain my cup. Joseph fills it again as the evening makes an obviously subtle transition from dusk to dark. The stars wink into place and the carpenter lets out a gentle sigh.

Pointing at the stars making up the constellation of the Ram, he dwells on a memory he chooses not to share. "The stars do remind me how creation makes us all so small. I do not often get to sleep under the stars but they are always glorious to me."

"*The heavens are telling of the glory of God; And their expanse is declaring the work of His hands*" I respond recalling the Psalms and their beauty as I have recited them to the stars. "God is truly blessing us but I wonder why he also leaves us in bondage to Rome. We have been cured of our idolatry. Rome installs rulers who push us away from God. The priests have lost their way. All of that seems to fade, however, under the naked stars."

Joseph eyes me quietly for a moment before continuing. "Nazareth has not forgotten what happened to your uncles and your mother. I do not know what versions of the story you have heard but I would like to ask unless it is a violation of our friendship."

Versions, I think for a moment. It has never occurred to me there could be a version other than the one my father told me. I relate to him what I know of the story and point out I have never heard anything different. As I say this, my heart floods with trepidation. The cornerstone of all I know is the story of the Romans who killed my mother. Just the idea there being another "version" of the events chills me.

Joseph begins gently telling me the other version; the one offered by the Romans and many witnesses in the market that day. Unsummoned anger rise in me as he explains many say my uncles attacked the Romans first. There were many witnesses who refused to bear false witness just to implicate Roman soldiers. He goes on to add that my mother's death was an accident and not due to malice.

The anger inside me wants to erupt. This cannot be true. I look at Joseph squarely, "My father has told me all my life Patrius killed my mother. He was there. He witnessed it."

Nodding in understanding, Joseph adds more to the story, "Patrius, Portimus, Longinus, and Maxim are my friends. They have been a part of our extended family for many years. Patrius does not speak of this. Longinus, however, came to me when there was some other Zealot trouble not long after we returned here from Egypt. According to him, your father was not in position to see who threw the spear that killed your mother. He is a Roman but he does not lie."

This seems too much for me. I drink more water and Joseph fills my cup again. "If it was not Patrius, then who killed her?"

Joseph lowers his head, "Only Patrius and Longinus know the answer. One of the other soldiers there on the day in question survived the incident but was murdered on the road to Jerusalem when carrying dispatches to Longinus. It was clear Zealots murdered him."

I think to run to the garrison and confront Patrius. Joseph sees the anger in my eyes and places a hand on my shoulder. "Patrius does not speak of these things and he is more dangerous than most realize. Longinus rarely comes to Nazareth. If you choose to speak to any of the Romans, speak with Maxim. He is hard as a stone but a real heart beats beneath his armor. He sees us as people to be treated with justice and sometimes even kindness."

All I can imagine is Joseph has somehow been fooled. Then the Proverbs rise in my mind, *"He who gives an answer before he hears, It is folly and shame to him."* This is why we memorize. This is why we learn. I nod to Joseph and thank him. I do not tell him I will speak to father first.

Awkwardly we talk about wine making and carpentry for a little longer. I am anxious to sleep. I am also anxious to know the truth. Joseph shows me to the place in his house where I will rest for the night. With a final look of compassion, he takes his leave of me. I find sleep quickly enough but it is filled with visions of anger and vengeance renewed.

I awaken early and choose to slip outside for some prayer under the violet sky of early morning. I sit on the bench Joseph and I shared the previous evening. My efforts to pray are hindered by my thoughts about my mother and her demise. Anger and hatred demand vengeance.

A sound from the other side of the yard wrests me from my brooding. It is the noise of wood on wood. Looking, I can barely make out a figure moving away from our wagon into the shadows of the houses nearest to Joseph's.

I know I cannot pursue the person but I rush over to the wagon to see what may have been of interest. Inventorying the things in the wagon as I go, there are few things that could be of value to a thief. I cannot be certain in the low light but things seem to be undisturbed. If this is the case, what the person may have wanted is more of a mystery.

Searching the cart, the few tools in the back and the harness for the donkey are all there. The bed is empty. In the front, however, there is a bundle not present last evening. It is large with a hastily scrawled note.

> Judas, Esther and I have heard of a spice shipment arriving in Joppa. We are leaving early to acquire more items that will benefit Veena and our business. We will be back either next week or the one after.
>
> Please give these cuttings and seeds to Veena with our love. Our hope is we can all prosper as we seek to serve God through providing good herbs and spices for his people. I remain your servant, Susa.

True to her note, the bundle contains a vast quantity and variety of seeds, cuttings, and plants. It is damp enough for the cuttings to survive the day. Nothing is labeled but I assume Veena will readily identify the lot.

My mood mollified by the kindness of Esther and Susa, I return to the bench to find my prayers are kinder and easier. I thank God for his further provision and imagine how pleased my betrothed will be at the gift. After an hour, the rest of the house begins to stir. I go to the well and draw water for them all as a kindness to my hosts.

When I return with the water, Mary and her daughters are already busy in the kitchen, James and Simon are tending the goats and donkeys, and Jude is feeding the chickens. Joseph and Jesus take the pails of water and put them in the kitchen.

We greet each other all around and I am thankful no one inquires about how I slept. Joseph suggests we load the wagon and then we can dine together before I travel back to Cana. He and Jesus move toward the door and I join them.

With three men working, it takes very little time to load the cart and yoke the donkey. I pay Joseph his asking price which is fair and yet low. He says they will bring the rest of my father's order when it can be acquired. He estimates two weeks. We wash and go inside for breakfast.

The morning meal is rich and friendly with this family. We talk of the wedding and James mentions he will be working on Veena's cart today. I almost wish to stay longer but I want to get the bundle of supplies to Veena. I tell Joseph about it and he smiles expressing his joy that we have been blessed.

I take my leave and turn the cart and donkey toward the city gate and the garrison. Maxim is standing by the garrison speaking with the Legionnaire on watch. He waves me down and asks if I will take a message to Amulius. I agree and tuck it into the sheepskin bag I keep for currying messages. All the way back to Cana I consider how I am going to discuss the death of my mother with my father.

Even though I am caught in a maelstrom of emotions vying for my heart, there is nothing but imbalance there. The difficulty of believing my father to be wrong concerning his passion is too much for me. If I have hated for the wrong reasons, then my anger is unjustified. My mind tries to tell me how guilty the Romans are anyway. I know I must find a way to settle this in my heart. I know there is a way but it seems beyond my reach.

Wagons, Wines, and Weddings

Arriving home in Cana, I have plenty of time to put the load of wood in the shed and clean the cart. There is no one at the house and I assume they are all out working the trees and vines. Taking a little time to refresh, I enjoy the coolness of the shed, wash off the road dust, and water the donkey.

As I look east from the shed, I know I need only walk up the hill to the groves on the higher ground to find my family. For the moment, however, I will enjoy the solitude. I have decided on an approach to father but it will need to wait a day or so. I want to celebrate the good things and the favor of God I found on the journey.

A cool breeze comes from the east off of Galilee, flowing up the hills, it brings the moist air so needed for the vines and trees to flourish. I can smell grapes and the musk of fertilizer. Deciding to walk up to the fields, I grab a jug of water in the event those working there are thirsty.

I find Tabitha, Jael, and Elon first. They are busily tending the rows where Veena has planted or will plant her herbs. The plot she has laid out is large and gets good sunlight. It also has one side that passes under the first row of olive trees for the plants requiring more shade. My nieces cry out in greeting but keep working. They know the work always comes first with father.

Veena is assisting father with erecting new vine arbors. When I reach them, as I pass out water to refresh them, father explains that Darrius believes we can double the yield of our grapes if we give them more space to grow. Laying aside the water jug, I proceed to help with the line of arbors. Whilst we work, I assure father all we wished to transact in Nazareth was completed.

As I tell Veena about meeting Esther and Susa, her delight distracts her from the work. When I explain the bundle they sent, she ties off her current beam of the arbor and with father's blessing, departs for the shed to retrieve her seeds and cuttings. She will have the cuttings in soil today and have plans for the seeds as well.

Taking advantage of her absence, I assure father the plans for the wedding can go forward. I also explain my transactions with the Romans and Joseph. I decide now is the time to begin the discussion about my mother. I feel my fear and anger vie for purchase. I look him in the eye.

"Father," I begin, "I need to ask you about something but I wish to do so with great love and respect for you. It will be difficult but if we speak the truth, we will prevail."

In my father's eyes I can see he is aware. He is certain I approach him as a man and not just his son. He is also certain I do this with respect for him. He simply takes a seat on the edge of one of the arbors and nods.

"This is difficult for me," I begin. "I know it will be uncomfortable for both of us. When I was in Nazareth, I spoke with Patrius. His account of events that happened when I was an infant differ from what we have believed all these years."

I see father stiffen. He knows I know more than I did. I am not sure what is truth and I need to understand. "Please father," I continue softly, "tell me the entire truth of this. I would honor mother by knowing the truth."

I have never seen my father weep. A single tear traces its way down his right cheek. "What truth would you know Judas," he asks?

"Patrius says mother's death was accidental." My voice shakes, "He says my uncles attached the Romans first. He made it clear you were not involved in the attack. He says Longinus ordered you spared or he would have killed us both."

Father looks straight at me. I can see the dam of emotion is about to burst. I cannot tell if it is his anger which I know so well or something new. He just stares for what seems like an eternity. Then his eyes change. When he speaks, he sounds almost young. "I loved your mother far beyond our marriage. I loved her from the first time I saw her at the market in Kerioth. I already knew the Romans were cruel and harsh. In my grief it was easier to lay all the blame on them. It was better to tell a one-sided story. I could not let her death be a tragic accident when there was such an easy target to blame."

I sat with this for a moment. I could tell father wished for some response from me. What he has just said threads its way through what was the truth until he spoke. Everything I have built my hatred of Rome and my commitment to Judea on is founded on a single horrible lie. My anger and sorrow clamor for control of my heart. My father deserves anger but he also needs understanding and compassion. Again, the Law echoes in my mind. It asks how I would wish to be treated if our roles were reversed.

"What does this mean in terms of our work with the Zealots, father?" I ask. This is the best way I can see to mitigate my anger and get at the heart of the matter.

Father chooses fact wrapped in pride, "Rome is no less guilty of the systematic murder of our people. Your mother would not be dead had they not killed your uncles."

Anger seizes me, "My mother would not be dead had my uncles not attacked the Romans who have been good to Judea since they arrived here. This General and his men treat us with respect. They are only violent with those who violate the law. Their rule over us is unjust but it has been allowed by God."

My father hangs his head. Without raising it he asks, "What then can I do to make things right between us? I have lied to you and I have failed to love God with all I am."

I sit beside him. I sit quietly. The thought comes to me as if suggested from outside my own mind. "Let us really build something good here father" I begin. "We can make good wine, grow great olives, and provide the region with herbs and spices. You can enjoy your family as they grow. We have friends in Nazareth and we can cultivate that as well."

He sits for moment longer and then looks me in the eye. "Yes, we will do as you suggest. Let us return this place to the height of fine wine and olive oil. We will host weddings and celebrations. You and Veena will build a fine spice and olive trade. Our good work will be our repentance for not loving others for so long."

Rising, I extend my hand to help father up. I begin, "Let us start by telling the family of our direction tonight. They will find peace in a clear direction for all of us. We have enough hands to make it all work."

"Then make it work we will, son. We begin today to build a legacy for you and your children that will be remembered throughout history. Your name will be synonymous with fine wine and fair dealings."

What my father says feels good. His announcement of both the marriage and our plans are loved by the family. We all enjoy the meal and some leisure afterwards.

Veena and I slip away for some conversation afterwards. All she can speak of is the plantings and seeds she has. She intends to plant everything in the next few days. She takes me out to the garden area where she has already planted the shoots and cuttings sent by her friends, Esther and Susa.

When father is sure no one is near the shed, he also visits the wagon I used for my trip to Nazareth. Whilst Veena and I celebrate the gift from Esther and Susa, father retrieves the one they have left for him. Under the wagon seat, in the secret place he made there years ago, he finds a bundle of the curved short knives used by the Sicarii. These Sicarii daggers are easy to conceal.

Simon takes the bundle of thirty Sicarii and hides them in his room. Later, when everyone else sleeps he divides them into three parcels to leave at prearranged places for the Zealots who need them. He keeps notes of all his transactions with the Zealots and adds this one to it. I will learn later it was no accident the sisters sought me out and insinuated themselves into our lives as friends of Veena.

I sleep peacefully believing things will be better for our family. My father's journal will only become known to me after blood is spilled and the future we plan to build for our family is hanging in the balance. It will be too late for some and irreversible for others.

In the morning, Amulius and Darrius join us as we lay out the rest of the garden and expand the vineyard. The plants already growing on the arbors become leafy in the warm sun. Darrius shows father, Judah, Elon, and Calah how to trim and train the grape vines on the arbors.

This day and many days to follow are filled with work and joy. Weekly travel to Nazareth finds me often speaking with Joseph and his family. Esther and Susa often send small gifts to Veena with me when I leave. Midway through summer it is clear our grapes and garden are doing well. The olive trees also seem bounteous. The trees we brought from Kerioth are growing well in the rich soil here. Father is discussing how we will graft the southern olives with northern ones to see what we get.

On a cool afternoon as we stop for some nectar and cheese to see us through the day's work, a call comes from the gate. It is Amulius and Darrius but they are not alone. With them are Joseph, Jesus, and James. They are in their wood cart and pulling Veena's new spice wagon.

All work stops as the family gathers to greet our guests and to view the new spice wagon. Veena's excitement is obvious. The wagon is far better than envisioned. Joseph has also brought the wood order I was to collect in Nazareth tomorrow. We unload the wood and place it in the garden shed to be used on father's project on the north edge of our land. He has not told me what it is for but he has had weekly loads of wood retrieved.

Joseph and father confer about something for quite a bit as the rest of look over Veena's wagon. The movable casks for the spices are joined so well they slide in and out of place easily. The excellence of the work is unquestionable. Together Veena and I pull the wagon to the shed and return to the throng in the front yard.

Father motions for everyone to be still. We all give him our attention. "Today is a day I have anticipated for some time. Joseph and his older sons are here to lend us his skill as well as deliver the wagon to Veena. With the help of Darrius, I have been quietly building a house for Judas and Veena to live in after the wedding. The family of Joseph will be helping complete the house over the next few days. I will ask the women arrange sleeping space for our guests and plan dinner accordingly."

I am overcome by the generous kindness of my father. We refresh ourselves and I return to the work on the arbors whilst father and Joseph go to work on the house with his sons. My cousins also go to the house with them. Veena and I set to work on the arbors and share our joy at father's gift. I also tell her about my talk with him and how receptive he was.

As we plant and prune others build. Soon enough the day is done and we all gather for dinner. Sari and Puah have prepared a feast for us all. We all sit under the large arbor closest to the house. The evening is warm and quiet. We dine and talk of the new house and the growing crops of grapes, olives, and herbs.

I notice James and my cousin Tabitha talk with an interest greater than the others. Perhaps there is something there. If there is, father will have noticed as well. Families spring from interesting places including Passover Bazaars and grape arbor dinners. We do not talk too late into the night because we will all have much work in the morning.

The house has been arranged to accommodate our guests. I am still sleeping in the shed. The young boys are sent to sleep in the wagon to make more room in the house. Our guests know not to protest as it would diminish our gift of hospitality. Calah and Elon think they are going to sleep out in the shed with me. Their mothers make it clear to them this is not an option. I think of them more as brothers than cousins. The recent news about their fathers will be learned by them one day. I hope I can ease their pain when it is.

Making a palate out of one blanket and covering with another, I lay down the older wagon to rest. This is the same wagon I rode in from Nazareth to Kerioth as an infant. The thoughts about my mother and her death weave their way into my sleep. I can tell I still struggle with the truth of it.

I am unsure how long I have been asleep when a noise outside the shed awakens me. Someone silhouettes the doorway. I stay quiet to see what unfolds. For a moment, I both fear and hope it is Veena come to steal a moment alone with me. It is not. It is a man but I cannot see his face in the shadow.

His voice whispers clearly, "Judas, I would speak with you if it is not a disturbance." From the tone I can tell it is Joseph or one of his sons.

Instantly wide awake, I respond, "I am here. Feel free to join me."

Walking out of the shadow, I can clearly see it is Jesus. "I hope I have not startled or disturbed you," he begins. "I would get your thoughts on the things happening in our two little towns. Perhaps since we are in favor with the Romans, we can do more to promote the peace."

Sitting up, I move over so he can sit on the edge of the cart. "Please join me. We can talk as much as you wish."

Jesus sits by me. "Eventually we will be traveling to Jerusalem again. I think anyone from this region is going to be under careful watch by the Romans. They know the Zealots are working out of Galilee. We are blessed with fair-minded Romans. This will only last so long."

I answer, "It is difficult for me to think of Romans as fair in any way. General Maxim does treat us well. His men follow his example here. Still, the events in Jerusalem remind us we are dealing with sleeping cobras. They will eventually strike."

He looks at me for a moment. "Perhaps, if we treat them well, as my Father does the Garrison in Nazareth, they will not have to strike. We have many things in the Law telling us how to treat strangers in the land. That they think they have taken our land does not change the Law."

"I cannot disagree," I nod. "Still, how will our behaviour impact the Zealot problem?"

"Our families will prosper here," says Jesus. "We can set an example. We can be devout Jews who do not cause problems. When our people were captives of the Persians, did not Daniel obey the Law and rise to be Rhab-Mage of the Parthian Magi? If we keep our faith and keep the Law where it applies to our guests, truly God will honor us as well."

"Again, I cannot argue with the truth you speak," I agree, "but God has been silent for so long. What we need is Messiah to come and make his rule the way of the world. We need to see his rule asserted over all our enemies."

"When the time is right, it will happen," he says. Can we agree for now we will work together to guide this region into peaceful acceptance that God has all of this under his control; his plans for us are to prosper us and not harm us?"

I shake my head, wondering how his words have cut so deeply to the truth of it. Between the house, this family from Nazareth, and the hope I see in Veena, I feel things can be peaceful if we work at it. Father has agreed to work here to make things good.

Jesus stands and moves toward the door. He turns, "Tomorrow we will finish your home and return to Nazareth. We know most of the families here and there. I am sure as your family begins to host weddings here, we will get to talk often. I look forward to seeing this all unfold."

He nods and slips out the door. I drift off to sleep pondering what could be if we were able to keep the peace. I dwell on how prosperous it would be if we found a way to live our faith without stirring up the cobras. Sleep settles over me.

I awaken in the morning refreshed. After washing my face, I join the two families for a robust breakfast and by day's end there is a small home on the eastern end of father's land. After Joseph's family departs for Nazareth, I return to working the arbors and garden. We establish a simple weekly routine of work tending the garden, the olives, and the grapes. Almost weekly I journey to Nazareth for supplies. I deliver messages for the Romans.

As summer slips away we harvest crops truly blessed by God. We hold a harvest feast and Joseph's family, Maxim and his Centurions, and Susa and Esther all attend. It is the first real celebration in our new home. We have so much to be thankful for and no one present questions this.

The Romans have obviously learned our customs. Maxim, Patrius, Portimus, Amulius, and Darius all observe the ceremonial washing and behave reverently as we pray. I see Patrius is uncomfortable but he does his best. The tables set under the great arbors, still heavy with dark ripe grapes, accommodate us all well.

We have earned our place in Cana. The other merchants count on us to deliver messages and materials to Nazareth for them. At dinner we discuss plans for Passover in the coming Spring. It seems our first pressings will yield a great quantity of wine for the market. Patrius is the first to remind us we will be delivering some of the wine to the Garrisons as tribute. Amulius laughs and quips we may as well deliver it to Patrius directly.

I must admit I care for these particular Romans. It is obvious they are close friends with Joseph and his family. Amulius and Darius have grown close to our family and even father seems to like working with Darius. At the very least he is pleased with the grape yield and the beauty of the vineyard, all due to the dedication and skill of the Roman.

When there is a lull in the conversation, Maxim clears his throat for attention. "I received word from Rome today," he states. "It is official; Darius is released from the military and invited to stay as servant to Centurion Amulius. Further, he is awarded a small stipend for his faithful discharge of his duties. It was agreed his injuries, whilst not life threatening, disqualify him from the Legion."

Wagons, Wines, And Weddings

Turning to Amulius he continues, "Since you wrote the request, Darius is left in your care Lieutenant. He can remain at the Garrison as long as there is room there."

It takes me a moment to realize this is a celebration. Rome is not known for care of the soldiers of her conquests. Darius is an exception and we are all thankful for it. The dinner closes and the Romans depart for the Cana Garrison. It is still cool enough in the evening to sleep in the wine shed. Father sees the children and our guests have places in the house. Veena and the women will sleep at our home far enough away to observe propriety.

Autumn arrives with a vast quantity of wine fermenting in the new skins provided by some local shepherds after their late summer culling of the sheep. In the wine shed the slow bubbling of the fermentation process sounds like rain. The skins all hang from the beams in the ceiling designed for that purpose. Darius checks on them daily.

The wine will be ready for tasing in late winter. It will be ready by Spring for sale at the market and delivery to the Romans. Most of my visits to Nazareth now are to curry messages of the Empire. In our garden shed rows and rows of herbs and spices hang drying to be sold in the Spring as well. It will be a busy year at the beginning and then we will have time together. The wedding is set for two weeks before Passover. Observing all propriety, Veena and I spend as much time together as we can. The cold winter nights will be warm again when Spring arrives and we begin to realize the hopes we carry. Leaving the anger and bitterness behind has helped me see the good in most people. It is true, however, even cobras sleep quietly in winter.

In the relative quiet of the winter months, Cana seems to sleep restfully. We spend our days caring for the wine skins, drying herbs, and preparing for the Spring planting. Father chooses to send a message to Shlomi's family in Jerusalem inviting them to the wedding.

My journeys back and forth to Nazareth is only every other week at this point. With less people on the road, it is not as safe because it gives opportunity to bandits. After the Festival of the Maccabees in Kislev, father asks that I take the invitation to Jerusalem personally. He explains he spoke with Amulius and one of the Centurions will be traveling there next week. If I go to Nazareth the day before, I am invited to travel with him. My mind races through the names of who it might be accompanying me. Portimus, Amulius, and Longinus are pleasant enough. Patrius is both irksome and dangerous. He has been neutral of late and perhaps there is a way to build on it.

When the Festival is over, I prepare for the journey. Amulius intends to go with me to Nazareth. Veena hands me a bundle of still warm seed cakes. She explains that none of them are for me but I am to give half to Mary and half to General Maxim. Checking I can see she has wrapped to sets of cakes individually and then again in a linen encasing them all. I am unsure if she does this for my convenience or to keep me from temptation. Either way, once she is sure I will not help myself to the cakes she hands me a smaller bundle and whispers they are for me.

I turn the cart toward the road out of Cana leading to Nazareth. Amulius exits the small Garrison before I can come to a stop. He is trailed by Palouse and Darius. The Centurion carries a bag and his pack. He also has the leather pouch he leaves in my care when I am carrying messages for the Romans.

He mounts the cart without ceremony and I consider it odd that he is riding with me rather than taking his own horse. He must see the surprise on my face. "My father has sent a new horse for me from Rome. It is waiting for me in Nazareth. Riding with you will be a new and anticipated experience for me."

I ponder that were this man not a Roman Centurion who could at any time receive orders to burn Cana to the ground, he and I would sound like fast friends. Some of the bile I have carried for so long tries to rise in me. This Roman, however, has never done me wrong. I respond as he hands me the messenger bag, "It is wise to have an extra horse here. Was there an occasion for the gift?"

Amulius shakes his head, "My father breeds the particular horses coming from Hispania. They are known for their skill in maneuvering and their beautiful flowing manes. Father is very good at horse breeding and has developed a strain both strong and durable. He even managed to keep the beauty."

Stowing away the messenger bag, I respond, "I can tell you are delighted and you are welcome to ride with me as opposed to near me."

We both laugh, take our leave of the other Romans, and depart. The ride to Nazareth is filled with conversation that is light but free. Amulius tells me of his time in Gaul and Hispania. I do not know of these places but his description of their lush greenness makes me wish to see them.

He also explains he arrived here because his commander in Rome did not like his father. Until Maxim arrived, he feared he would spend his days as just another overlooked Legionnaire. He says he begins to see why Maxim cares for the people in this land.

I must confess I struggle with his words. One part of my mind sees these kind Romans as a deception puts us off our guard with the rest of them. The Law, however, requires love and kindness of me regarding them. Even though I have chosen to try and be good to these Romans, the larger picture still vies for my anger and attention.

The Centurion must have seen the trouble in my eyes, "What is it Judas?" he asks. "I see trouble on your face and would know how I may help."

Again, anger tries to repress the love and kindness. Still, I can tell he is being genuine. "I still struggle with what happened to my mother and the thought of befriending those who were a part of it. My belief, however, requires me to forgive and that I be good to everyone. We are obligated to be good to strangers in our land."

Amulius nods his understanding, "We are all aware of the death of your mother. Longinus still grieves over it at times. He and Maxim are honest men. Were it not true that it was an accident they would be honest. I know it is hard to carry but the truth must be what we embrace."

I know he is right. Then he continues with words making me suspicious again. "My greater concern," he says, "is the Zealot activity will be what defines your people in Rome. The Senate and Caesar have no love for this region as it is. That such a small state causes trouble impeding commerce is something they will not long tolerate. The reason Maxim is here is to stop the Zealots. He and Portimus, his first officer, are planning to find a way to stop them without violence but it may not work."

"I know my people," I reply, "they view any form of occupation or bondage as an affront not just to them but to our God. He gave us this land forever. Ever since he did, foreigners have tried to take it. There are those among my people who will die to fight for our God. They cannot be mollified."

The Centurion nods his understanding. He changes the subject and offers me some water. I silently agree and do not pursue the thread of discussion. I recall the two seed cakes Veena gave me and pull them out from under my seat. We each eat one, savoring the sweetness. Again, I feel this man could be my friend were things different.

The rest of the journey is silent but there is no tension in the air. As we approach Nazareth, the Centurion speaks a final thought, "Talk to Longinus about this. You will be able to see the truth of it. I will not speak of our conversation with anyone. It is the least I can do to repay your honesty."

The arrival at the Garrison in Nazareth has become common to everyone. Instead of going to Joseph's home straightaway, Maxim has had a lunch prepared for us. Patrius, Longinus, and Portimus are all present. As we dine on boiled eggs, cheese, and goat stew, I quietly pass the bundle of seed cakes to Maxim. He knows at once what they are and sequesters them under a fold in his cloak lest someone suggest he should share them.

The meal is a short one and Maxim proposes we not depart for Jerusalem until morning. I infer he is going with us but that is not his implication. He explains Longinus and I will take a cart loaded with armor and arms that has come from Joppa. I am to accompany him, deliver some messages, and return here with the cart which will be supplied with food for the Garrison.

It is simple enough. It will also give me the chance to speak with the Centurion Commander as we travel. My mind tries to suggest all this has been arranged by the Romans because somehow, they know of my father's past. My spirit says it has been arranged by something higher. I express that I am aligned with the plan and ask permission to visit Joseph and his family.

Maxim asks I remain here. He says Joseph should be by later in the afternoon with the wagon we will take to Jerusalem. I realize when he employs "we" he does so because he includes his support in every errand his gives to his men. He journeys with them even when he remains behind.

I choose to sit outside and rest through the afternoon. Mulling over the Law of Moses and that which we are to obey concerning strangers and sojourners, I speculate on who I will ride with to Jerusalem. As the afternoon deepens toward evening, I hear the cart before I see it approaching. It is larger than mine but just as rustic.

The man pulling it has a yoke turned the wrong way on his shoulder so the space for the ox's neck can drape over it. The carpenter pulls the cart with ease expressing the strength that is not obvious when there is no exertion. That this one man can pull a cart meant for a pair of oxen also aids in telling the tale of his strength.

Still, there is something odd about the beam of the ox yoke over the carpenter's shoulder chills me. I rush to help in the pulling only to find behind the wagon there is someone pushing as well. Jesus is the one under the yoke and Joseph is behind the wagon. Jesus says nothing but Joseph calls for me to help push.

The Roman cart is a heavy one. The timbers are reenforced with brass to make it defensible. The sides have metal sheeting on them and are higher than most carts. We push and pull it to the front of the Garrison. Four Legionnaires, Joseph, Jesus, and I transfer the items destined for the Jerusalem armory to the cart under Maxim's direction.

The items are wrapped in cloth drenched with thick oil. Their weight makes it clear this armor is iron and not the softer bronze. This armor is intended for battle or at least for real protection. I ask as we are loading the last of it, "Why so much armor for Jerusalem? I thought things were peaceful there. "

One of the Legionnaires growls at me, "One can never count on peace where Jews are involved. The Governor has asked for and

Wagons, Wines, And Weddings

been granted extra Legionnaires for the Jerusalem Garrison. Rome will bend this nation to its will or this nation will be broken."

It is the voice of Longinus that cuts off the soldier's rant. "We will not insult a guest of the General who volunteers to help us load the wagon. Your personal feelings about the locals is subject to your duty to Rome. I am certain you do not wish to offend our friend Judas. If you do not care about that, consider you offend me and the General."

The Legionnaire snaps his head up and signals his understanding. I can also see the anger in his eyes. There is no doubt this soldier is obeying against his will. It is clear the man would do anything he could get away with to the Jew of his choosing. I quietly hope I am never alone with him.

After the cart is loaded, two oxen are brought from behind the Garrison and yoked to the harness. Two horses are also brought around. I feel confused until Maxim explains that two of the Legionnaires will accompany us as part of the transfer of soldiers to Jerusalem. He points to Carious and Palo, introducing them to Judas. Both had helped load the cart. Palo was the one who had words for Judas and was reprimanded by Longinus.

Both are older soldiers and have been at the Garrison since I began currying for the Romans. Longinus is in real, not ceremonial armor and carries his odd-looking spear. I am sure it is the one father has described often. Unlike the Roman Pilum, this spear is longer and has a haft tapering at the head. The metal of the tip is not like iron or bronze. It shines like silver and has a broad leaf shape. Just below the tip I can make out writing in silver inlaid in the wood. The little Latin I know serves me well. The single word on the spear is *Fatum*; Destiny.

The Legionnaires take their place ahead of the wagon as Longinus climbs into it to sit next to me. It is clear he intends for me to drive the oxen. After a few words of good wishes from Maxim, Patrius, and Portimus, we bid our farewell. At the last moment I recall my own duty and pass the bundle meant for Joseph to him.

As we pull away, I ponder that behind me are Romans who treat us well even though not all of them love Jews. Ahead of me is one who would not treat me well no matter how he feels. Longinus will see to it there is no difficulty but just how careful would these Romans be were my protection necessary?

We arrive in Sychar just as the sun falls behind the hills to the west. The inn is always welcoming to Longinus. His wife, Syrah used to work at this inn. Nahum, the innkeeper is up in years and his son, Syrus does most of the work now. He is elated to see Longinus.

"Longinus, you are riding in a wagon," he exclaims. "Are you injured? Do you require aid?"

I can hear genuine concern in his voice. The two Legionnaires dismount from their horses and try to hand Syrus the reins. He ignores them, moving to the wagon. Palo looks irritated but keeps silent.

Longinus grins at Syrus. "I am quite well, thank you friend. I am riding because my horse is in Jerusalem. I helped deliver a new horse to Amulius in Nazareth. My friend Judas was kind enough to drive our wagon to Jerusalem and will return it. How is Nahum?"

Syrus returns a comforted smile, "Father is slower but doing well. He will be glad of your company and news of Syrah. Let me show you in. Are the Legionnaires staying as well?"

"Yes," replies the Centurion Commander, "put them in the small room near the baths if it is available. Judas will stay in my room. Is any of that an inconvenience?"

Syrus shakes his head indicating it is not. From his pack Longinus produces a small bag of coins. Tossing it to Syrus he explains, "Maxim wanted to be sure we stayed ahead on our account. There may be a great deal of traffic in the coming weeks. My room must always be available to any of the General's council. You may, of course use it for someone in great need if it is empty."

The young innkeeper nods his understanding. He whistles and a young boy exits the inn. Longinus considers Syrus was the same age when he first arrived here wounded and weary. The care he received from Nahum and Syrah back then set him on the path to where he is now. Syrah, now his wife made her interest in him clear and he returned that interest making the inn under the protection of Maxim and his men by fiat.

The boy takes the horses and the cart. The four of us follow Syrus into the inn. Nahum, seated behind the raised counter where food is set out from the kitchen, waves cheerfully at us. I remember him from my journeys back and forth to Jerusalem. I recall my father telling me this is where he met Longinus and Patrius. Being in closed quarters with the Centurion Commander is not what I would choose but is obviously going to be thrust upon me.

At the door to the room intended for Longinus and I, Syrus suggests the four of us wash off the road dust and come to the common room for dinner. We agree and the two Legionnaires turn to follow Syrus to their room. Longinus and I enter the room familiar to him and unknown to me.

I notice he chooses the bed facing the door. He props his spear up in the corner where he could easily reach it from the bed or the chair. The spear that killed my mother leans in the corner of a room I will share with the man who threw it. The man seeks to be my friend but by definition he is my enemy.

He is a Roman Centurion charged with reining in all Jews in the region. He is Centurion Commander of the Garrison in Jerusalem. He is one of the leaders in the quest to destroy the Zealots. All of this is true but the man is good to me. He is kind to others. After dinner I must speak with him.

A young woman, Deborah brings some hot water and a basin to our room. Longinus and I wash and then repair to the common room. The table closest to the service area is empty. Longinus points to it. We are seated and soon joined by Carious and Palo. As they are seated, the girl who brought water to our room gives us a large jug of wine and four cups.

As we pour our drinks, she returns with a platter of goat and vegetables as well as fresh warm flatbread. Without thinking I begin the prayer of thanks and am halfway through it before I realize the two Legionnaires have begun eating already. I finish the rest silently and allow the Centurion to serve himself before filling a piece of the flatbread with hot spicy goat and roasted vegetables.

We speak little and eat well. Longinus takes the last piece of bread and uses it to soak up the juices from the goat. He raises his hand for attention. "Judas," he begins when he has everyone's attention, "I would honor you and offer the last morsel as a bid for peace between my family and yours. I do it in front of my soldiers so you have witnesses."

He pauses and looks at his men. I do not realize it but his voice has carried and the entire room is listening. "I know," he continues, "I have cost your family much. I would make amends by seeing to the future safety of you and your kin. You should not have to pay for the crimes of your family. You serve Rome well even when you are not compelled to do so. Accept this honor and let us have peace."

Longinus proffers the morsel to me and I feel I can do nothing but accept it. The stranger in our land seeks forgiveness and peace.

I honor him by accepting it. The Legionnaires seem unimpressed. I notice the silence in the room and look around as I enjoy the sop. Sitting on the other side of the room, in the corner closest to the door, are Esther and Susa. Esther catches my eye and smiles.

Returning her smile, I gesture for them to join us. Susa shakes her head no. I let it go and return my attention to the table. The sound of talking guests rebuilds as people dismiss the diversion of a loud Roman and return to the various stages of their meals.

We finish our wine and at a word from Longinus return to our respective rooms. As we sit together, a little wine in our heads and some discomfort in our situation, the Centurion Commander speaks first. "I know you have ample reason to hate me. I wished to break the silence of our situation publicly so the private conversation would go more easily."

I nod in understanding, wishing there were more wine but pouring water for both of us. "There are things changing in me," I reply. "It seems this may be one of them."

Longinus continues, "I have done worse things since I accidentally killed your mother. I treat your people well in hope I can find redemption for the things I have done. I am not like Patrius; hating anything not Maxim or Rome. I am not like Portimus, full of faith and conviction in this God you follow. I long for freedom from my guilt but I also love Rome."

"I understand your plight," I begin. "God says I must care for the stranger in our land but he used to have us destroy the enemies of his people. We left our idolatry but my people are oppressed by your people. We must treat you well to honor the God that we pray will send Messiah to destroy you. It is a puzzle."

The Roman actually smiles when I say Messiah. I wonder if he thinks me foolish and he reads that on my face. He dispels the notion with his next words.

"I know of this Messiah you yearn for." He takes a long drink of water between statements. "I first came here when I was young with the Magi from Parthia who were seeking him. Maxim conducted them safely to Jerusalem. They testified they had found him and we worked to keep him safe from the former Herod. If the story of your Messiah is true, then he lives and would be close to your age."

I am shocked this man would be so sincere concerning our beliefs. "What else do you know of him?" I ask.

Longinus smiles again, "More than I am permitted to say. I have likely already said too much but Maxim would allow it for you, I think."

My mind races. These few Romans are good to us. Now they speak of Messiah as if he is real. It breaks on my mind that if the Redeemer is at hand, the Zealots will not be needed. They should be ready to aid him but if Messiah is my age, when will he act?

I look Longinus in the eye, "For the sake of our family and for the sake of Messiah, I will forgive you of all that has passed between our families. We will be friends if you wish it. I cannot speak for my father but I see the Centurions with whom we do business treat us honestly. That is enough to begin."

He looks deeply into to me for some shadow of deception. He answers, "That is enough for me. We are friends. Further, at my word Maxim, Portimus, and Amulius will be as well. All I can say for Patrius is he will not allow harm to you and yours as long as Maxim restrains him. He has his own tragedies to tell, but he was down the darker path before your mother's death. That he did not kill your father that day shows that there is something in him holds hope."

I take a drink of water and fill our cups again. It gives me a moment to collect my thoughts. "I will say nothing about our conversation to anyone. I would, however, ask if you can tell me anything else about Messiah. We hold this hope so tightly."

"I can tell you only this and nothing more," rejoins the Commander, "we have held this secret for twenty years. We have dealt with others who claimed to be your Messiah and their actions brought them all to a bad end. Save Amulius, the rest of us have watched over this knowledge with our lives. I cannot say I believe the man is who he is portended to be. I do believe the secret we protect serves both Rome and your people. For now, that is enough for me friend."

I can tell by the way he says the last he will speak no further on the matter. We talk about travel and the growing unrest in some areas. Longinus speaks of the Zealot problems in the south and rumors they have a growing influence in Galilee. We turn to our beds but my mind is racing.

I wonder if Messiah could truly be among us. I ponder what it would mean to find him and serve him. I pursue the idea of helping Messiah overthrow Rome as I enter sleep.

When I awaken Deborah has already delivered a hearty breakfast and word that our wagon and horses wait for us outside the inn. We dress and eat then meet the Legionnaires outside. Syrus is there to bid us good journey and we make the turn south out the gate. The Romans ahead of us are quite different from the one beside me. By day's end I will be pondering if that variance makes all the difference.

Syrus has included food for us and it will not be necessary to stop on the journey to Jerusalem. Carious and Palo are engaged in some deep conversation. At Longinus' signal we stop in the shade of a bluff to distribute the food. He calls for the Legionnaires to ride back to him and they turn to comply. Even these Romans will not refuse good food from a good source. The arrow that passes through

Carious' neck nocks him backwards off of his horse onto the ground. The one intended for Palo misses narrowly imbedding itself in the hindquarters of his mount.

The horse jumps forward and sideways at the same time. Palo, taken by surprise, falls as the horse bolts out from under him. Both horses flee north, back toward Sychar. Before anyone can respond two ropes fall down from the bluff and four figures hurry down them.

Longinus responds like the Centurion he is. Faster than I can follow, *Fatum* is in his right hand and flying upwards at the descending figures. It sails skyward and into the uppermost man on the rope nearest us.

The spear catches the man squarely between his shoulders and his arms flail out away from the rope. He falls, hitting the other descending man and both of them plummet to the ground. The unwounded man has his wind knocked out and does not recover before the quick thinking and acting Longinus can advance on him and dispatch him with his gladius.

The two attackers on the other rope see their companions fall They pull themselves back up the rope, realizing they have underestimated their quarry. Palo, having gotten to his feet, picks up his pilum where it fell. He launches the heavier spear at the ascending foes and clips the shoulder of the lower one.

The voice that cries out is female and she manages to keep ascending to the top of the bluff. The other attacker pulls her to safety and they both disappear over the edge of the rim. Longinus orders me to watch whilst he sees to his men.

Carious is dead. The arrow pierced the vein in his neck. Palo's right arm hangs limp at his side. It then occurs to me he threw the pilum with his left hand; his off hand. Longinus orders Palo to the wagon and he moves to the bodies of the fallen attackers. Retrieving Fatum, the Centurion inspects the dead men.

I can only hear a single word escape his lips. He says it like the foulest curse one can utter, "Zealots." He lifts a Sicarii dagger from the body of one of the fallen men. Palo begins to move up the road north in search of the horses. I stop him, suggesting he stay with the wagon whilst I search for the horses.

Whilst I walk, I ponder the female Zealot. It was either Susa or Esther. This to my mind means the others was likely one of them as well. They were at the inn but would not communicate with me.

I find them not too far up the road. The wounded one is wide-eyed and difficult to approach. I catch the other one by the reins and turn him south. Guiding the horse very slowly, I see the other one begins to follow. Within half an hour we are back at the wagon.

Longinus has not been idle. He has the body of Carious and the two dead Zealots loaded into the wagon. Palos sits in the front of the wagon keeping all pressure off of his wounded arm.

Without a word the Centurion approaches horses. He ties off the calm one and produces something from his hip pouch. The horse immediately nuzzles his hand and takes the offered dried apricot. Producing a second one, Longinus moves away from the first horse. Neither I nor the horse realized the Centurion had tied the horse to the back of the wagon whilst is was distracted.

The second horse smells the apricots Longinus holds at arm's length on the palm of his hand. Not risking a movement, I watch as the wounded horse, blood thinly trailing down its left hind quarter, moves tentatively toward the man. Longinus says something softly in Latin. The horse moves closer and Longinus draws the apricot toward his body. At the same time the animal takes the fruit from his right hand, Longinus grasps the reins with his left.

As the frightened beast devours the fruit he is tied to the back of the wagon as well. In the calm of the moment, the Centurion gently guides the horse to the ground so the wounded flank faces upward. He signals for me to come.

It takes a moment for me to realize I must move. Gesturing to the horses head he motions for me to hold it still. Straddling the horse's hind quarters, he quickly pulls the arrow out and holds down the animal until it quiets again. The entire time he has not stopped speaking to the horse softly in Latin.

Once the horse is calm again, Longinus signals to me and we both move allowing the horse to stand. In some odd twist of trust, the horse allows the Centurion to clean and dress the wound. I water them from our waterskin whilst Longinus turns his attention to Polus.

Walking up to the wagon front, he sees the Legionnaire still cradles his arm gingerly. For the first time since the attack Longinus smiles and there is mischief there. Placing one strong hand on the shoulder of the wounded man, the Centurion pushes the arm up and across the chest. A dense pop erupts causing both horses to jump a little and one of the oxen to bay.

Palos lets out a yelp more of surprise than pain. The pain comes next. He can move the arm again but it will take some time to heal. Longinus pulls a strip of cloth from his pack. He fashions a sling and immobilizes the arm tight against the Legionnaire's chest. The soldier points upward to the bluff, "What about my pilum?" he asks.

Longinus grunts, "You can have Carious' pilum. He has no more use for it. Unless, of course you wish to climb up there and get yours." Turning his attention to me, the Centurion continues, "Palos will need to ride with you and I will ride and guide the horses. Try not to hit too many rocks."

What he says is funny to me but I dare not laugh. Three people are dead. One of them, a Roman, died at the hands of Zealots. There will be more blood before this is done. Then there are the two who

Wagons, Wines, And Weddings

escaped. I wonder if the sisters will trail us. Following to attack again is not unusual for Zealots.

I nod to Longinus and we proceed down the road to Jerusalem. After a short time, Palos turns onto his uninjured side. He rolls his cloak under his head and is soon sleeping off the pain. I do try to keep the wagon on the worn smooth path created by centuries of those journeying to Jerusalem for feast days.

It surfaces in my thoughts I am caring for a wounded Roman and that they fought off Zealots. My father could have been among the attackers were we further north. The Zealots thought they had found an easy target but any one of Maxims' Lieutenants could best four common men. Something about this puzzles me but I have not yet reasoned it out.

I think as I ride and Polus sleeps. Longinus rides ahead far enough for us to be warned should he encounter any further trouble. He guides the horse with his knees, holding his shield in one hand and Fatum in the other. Anyone seeing him now would think twice before daring an assault. Thinking of the spear throw that felled the Zealot, I realize this man could not have intended to kill my mother. None of the facts support intent relative to the man in front of me.

I am still turning all of this over in my mind when we reach Jerusalem. Arriving at Herod's Gate, Longinus calls for the Legionnaires guarding it to take Palos into their care and lead both of us to the Garrison. They know their Commander and obey him instantly. Two of the four guards move to the wagon. Longinus rides ahead to the Garrison stable to see the wounded horse receives care.

When I arrive with my escort, they ignore me but rush the injured Legionnaire into the Garrison. It seems everyone but me has neglected the three dead men in the back of the wagon. I admit to being a bit concerned over sitting in a Roman wagon by a Roman Garrison with a dead Roman and two dead Zealots in a wagonload of Roman armor. If the wrong Legionnaire comes along, I might join the corpses before getting an opportunity to explain.

I have just begun to pray when Longinus returns. The two soldiers also emerge from the Garrison. Gesturing toward the back of the wagon the Centurion speaks, "See to the legionnaire in the back, unload the armor, and dump the Zealots in Gehenna." Pointing toward me he continues, "This is Judas of Cana. He is my honored guest here. See to it all the Legionnaires know this as well as the Temple guard. Should anyone even insult him they will serve a month in the valley as guards."

Even I know of the stench of Gehenna. All Jews avoid the valley and for Longinus to send the bodies there is a gravid insult to the dead. I assume he knows this. I know I will never go near the place. He gestures for me to get down and I follow him into the Garrison. He assures me Palos will heal.

He orders one of the Garrison slaves to prepare a meal for us and asks after the senior Legionnaire. The slave, from some tribe I have never seen nods and responds in a language sounding like Latin but is not. Disappearing down one of the two long hallways a Legionnaire with a tunic full of service stripes soon exits from the same.

Saluting Longinus, he speaks, "all was quiet here until you brought us a wounded soldier. Welcome home Commander. The Spaniard said you wished food. Are you not returning home to dine with Syrah?"

"We will eat here so you can take down my report," orders the Commander. "Judas and I will then rest at my home. Send someone to Syrah to tell her to expect us. We will clean up whilst dinner is prepared."

We wash and eat. The report he gives to his aid includes the suspicion the attackers were Zealots. Longinus delivers the information with clear and honest detachment. He pauses a moment when detailing the death of Carious. I can see the hurt in his eyes. Even the soldiers that are less than good men matter to him. He cares for every soul under his command.

Once Longinus completes his report, he repeats the order demanding the wagon be loaded with the list of supplies he passes over to a Legionnaire. He commands it to be ready for me to go by second hour so I reach Sychar long before dark.

The senior Legionnaire assures his Commander it will be done. Turning to me Longinus motions toward the door. We walk up the street from the Garrison to a few small houses quartering the most senior Roman officers. No one in Jerusalem outranks Longinus. He has a small house but it is the best of the five that are there.

Syrah is delighted to have Longinus home and to see me. She remembers me from years earlier at the inn in Sychar, I was the infant with a grieving father. She met Longinus then. He returned wounded from Nazareth. She wonders how our destinies became so intertwined that as an infant and now a man I am with her husband, the man who killed my mother and we are friends.

We talk for a bit but the events of the day make me weary early. Before going to the room they have provided for me, I get their promise to come to Cana for the wedding in the springtime. It is a chill mourning when Longinus and I walk to the Garrison. The wagon is loaded and ready. Syrah has sent along some warm bread, dried fruit, and tender lamb. A fleece and a cloak are on the wagon bench to keep me warm as well.

It is not likely the day will warm. Winter has arrived in earnest. I bid farewell to Longinus. The day will be a good one to travel as most will not wish to in the cold. I am on the road for an hour when the thoughts of the last couple of days assault me. Men I am supposed to hate have protected me and provided for me. Zealots, my people, have attacked and killed in front of me. The men might not have spared me in the attack.

My father would have sided with the Zealots. Depending on the circumstances, I would have as well. The moments where these few Romans are acing good and just keep accumulating. The evidence is they are still usurpers and conquerors but Maxim and his Lieutenants seem to move among the chaos with honor and integrity.

As I think and pray, I ponder Longinus' words. Could it be true Messiah is among us? If so, I must find him. I must do all I can to support him. I know once I have proof Messiah is here, I can help him overthrow our oppressors. I must begin to seek him. I must know him.

※

The journey back to Nazareth and then to Cana passes easily. So do the next few months. Winter gets colder and then begins to fade away to Spring. There are more trips to Nazareth and more work on the house meant for Veena and I. When the first leaves erupt from the olive trees and grape vines, it is time to begin our outdoor work.

Four weeks before the wedding which is six weeks before Passover, Veena and I will hold our wedding feast. Passover is the latest in the year it can be which means there will be an early harvest of flowers and herbs for market before we journey to Jerusalem. We put in new plants for the garden as soon as the danger of cold has passed.

Darrius comes the same week to see to the new growth on the grape vines. He takes Calah and Elon with him and teaches them how to prune the vines for the best branching and growth. The retired soldier reports we should have a great grape harvest this year.

Wagons, Wines, And Weddings

The trio inspect the wineskins in the hanging shed. Darrius declares them ready for sealing into jugs. We all gather in the middle of the afternoon and begin the process. By sunset we fill and seal almost two hundred earthenware jugs with sweet wine. After we expend all the empty jugs, we fill two large jugs having wooden seals. These are as large as the urns kept by the door of every Jewish home for washing the dead. The ones I fill are earthenware but those for the purification of the dead are stone, The stone ones absorb nothing so they are always pure. Darrius will take these to the two large urns to the Garrison.

We lay down the sealed jugs to rest and father invites Darrius to dine with us. During dinner he says our grapes should be robust enough to make Sharon wine. This rich dark red vintage is prized everywhere, It is highly prized and will bring a good price at market. He suggests we should have at least one hundred wine skins and we prepare for up to five hundred jugs of wine.

Father having also inspected the olive trees; believes we will have nearly fifty barrels of olives from the harvest in the fall. We have twenty barrels from the previous year will sell at the Passover market. The year opens with great hope.

The wine we preserve will have laid down just long enough for our wedding feast. The weeks leading up to it seem to pass like the flowers on the olive trees. The pruning worked and the grape vines send out long healthy shoots which flower as well. Father has erected a series of bee hives among the vineyard rows and olive trees.

The week of the wedding arrives and the land is alive with green and growth. The grove, garden, and vineyard dance with the bees gathering the nectar that will become honey in the harvest.

Our small town is bursting with life as well. Guests begin to arrive in Cana and the town stirs with the reopening of our vineyard as a place for marriage feasts. To father it is fitting the first wedding of that resumption is his son's.

※

The coolness of morning before sunrise is one of my favorite moments of Spring each day. The ruddy dawn and my time at prayer combine to begin what should be a perfect wedding day. Cana is filled to capacity with friends and family from all over.

Some wedding guests will still arrive this morning. I am secluded in the house father built for us. All of the women are staying the main house. This rare night alone was one of thought and insight. The peace of our times is truly only a veneer.

The attack on the wagon when I journeyed to Jerusalem was no isolated incident. Over the weeks we have had reports of further attacks by small groups of Zealots moving very quickly to strike and retreat. Those killed have not been looted. Even the finer horses have been left behind. The Zealots are killing to send a message for the Romans to leave.

Anyone knows this message will not be heard by Rome. It will be resisted and eventually repulsed should it take an entire legion to quell us. It is not the day for it but I long to speak with Maxim and find a way to avoid trouble for Cana like there already is for Nazareth. Apparently, there is Zealot leadership hiding among the people of the city in which General Maxim resides.

True dawn brightens and with the song of the birds I hear the sound of mallets driving pegs carried on the light morning breeze. That would be the sound of Joseph and his family assembling the wedding arch. They must have arrived late last night after I retired to the house for my solitude.

Wagons, Wines, And Weddings

Walking out of the sunrise, a figure crests the hill moving toward me. It could be any of Joseph's sons as they are all similar in appearance and bearing. Except for Jesus their shoulders, hair, and stride are very alike. Before I can distinguish who it is, Jesus calls out to me, "Good morning Judas. Perhaps this is a good day for a wedding. I have brought you some bread and roasted lamb from your aunts. They say you need to eat as it will be some time before the feast."

Again, even his words draw me. I return his greeting, "It is indeed a good day to marry. I hope when you take a bride, your day is as beautiful and clear."

Handing me the basket, Jesus takes a seat beside me on the bench outside the house. He also has a jug of fresh grape juice held over from yesterday's pressing. He smiles saying, "Darius is acting the steward from first light. He added this to your repast insisting you share in the delight he finds in these grapes even when they are still."

We offer a prayer of thanks and break our fast together. The conversation is on the wedding and what lies ahead for our family. Jesus offers that God seems to be blessing us and this pleases him. I rejoin that their carpentry work also sees God's blessing. We talk for a bit about the abundance God provides even in the midst of our nation's trouble.

The conversation stays light and Jesus offers another prayer of gratitude after we are done eating. As he begins to take his leave of me, he looks me in the eye, "I have asked your father and gotten permission to return for you when it is time for you to arrive. You and I will be friends for rest of our lives, I think. I would be honored if you would allow me to be your man for the wedding."

I am delighted this honorable man thinks so highly of me. I have no brother to serve in this role and assumed father or one of my cousins would. The answer is simple, "Yes ,my friend. I would be filled with joy to have you represent me. We shall see all things properly fulfilled for this wedding."

After Jesus departs, I bathe and dress for the wedding. I find myself thinking again about how much I respect this family from Nazareth. Jesus is my age and all of his siblings are younger. They all work hard. It is simple to see Joseph and Mary are both proud of them. I know I have seen Jesus' brother James and my cousin Tabitha share close looks more than once.

I think in a few years, if that continues, I will suggest the match to father. He will be responsible for finding husbands for his nieces. If there is already an affinity there it can only help. I know because I marry for love, the life we have will be richer. After dressing I rest and even nap for a bit.

At the noon hour I hear the sound of both animal and human footsteps. Jesus has come for me with the donkey foal intended for me to ride to the feast. I think this bit of ceremony foolish but father will have it this way or none. He sees in it the portent of Messiah and wishes to embrace that symbolism whenever possible. One would think he would rather see Messiah on a war horse dispatching Romans but today is a day of peace and so I ride the foal.

When we crest the ridge leading down to the main house, the view of it is obscured by the tall rows of grape arbors erected by Darius and my cousins. It is not until we reach the edge of the hill, I see how our front yard has been transformed. The wedding arch and a long white linen are on the main path to the house. A circle of posts that could hold up a tent are placed in case the weather should turn damp. It is not likely it will rain.

Rabbi Esau and Rabbi Samuel walk to greet us, praying a blessing over me as I alight from the foal. Jesus' brother, Simon comes to lead the donkey away and I follow the rabbis and Jesus to the appointed place by the arch. The guests are all arrayed around the path in the yard. All grows silent as Veena emerges from my father's home. Mary, Puah, and Sari accompany her.

Veena is completely veiled and the flowers adorning her veil are all her favorites. I am certain she has grown them all. They are from the seeds and shoots provided to her by Esther and Susa. I see the two sisters to the right of the path. I push away the thoughts of them as Zealots tempting me to distraction. I can hear the sound of small bells as Veena slowly walks the path of white linen stretching between us.

I think for an instant what an act of love it is that the women have put out white linen for her. They all know of her abuse in the past but have lain it aside out of love and respect for who Veena has become to them. I consider God would be pleased my family puts love for others above the institutions created by men.

Jesus touches my elbow and subtly gestures for me to look at Veena. Beneath the wedding veil flowing from the crown of her head to the bells on her ankles, I can see a hint of crimson from the gown she wears beneath the veil. The contrast against the white linen is bold and beautiful. Isiah drifts into my mind, *"though your sins be like scarlet, they shall be made white as snow."*

Before I have any more time to ponder, Veena is at my side. With a look from my father, the rabbis begin to evoke blessings over all of those present, including the Romans who have come from Nazareth and the Garrison here. There are prayers for faithfulness to God and each other. The prayers become more refined until Rabbi Esau speaks a final blessing over us uniting us before God.

I hear Jesus, standing to my right whisper something I cannot understand but I know he is praying for us as well. My heart captures in this moment the vast sea of blessings on which I am adrift. I have a bride and she is all I could hope to have. I too whisper a prayer of gratitude as I accept this life bond with all I am.

The women complete the formal removal of Veena's veil and we are both placed on the wedding bier for the short procession to the tent erected behind the house for the feast. After we are delivered, the guests will all join us.

The curtains are drawn on the bier and Veena and I share our first kiss. It is filled with all the tension we have withheld for the months since we first knew we loved each other. For the first time I understand why we have laws to keep us distanced. Had the trip to the feast not been a short one, someone would have been embarrassed.

The feast is filled with wine, songs, and joy. The wine is the best I have ever had and one can see the pride in Darius as he receives the compliments of the guests. Even the latter wine is good quality. The food matches in quality and quantity. I know some of the dishes served were prepared by Esther, Susa, and Veena. Perhaps only the Romans have tasted their like. None of them disappoint.

It is the joy that is so filling. I gaze around at the many people and preferences represented at my wedding. I find it fitting for us to celebrate with friends who are not alike but care deeply for each other. Patrius is even at peace for the day. I am sure the quantity of wine Amulius pours down him helps. Both Longinus and Portimus have sent gifts with their regrets at not being able to attend. Portimus has returned to Rome on some errand known only to Maxim and the Emperor. Longinus is in the southern part of Judea quelling an uprising.

The evening arrives and the foal is brought around for me to lead Veena to our home. Amidst the cheers and well wishes of our family and friends, we begin the short walk up the hill to our home. Once we are out of sight, we both care nothing for protocol. The passion of our love is fully kindled by the time we reach the door of our home. That it is fueled by love and nothing else makes the home fires burn with greater intensity. I had not thought I could love this deeply and I will do whatever is necessary to keep this love alive.

The Funerals and The Pharisees

It astounds me how quickly eight years slip through the glass. Each day has its own joy and sorrow as the grains of sand measure out our lives in pursuit of love for the LORD our God. All is good for our family. The vineyard, the grove, and the garden all provide momentously for our needs. We have enough to be wealthy and to share generously with others. My cousins all grow and learn. Soon I work only to oversee the labor of my younger family members. It is not that I will not work but the management of the work is labor enough now.

Father has begun to take messages north for the Romans from Nazareth and I continue to transport them south. The Garrison commander, Amulius has passed over a few promotions so he and his servant Darius can remain in Cana and with our vineyard.

The only dim spot in our bright lives is Veena and I do not yet have children. She sometimes feels a deep sadness about it. I never feel she has failed us. I was happy to have her as my wife and the prosperity we share is abundant and joyful. Just a few weeks before Passover, we sit as a family with father and the aunts planning our work to be ready for the feast.

Both father and I had messenger trips for the Romans and Veena was going to oversee the food preparations for the bazaar in

Jerusalem. Her wagon had served us well over the years and she had a large group of merchants who anticipated her wares and brought good coin to buy from her. She has also sent Joseph and his sons much business. Other merchants now have wagons similar to hers.

The relative peace of the years is true but there has been increasing Zealot activity as well. It is mostly to the north and outside of Cana and Nazareth the unrest receives increasingly harsh Roman responses. Tolerance for the common Jew wanes as the Zealots wear thin the patience of Rome.

The early spring morning when I take my leave of everyone is bright and warm. Darius is already among the arbors. Veena and the other girls, now almost women tend the garden. My aunts care for the house, the chickens, and the livestock. The cousins tend the olive trees and the heavy work of caring for the buildings and fences. The saplings from Kerioth are now full producing trees yielding plentiful rich olives.

Father and I take our wagons to the Garrison. Amulius meets us at the gate and hands over satchels with letters, water, and some dried fruit for our journey. The Centurion is still very good to us. By example from him so are all the soldiers at the Cana Garrison. Once a traveling merchant tried to cheat my Aunt Puah at the Cana market. Her cry of foul was answered by three brutish Legionnaires who made it quite clear that disrupting the women of our house was considered and insult to the Empire because our family serves the Empire.

There are other benefits as well. We received a better, lower rate on our taxes because of our favor with the Romans. I know father would not have approved of this so I pocketed the difference and used it to help others who could not pay all that was required of them. I know Amulius is aware of this. I think he approves. I use the extra coin for good and help others. I am sure it is alright.

The Funerals And The Pharisees

Father and I ride to Nazareth taking in the beauty of the spring day. When we arrive there, Maxim has a small mid-day meal for us and a larger collection of letters and missives headed both south and north. Some are headed all the way to Rome.

I will stay in Sychar over night at the inn near Jacob's well. They have become so accustomed to seeing me they regularly send messages with me to Longinus' wife, Syrah. Their sons are the delight of the aging Nahum and more than once he has made the journey with me to Jerusalem to see his grandson.

Father will head north to Ulatha and then back through Capernaum. Whilst we are eating, Maxim expresses that Patrius must accompany father as he carries a report only meant for Phillip of Antioch. Father hides his hesitancy well but I know his looks and something is not right. Still, he has grown comfortable with our local Romans and hardly ever refers to them as cobras any longer.

We take our leave of Maxim and I drive my wagon the short distance to the great road running from the salt sea to Syria. There, in Damascus the road joins greater trade routes running to Parthia and Rome. Father and I part ways at the road and he and Patrius travel north.

I will reach the inn at Sychar before dark. It is a lovely day and I focus on what our family will accomplish this year. I have grown used to the nice room at the inn and the good treatment I receive there. Syrus, Nahum's son cares for the inn well since his father has grown old. I know the welcome there will refresh me as much as the food and bath will.

The road is easy and the donkey's drawing the wagon are content. It is quite still as I pull into the path and under the arch at the entry to the inn's yard. I can see women gathered at Jacob's well to collect water for the evening. This place is one that gives me relative peace.

Stopping the wagon by the door, I climb down and walk into the inn. Uncharacteristically, the main room is empty. I do not recall ever coming here when either Nahum or Syrus were not here to greet me. Further, there are no guests in the common room even though it is near dinner time.

I think to call out but then wait to see if someone comes out from the back. The quiet is too noisome for this place. Then, I hear a din of sound coming from the garden behind the inn. Passing through the kitchen, I exit the back door. There are several people in a rough circle standing where the fig trees grow.

As I approach, I can hear someone weeping. Once I can see past the standing group, I see Syrus kneeling over someone who is on the ground. I see the man on the ground is Nahum and by his colour things are not good. Syrus looks up at me, relieved to see a familiar face. "Please Judas," he asks, "my father has died here in the garden. Can you help me?"

Most of the people around us are obviously guests of the inn. I am the only Jew here. I look to two men, obviously Persian and very strong. "Help Syrus move his father into the inn. He will show you which room."

Looking to the other two men standing there, I ask, "Please get the four large jars by the entry door and use my wagon out front. Take the jars to the well and fill them with water."

To the weeping woman I say, "Go to the well with the men and get the women there to help you draw water. If I remember correctly, Samaritans observe the same custom for washing the dead as we do."

One of the young men answers back, "Who are you to give us direction, Jew?"

I am wearing my courier bag with the insignia of Maxim and the seal of Rome on it. I answer, "I am a courier of Rome and aid to

General Maxim. Shall I send word to him you refused to help the family owning his favorite inn when they were in distress?"

The man who spoke pales. The woman speaks, "I am Photina and I live here. This is my new husband, Barnabas. He is full of spirit but not always wisdom. This is his brother, Cephas, he is strong but a little dull. We will do as you request."

The two Persians heard all they needed when I said Roman. They help Syrus lift the body of Nahum and carry him inside to his own room. They lay Nahum in his bed and leave. In less than half an hour Photina and her brothers return with the water. After unloading the urns, they directed the inn's stable boy to put away my wagon and to tend to the other guests who have just arrived.

I offer to stay with Syrus whilst he begins the washing ceremony. He gratefully accepts. I am sitting, knowing he does not want me to assist. I hear Photina talking to two other women. They enter the room. It is Esther and Susa. They begin to help without asking. Photina leaves saying we are to remain here and she will see to the guests.

Word spreads throughout Sychar and friends of Nahum come to mourn, help with the inn, and bring prepared food. I remain an extra day as do the sisters. We care for the inn as it has so often cared for us. We comfort Syrus and I promise to get word to Syrah and Longinus in Jerusalem. In that promise lies a threat I cannot see at this point. I sleep and our two wagons are ready in the mourning. We depart knowing the village will care for Syrus and when there is opportunity, Longinus will see to his needs.

Traveling with the sisters to Jerusalem gives me a sense of safety I only feel with soldiers by my side. I know well the sisters are trained in the way of the Sicarii. Once the road widens, we drive our wagons next to each other. I am always impressed with the articulate and intelligent conversations the sisters provide. Both of them, but especially Esther are fervently committed to our faith. They also possess strong views about Rome and the occupation of Judea.

They admit the current Roman leadership is "docile" enough but the Legionnaires still take advantage of the people. Susa offers, "We all know it is only a matter of time before a new Roman official or even Caesar decides more than compliance is required of us."

Ester joins in agreement, "It will come to violence sooner rather than later. There is no real oversight of the tax collectors. They are encouraged to cheat us for their livelihood. It becomes harder each season to make an honest living."

I answer, "We must admit Maxim and Longinus have done much to stabilize things. I agree we should be free and only under God's rule but at least we have a measure of mercy from him in these men."

I see a slight blaze in Susa's eyes as she responds, "Cobras in baskets are still cobras. They will eventually awaken. These Romans will bite us when we least anticipate it,"

Fighting to keep the chill in my heart from showing on my face, I respond, "We must be always vigilant. We must always know the nature of our adversary. The Lord will deliver us in his time. Perhaps Messiah is already on his way."

Mention of the Messiah sends both women and the conversation in the direction I desire. We talk of the hope and joy of the King of Kings coming to take our movement on his shoulders. In my mind, however, I am concerned. It alarms me these women just repeated the phrase, the metaphor father uses only among our family. Using the skills I have learned watching father over the years, I say nothing. I only nod.

The Funerals And The Pharisees

I use taking a drink from my water skin to avoid conversation. Then, after a pause, I express my concern Veena has not yet been blessed with children. These women have known her much longer than I have and it is the right diversion. I make it clear I am not disappointed in her and do not blame her.

Susa again speaks first, "It would not be unusual for someone who suffered the treatment she did to be wounded beyond child-bearing. I know you will not shame her over this."

"Even if he does not," rejoins Esther, "women will shame her out of spite. There will always be talk about barren women. It is one of the reasons we have remained unmarried. We will find our own way."

Susa nods in agreement with her sister adding, "This is yet another cause to rid our land of Romans. The Sicarii are the way, Judas. They will bring down the Romans here and if Messiah comes, they will be ready to stand with him."

At this last, I can see Susa has said more than her older sister wishes. They both fall silent but the lot has been cast. Perhaps they are just energetic supporters. They think they are good Zealots and that is not a good thing.

As I look around in silence. there is a large bend in the road with a bluff on one side. I recall this bend from years ago when I traveled to Jerusalem with Longinus and two Legionnaires. Up near the top of the cliff, still embedded in the side is the point of Palo's pilum. The haft has long-since rotted away.

I have thought of that day every trip to Jerusalem. Today, however, I recall Palo wounded one of our attackers with that pilum. It surfaces to my mind, making some sinister connections that the wounded Zealot was small, agile, and cried out in a female voice.

When I look back at the sisters, they too are looking up at the cliff. Susa notices me looking at them and taps her sister who looks away. It makes sense but it is also unbelievable. Women who work as Zealots is both a perfect deception and an advantageous way to work in secret.

As we finish our journey to Jerusalem in silence, it all falls into place for me. Father is still working with the Zealots. He travels north with the best cover possible. As a courier for the Romans, no one is going to question his having missives and scrolls. As one connected to all the Zealot leaders, he can help them be organized and better understand Roman movements. The sisters have been close to father since Veena introduced them. I live in the midst of the rebellion and have been unaware of it until today.

❧

At the Jerusalem gate I use my station to see the sisters pass without any harassment. This serves to at least let them think I support them and will not turn them in. When I arrive at the Garrison, Longinus is there. I ask at once if we can go to his office. He agrees seeing my concern.

I deliver the news about Nahum as gently as I can. It is clear he loved the man and after putting away the satchel of communique, we eat and wash then depart for the short walk to his home. I will hold what I have surmised of Esther, Susa, and my father for now. I am uncertain what to do and once again, uncertain of where I stand.

Those problems quickly recede from importance as we tell Syrah of the passing of her father. Her grief is instant and steady. Her tears flow but she still insists on treating me as a guest. With some effort, Longinus and I convince her there is no need for it. We have eaten with the soldiers and bathed as well.

Longinus calls the house steward and sends orders to the Garrison to have my wagon and his horse ready for early departure tomorrow. He also orders there be provisions laid in to fill the

The Funerals And The Pharisees

larder at the Sychar Inn. The steward of his house is handpicked and a freed slave. The man is loyal to Longinus and will be for life. All will be seen to and more. The three of us go into the Commander's sitting room to allow the grief to have its place in the night.

The steward returns from making the arrangements and informs me the servants have readied the guest room for me. I leave Longinus and Syrah to grieve together in a way only couples can. We will talk further on the road back to Sychar.

The Steward honors Longinus. The room is complete with food, fresh water, and what he tells me is the finest wine in the region. He points out the basin and towel for washing and bids me rest well.

I pour a large cup of wine and sit at the table. I wish to think and I take a deep pull from the cup. I smile as I realize the wine is one of ours. Of course, Longinus would have it in his house. Still, I need to ponder what I have concluded about my father and the sisters.

Drinking a full second cup of wine makes me realize I am more interested in not thinking about the situation. As the wine begins to put the faintest buzzing in my head, I choose I will put away thinking about this until tomorrow. Allowing the wine to seep into me, I prepare to sleep and take advantage of the luxury in which I will do it. All trials and tribulations can wait.

Morning arrives with the Steward visiting me the moment I rise. He leaves fresh fruit and water ask me to let him know when I have completed my morning prayer and broken my fast. As he exits, I see he has provided my clothing, cleaned and scented with myrrh. I pray, including Longinus and Syrah in my prayers. After eating, I dress and just as I go to the door to call for the Steward, there is a gentle knock.

It is Longinus, "Good morning, Judas," he smiles wanly. "I trust you slept well and all was to your liking."

Attempting to start things lightly I inquire, "Where did you get that marvelous wine in my room? It is one of the best I have had."

He does not get it and offers, "I will find out from the Steward. He chooses the wines for our guests. He will know where to get it and I will have him send you some."

I realize he is still lost in the numbness of grief. This group of Roman officers with whom I have made friends have all been cared for in some manner by Nahum. His passing cannot be easy for any of them.

The Steward appears as we are talking and Longinus inquires, "Judas was asking about the wine we provided for him last night. Can we get a small cask of it for him to take with him back to Cana?"

The Steward looks confused for a moment. "Master Commander," he answers, "That wine comes from the Iscariot vineyards in Cana. It is part of the wine they gift you each year. You say often to serve only our best wine to your guests."

The Steward's innocent honesty draws laughter from both of us. "Steward," chuckles Longinus, "This is Judas Iscariot, son of Simon, owner of the Iscariot vineyards in Cana of Galilee."

The Steward stands dumfounded. I can see he is working out whether he has erred or caused offense in some way. I rush to his aid. "You have honored me by serving my own wine thinking it the best there is. I am grateful and you need not send any back with me."

I can see the laughter was good for Longinus. The Steward turns to him, "The wagon, loaded with Garrison supplies for Nazareth and Cana, your horse, and another worthy horse stand outside ready to depart. I have been to the Garrison and collected any dispatches needing to go north. The officer of the day knows of your departure and I have sent word to the palace as well. I also took the opportunity last night to dispatch a messenger to ride straight through to Maxim and inform him of the situation."

Longinus eyes soften as he realizes just how capable and faithful his steward is. He knows this former slave could command the Garrison himself if needed. He finds a way to put Longinus' family first in all things. Nodding his approval, we meet Syrah in the main room of the house. She is dressed in mourning clothes and exits the house with us. Syrah chooses to ride with me and we begin the journey back to Sychar. The beauty of the day seems to mock the sorrow of my fellow travelers.

Our arrival at Sychar is quiet. Syrus greets us in the main room and he shows me to the guest room reserved for the Romans. Syrah and Longinus will use her room her father had kept for her here. We all remain for two days. It is decided Syrah will stay longer. She will help find some suitable workers for the inn. Longinus and I will journey to Nazareth to seek guidance from Maxim.

On the morning we are to depart for Nazareth, Esther and Susa arrive as we are about to leave. They give no hint they understand what I have surmised about them. I consider the time to reveal what I know is when we take counsel with Maxim. Longinus has left the extra horse for Syrah in case she chooses to join him in Nazareth.

We will not have to take the news about Nahum to Maxim. The messenger will have delivered it ahead of us. The letter asked word be taken on to Cana as well. I consider as we ride north what an impact this kind Samaritan man had on so many travelers. I realize I will miss his simple kind way of seeming inept but always rising to the challenge. I hope Syrah and Syrus can keep the inn flourishing.

Riding next to Longinus, I think to tell him about the sisters and my father. It would keep me safe if things go badly. It is also a betrayal of my family and my people. On the other hand, it may be the only way to save my family and my people. The choices bring only distress to my thinking. I must do something but I am frozen by the trepidation. Not for the last time I wish for the rumor of Messiah being born to be true.

Longinus and I speak little before arriving in Nazareth. He is still wrestling with his grief and I with my fear. The Garrison is watching for us and I see a Legionnaire move quickly into the building when he spies us on the road. By the time we reach the gate, Maxim has exited to greet us. Amulius joins him. Apparently, word has reached Cana and he has come to await his friend and fellow Centurion. I am greeted warmly and immediately forgotten as the Romans close ranks to care for each other. They may be brutal to their enemies and hard on their servants, but they are kind and good when they care for each other.

Whilst I am watching the Romans, three more Legionnaires exit the Garrison. Approaching the wagon, one of them barks out an order, "What are you waiting for Jew? Unload the supplies for the Garrison."

It takes me a moment to understand he is addressing me. Before I can muster a response, Longinus turns to look at the three soldiers. Rising up to his full stature, he responds to the men. "My friend Judas will be glad to pull the wagon closer to the Garrison to ease your unloading but he is not responsible to do your work. Remember his face and never speak to him that way again."

I can tell they will remember me from their look. I can also tell it will not be fondly. It does not matter. I drive the wagon over to the Garrison door leading to the supply room. The gate guards give me plenty of room to get through. They know me and even though they are not friendly, they understand the service I provide to their leaders. They even follow and assist with the unloading, providing a barrier for me even if they do not intend it.

After the wagon is empty the two gate guards walk back to the road with me. They see me out and I take my leave of my friends. It

The Funerals And The Pharisees

is early enough for me to make it home before dark. That is what I choose. I do not know when father will return from his circuit north but it is a waste of time to wait.

Driving back to Cana, the things I know churn over in my mind. I do arrive before dark and the family welcomes me warmly. I share the news about Nahum at dinner and then Veena and I go to our home. Only there do I finally feel at ease. As we sit together, I unburden my mind regarding the things I have surmised about Esther, Susa, and my father. Veena is surprised and expresses her fear it may all be true.

We retire and whisper in the dark about what it means to our family if father is a Zealot or is helping them. I drift off to sleep a little easier having shared my secret. Had I known the magnitude of the danger; I would not have slept at all.

❦

Father returns two days later. He is well and the journey was mostly uneventful. One of the smaller Roman outposts they visited is unreachable by horse or wagon. Patrius required father to carry his pack to the outpost and back. Whilst there he was not allowed indoors and treated with disrespect by the soldiers there.

His anger is justified but it is also clear there was insult but no harm. Patrius cannot know he has torn open the wounds from thirty years ago in a way that will change us all. The reasons for forgiveness and peace are about to become all too evident in their absence.

It takes a full week to quell father's anger. I get word to Amulius we will not be going to Nazareth until after Passover. He has heard of the incident from his fellow Romans and he understands. Word also reaches us all of a Zealot uprising in Caesarea Philippi. This is near the north end of father's route and occurred a full week after he was there. Word goes out as Passover approaches, there will be increased squad patrols on the main trade roads. The ugly side of Rome will be quite visible as random searches and inquiries become the normal cost of movement in Judea.

Amulius asks me if I will consent to a trip to Nazareth the week before everyone journeys south for the great feast. I consult with father and agree. The Centurion asks on Thursday and I am meant to go on Friday. This will mean I must spend the Sabbath in Nazareth or be in danger of violating sunset by not getting home in time.

Darrius accompanies us and rides in the wagon with me. I soon forget the tension as I journey the day with these two men who do not share my faith but are always kind to me. Darius and I have spent many days working side by side in the vineyards and I have learned much from him. We talk of the rich cache of wine we are taking to the Passover Bazaar. Our family also has barrels of olives, casks of olive oil, and a small fortune in herbs and spices to trade.

The year has been bountiful and I will not forget it. We have the kindness of these Romans as well as the provision of God to thank for it. Father seems to have already forgotten. We arrive at the Nazareth Garrison and I quickly take my leave of the Romans. I travel the short distance to Joseph's where I am welcomed by Mary and assured staying for Sabbath will be no problem whatsoever.

She explains Joseph is still in the carpentry shop finishing and important project. Salome, the eldest of Joseph's daughters sees I am given water to wash for the Sabbath and to refresh my thirst. Maria, her younger sister sets the table and the four brothers move food from the kitchen to the dining area for their mother.

I offer to help after washing but Mary insists I should act like a guest for a change. She promises to let me help with breakfast before I leave on Sunday. No one will work tomorrow. A slight chill enters through the window as the suns caresses the horizon to the west. All is ready and Mary begins to light the Sabbath lamps.

Mary turns to Jesus, "Go to the shop and get your father. He needs to wash before the sun sets so we may begin the Sabbath on time."

Jesus immediately smiles, "Yes, mother. I will bring him if I have to carry him back. If he is working on one of his more artful creations, it is the only way to drag him from it."

He is out the door too fast for me to offer to accompany him. He also does not return before the sun sets. Mary keeps watching the door; wondering what is keeping her husband and Son. Jesus finally returns but without Joseph. He is holding a beautiful olive-wood cup. His face is stern and sad all at once.

"Mother," he begins, "We will have to wait to begin our Sabbath." A tear slips down his face as he says, *"Barukh atah Adonai Eloheinu melekh ha'olam, dayan ha-emet."* (Blessed are You, Lord, our God, King of the universe, the Judge of Truth.)

Everyone knows Jesus has just announced the proclamation of death. He is telling his family their father has died. Mary begins to move to the door but her Son restrains here. "We must obey all things mother." He looks at me, knowing I will help. "James, our friend Judas, and I will take turns seeing he is not disrespected. He will not be alone but we cannot do more until tomorrow night."

Mary looks at her Son, knowing he is correct but wanting to go to her husband. She instead leans into his embrace and he comforts her as best he can. There is a change in that moment I cannot identify until much later. Part of it is Jesus has just transferred from the eldest son of a respectable carpenter to the head of a household with all of the responsibilities for its care. So far, he is bearing them well.

I volunteer to go to the shop first and sit with Joseph. The carpenter is lying on his work table looking as if he is only sleeping. The pallor of his cheeks betrays the truth. Already the ashen color of death saps away the rich brown that filled this man's always kind face.

I can hear Jesus begin to chant the Sabbath prayers as they are carried to the shed on that same chilling wind accompanying the sunset. *"Baruch ata Adonai, Eloheinu Melech ha-olam, asher kidshanu b'mitzvotav vitzivanu l'hadlik ner shel Shabbat."* (Blessed are You, Lord, our God, King of the universe, who sanctified us with the commandment of lighting Sabbath candles.)

I cannot hear the rest clearly but I know the children's blessings and join in them from afar. I wonder how Joseph is so neatly placed on the work bench but choose to pay attention to the Sabbath prayers instead. A deep loneliness creeps over me as I ponder, I am participating in the custom of family but I am alone and sitting with the dead.

Hearing the pain in the voices coming from the home, I dwell on the depth of faith this family shows in observing all they are commanded even on the knife edge of their loss. Hearing Jesus lead his family in the Sabbath prayers I am reminded of the prophet Ezekiel:

> *"And the word of the Lord came to me, saying, 'Son of man, behold, I am about to take from you what is precious to your eyes with a fatal blow; but you shall not mourn and you shall not weep, and your tears shall not come. Groan silently; do no mourning for the dead. Bind on your turban and put your sandals on your feet, and do not cover your mustache, and do not eat the bread of people.' So, I spoke to the people in the morning, and in the evening my wife died. And in the morning, I did as I was commanded."*

Not long after the prayers have stopped, the family keeps to custom, offering the songs of the Sabbath. Once they painfully complete the joyful music, James comes out to the carpentry shop with food for me and a small jug of wine. He offers for me to join the family and he will remain with his father. I honestly tell him he should be inside with them and I am content to honor them all by remaining with Joseph.

As I eat, I consider how hard this will be for them not only because of the loss but because of the proximity to Passover and the work they must need to do to be ready for the journey to Jerusalem. The Law makes no provision for these events. There is no place in it for the spectacle we make of death. I sit with what Joseph has left behind until almost midnight. At his insistence, I allow Jude to relieve me. I can see the pain in his eyes and long to comfort my friends.

When I enter the house, I pass the four large water jars like the ones at the door of every Jew's house. They will be used after the Sabbath for washing Joseph's body. They are used only for this in any faithful home. Cleansing death has no part in any other area of our lives.

Jesus is still up and offers me some wine. I take it and we sit together quietly for a bit. The table is clear except for the olivewood cup in the middle of it. It is beautifully carved and sealed against moisture. Properly cared for, it will last for many years. He sees me admiring it, "Mother said father was making it as a gift for me. He wanted me to have a special cup for celebrating the Sabbath when I am not here to do so with family."

"It is graceful and strong," I reply. "It will serve well for the wine of joy and the wine of sorrow. It will help you remember your father often."

We speak no more. There is nothing to be said in the rawness of this night. With a nod of understanding Jesus shows me to an empty sleeping mat in the room where his brothers rest. The morning will bring uncomfortable waiting. The day of rest will be a restless one.

Around lunch time, Maxim and Amulius come to the house. It seems it is their custom to sit during the afternoon with Joseph and Mary to discuss the week ahead. I do not claim to understand the affection the Roman General has for this family but that custom will aid them today.

Informed by Jesus of Joseph's death, Maxim immediately orders Amulius to dispatch soldiers to Cana to inform my family and to Jerusalem to tell Longinus. This will be the second time death has brought Longinus north from his command. None of us doubt he will come. He has trained his officers well and the legion guarding Jerusalem is capable and efficient. They can spare their commander for the sake of his friends.

It is a mercy from God these Romans can travel when we cannot. None of them are bound by the Law. The ones who understand our Law know what we need and set to work providing it. A Pharisee would find problems with our compromises but Amulius returns with Patrius and they begin filling the water jugs by the door of Joseph's home. As I watch them work, the reality of Joseph's death pours over me. He has been a friend to us since we moved north from Kerioth.

In contrast to the custom, Mary and her daughters weep quietly. James and Jude go out to the workshop to allow Simon and Joses to be with their mother. Maxim is also sitting with Mary but seems more like a tired old man than the Commander of all the forces in Judea.

The Funerals And The Pharisees

Jesus comes to sit by me. "Many things will change now, Judas," he says. "We will take time to honor my father and observe the Passover. Then, I must begin to do things to change our world."

I assume he is talking about taking over the carpentry. I offer support, "I know Joseph has trained all of you well. The business you have will continue on. We will be needing forty more grape arbors according to Darius. That is only for this spring. You know our family will care for yours in whatever way you need."

In the depth of his sorrow, Jesus smiles at me. "I would speak with you and your father after we have buried mine. I have an idea I think would seem to favor both of you."

"Of course," I answer, "we will do whatever we can. We are your friends."

Maxim interrupts us to address Jesus, "I would like to put some Legionnaires at your gate. They will not hinder or harass anyone but you are all loved and the press of mourning neighbors will be great. You know this city likes to mourn."

Jesus gently looks at the Roman General he has known all his life. "You show us great kindness. I will not reject your offer and you must agree we are allowed to feed whichever of your soldiers you send. We will feed Amulius and Patrius as well."

"If it means getting to eat with your family, I may stand watch myself," offers Maxim. "I will arrange it and I will send for a couple of stewards to help with food as well. As I said, they love your family and Mary will not need to make a meal until after Passover."

Turning to me, Maxim adds, "Consider your courier duties suspended until you are ready to take them up again. Your freedom to help Joseph's family is another gift I can offer to my friends."

Jesus and I both thank him. He wanders off and we pass the afternoon with the remainder of his family talking over our memories of Joseph and the way he has been a good husband, father, and friend. Sunset arrives and we begin the proper preparation of Joseph's body for burial. My family will arrive in time for tomorrow's funeral but none of the carpenter's close relatives are near enough. They will come later in the week.

After the funeral, the people of Nazareth begin to bring food to care for Mary, now a widow and her children. My father, my aunts and cousins, and Veena all help to direct the stewards from the Garrison. The soldiers currently on duty at the gate to the walkway are both well fed and pleased to have it.

All over the yard and house one can pick up on snippets of conversation concerning the kindness and generosity of the carpenter and his family. As evening approaches, Jesus, James, father, and I gather in the carpentry shop to speak.

James pours some sweet wine brought from our home by father. In addition he has some cheese given to the family by a dairy farmer whose cattle shed Joseph had often repaired. We have had a filling meal but the sweet wine and soft cheese seem just the thing.

Jesus does not wait to begin, "I am aware you think I wish to talk about the carpentry work. That, however, is only part of it." Looking at James, he continues, "I know you know all you need to take over and continue our family carpentry work. I need you to do so."

James begins to speak but a twinkle in the eyes of his elder brother stops him. He looks at all of us and begins to unfold his plan. "It is time for me to move into what I am called to do. With the blessing of the Father and the power of the Spirit, I intend to gather the people we need to establish a better rule of the Father's Kingdom in Judea and eventually in all of the world."

He stops speaking, allowing the import of what he is saying to settle on all of us. He does not let us speak yet, however. He continues, "My cousin, John is calling for repentance and baptizing along the Jordan. My plan is to go to him after Passover and begin to

The Funerals And The Pharisees

teach about the coming Kingdom. My wish is for James to manage the carpentry and care for the family. I want you two, Simon and Judas to help me begin to bring the Kingdom promised to Abraham, Isaac, and Jacob."

Father squirms a little. I am sure he is thinking Jesus has somehow discovered he is a Zealot. We both can hear the subtext that is part of any plan the bring the Kingdom of God to earth. It is what all Zealots believe would be the climax of overthrowing or ousting Rome.

My father speaks for both of us, "If you truly have a plan, I can provide help in bringing the Kingdom. My son and I have longed for this. I can find many friends who would support you. I would ask, however, what you think would make you succeed where so many have failed?"

"All I ask," responds Jesus, "is for you to come with me for a bit and see if you can follow the lead I will offer. I know Darius can manage the vineyard for you. We can return to this region as often as necessary at first. It does not matter where we begin since our goal is to reach the world."

I look at father who seems younger, more eager. He answers Jesus, "We will go with you for two weeks after Passover and then give you our decision. We have a wedding to host the second week and must be in Cana for it. You and your family must come as my personal guests."

"It will leave us little time to see John, but I agree," says Jesus. James pours us each another cup of wine and we enjoy it with the cheese. As we are doing this, James speaks to Jesus, thinking he is unheard by us.

"Brother," he begins, "you are the eldest and head of our family. I must respectfully insist, however, your place is here helping us."

"James," answer Jesus, "you have known I was sent here for other purposes your entire life. Resenting my stepping into those purposes will not help anyone at this time. We can discuss this further after we bury father. For now, let us leave it rest."

The Baptist in the River

Later in the week relatives and friends begin to arrive. Longinus and Syrah come. With them is a young man from Antioch, a Greek. Apparently, he is a friend of Portimus and known by Maxim and Patrius as well.

Veena, Father, and the family have journeyed back to Cana and will collect me on their way to Jerusalem for Passover. We have made this journey for enough years now everyone knows the routine for preparation. Darius will fill my place with father so I can stand in stead for Joseph. James is already running the carpentry shop well but will take a few months of rest for his family after the feast in Jerusalem.

The week we are to leave for Passover, Maxim shares a letter from Portimus introducing his friend Lucius, the physician from Antioch.

From Portimus Rapier, Envoy of Emperor Tiberius Caesar,

Greetings to All my Friends in Judea,

Things go well here in Rome but word reaches us of the unrest in Judea. I have sent my friend Lucius to care for Maxim and his men as well as to see to the care of my

Judean friends. The last wine sent by Maxim was some of the best I have had. I also value the chair made by Joseph and James. It is the one I use daily at my desk for writing letters and tracking troops. I miss you all and will journey to Jerusalem and Nazareth as soon as my duties allow. Tell Jesus and his family I mourn the loss of my friend Joseph. Remember to keep all things peaceful and do not allow Patrius to drink too much.

> Portimus Rapier, High Commander of the Praetorian Guard

I listen as the Romans talk of our friend and all wish he were with us. We all hope he is able to navigate the mercurial politics of Rome and return to the simpler agonies of Judea soon.

All is ready four days before the pre-Passover Sabbath. My family arrives mid-morning and we all set out for Jerusalem. We will journey to Sychar, stay the night there outside of the inn and near the well. This is our custom so the inn can serve guests who pay more and understand less. The road is not yet busy with travelers but will be by the end of the week. We will be in Jerusalem in time to celebrate the Sabbath and be set up for the Bazaar.

After unloading some chairs Joseph made as a gift for Syrus and the inn, we rest. Refreshing our animals and filling our water skins from Jacob's Well reminds us all of the long history of our people and the promise of a Messiah. Father and I speak late into the night with Veena about our plan. My father confides he has already sent word to his compatriots about the possibility of a new voice for our cause. No one has mentioned violence yet. We will not have to wait long for violence to announce itself.

By the time we arrive in Jerusalem, the gates are busy and bustling. We choose our stalls at the center of the city just a short walk from the Temple. As Jerusalem has grown, the trade center has remained open for the many feasts during the year. It is always busy but the ten days before Passover see it swell to eight times its normal population of traders, vendors, and craftsman. Add the truth that every faithful Son of Abraham journeys here with money to spend and you have the makings for a very busy trading week.

We set up next to the carpentry stall which is shared by three carpenter families. Our friends, a local carpenter, and a group of young men, all brothers from Capernaum. Jesus and his brothers make friends easily with the brothers from Capernaum. They already know the local carpenters. News of Joseph's passing gives them all a moment of pause.

Shlomi and her family visit us as soon as the wagons are settled. She must be led by her granddaughters as her sight is gone. We take our first meal in Jerusalem as the night descends and the Bazaar is lighted by dozens of family fires. I notice the young Greek is always asking questions and taking notes with whomever he converses.

The Romans we know pay us a visit and Longinus buys several plantings from Veena for Syrah. Veena promises to visit in the morning once her wagon is ready for the Sunday after the Sabbath. She will stay with Syrah until she must return for Sabbath dinner. The Commander of Judea promises Syrah will be pleased and she has prepared something special for our Sabbath meal.

Patrius chooses to spend his time at the Garrison drinking with other soldiers. The rest of us talk around a fire until it is past time to retire and rest. By morning the court is filled with vendors, animals, and the noise of people bartering and bargaining. At noon father goes in search of something new for lunch. He claims every year that the first day of the Bazaar yields the best variety. By sunset the noise will cease as the city observes the Sabbath before Passover.

An hour after he leaves, all the available space is filled with sellers from all over Judea and further. Father returns to us with some roasted goat on skewers from a vendor. We use the morsel to see us through to dinner. He tells us C'Mot is from the Ankh region of Egypt and newly relocated to Jerusalem. He helped C'Mot with the vending registry and was able to get the roasted goat at a cheaper price for it. Since the Egyptian has no friends or family here, father has invited him to eat the Passover meal with us.

The goat is tender and oddly spiced. It is enough to carry us through the final preparations for the busy week of buying and selling. The women of our family and Jesus' have combined their efforts and prepared the Sabbath meal for us all to share. Only Veena is absent from the effort as we all agree her spice business serves us all better. Esther and Susa have put their wagon to the left of hers. Between the two spice wagons there is business all day because others seek their herbs and spices for their Sabbath meals.

They have to send people away as sunset approaches in order to cease work in time to obey the Law. As the sun's light diminishes on Sabbath eve, the glow of cook fires and heat fires dot the cool spring night throughout Jerusalem. I ponder how this night truly signifies the coming night next week unlike any other in our year.

Again, we sit and talk late into the night, knowing we will have all of tomorrow to rest. The new, non-Jewish vendors will open tomorrow. Unless informed by someone who understands my people, they will wonder why they have little business when there are so many present who are wanting to buy. The women will sleep with Shlomi's family. The men remain with the wagons because thieves do not usually respect the Sabbath.

The Baptist In The River

The Passover week is eventful and lucrative for us all. Beginning on Sunday, the entire day is filled with busyness and business. Jesus and I take time daily to visit the temple. The practices robbing people in the name of God has been improved upon by the Pharisees. C'Mot is with us on Monday and observes they have created a business out of our religion as ingenious as the way the Pharaohs use slaves to build their cities.

Whilst regaling us with stories of his travels in Egypt, we learn his home, Ankh is near the tomb of Tut Ankh Amun. The village is east of the tomb and west of the Red Sea, along the Nile. It is known for providing more pork to the kingdom than any other village. C'Mot confesses he left over some misunderstanding regarding prices and provision. He left the pork business altogether since it has no future here in Judea.

Whilst Jesus closely observes the Temple trade, C'Mot continues to explain his trade to me, "I was raising goats in the south to sell for milk and meat. A heard of goats is too much work so I processed them and sold the meat. Then I saw some Parthians roasting the goat on thick skewers and eating it right off of them. I thought that with the right herbs and vegetables I could provide good goat for others."

I am impressed with his simple idea and agree he should bring us lunch for the remainder of the week. "Bring us enough for everyone," I ask. "We will be working all day at the wagons and if the women do not have to prepare a meal, they too can work harder. I know my aunt feels pulled away when she could help with the selling."

"Since you have been so kind to me, I will give you a family price," says C'Mot. "I am thankful to find friends in a strange land. Your help with the Romans was timely and protected me."

"One must be careful when dealing with Romans," I reply. "There are a few good ones but for the most they are dangerous and deadly. I think Egypt fares better than we do, so make it known you are an Egyptian to them."

As I say this, Jesus rejoins us. "Yes, be careful of the Romans. Also, be careful of the Priests and Pharisees. Those entrusted with our Law seem to worship their own wealth over the worship of the Father."

I hear the intensity in the carpenter's words. It is deeper than it was even in our discussion at Joseph's funeral. Jesus continues to speak, "The way to freedom is found in being honest with others. We must not cheat each other or we rob God. Every coin exchanged or taken by the Temple should be clean enough to dedicate to the Father. Our prayers can only be pure if we arrive at the place of prayer with honesty."

He turns as he says this last and returns to the wagons and work. Something, however, is very different about my friend, Jesus. There is authority in his words but it does not overshadow the humility that has always been there. I bid good day to C'Mot and return to work as well. The odd little Egyptian is good to his word.

As we work each day, C'Mot comes around noon with fresh hot skewers for each of us. He has discovered our individual taste by the second day. Combining that with the herbs and spices he has bartered from my wife, each of us receives a mid-day meal tailored to our liking. The price he charges is fair and we are sure we have gained a new friend.

When he joins us for the Passover meal, he brings a roasted lamb he assures us was prepared and cooked in the proper way. Without telling us he had arranged this with Mary, Puah, and Sari as an act of gratitude for our including a stranger in our Passover meal. Esther and Susa join us as well. The large group is just one of the things for which we are grateful as we celebrate our people's liberation from bondage so many centuries ago.

During the meal, C'Mot notices the attraction has grown between Calah and Salome. When he points it out to my father, he smiles. Turning to Jesus he suggests he had intended to speak to Joseph about a possible match. Both men smile and agree to speak of it later.

C'Mot leaves after the meal explaining he must prepare his skewers for tomorrow. Even though it will be quiet again, there will be those who have not brought enough with them and he is not restricted by law from selling to them. Father thinks to chide the man for enabling others to break our Law but a sharp look from Sari reminds him the vendor is a guest.

By Sunday we have sold all we brought with us and purchased the things we need to work for the remainder of the year. Father, Jesus, and I will take our wagon to visit John at the Jordan. The rest of them will begin the journey back to Nazareth and Cana. We are not worried because Maxim, Amulius, and Patrius will accompany them as well. Maxim offers to allow the sisters to accompany them but they explain they are headed south to do some trade in Kerioth. The road north will be crowded but there will be no interference with the travel of our families as long as they are with Roman officers.

We journey to see John due to the stories reaching our ears of his fire and fervor. It is said he opposes the Pharisees publicly and they cannot answer him. Some have said he even speaks against Herod. There are rumors he is the Messiah. This matches the stories we have heard saying the Messiah is among us. Jesus simply wishes to see the cousin he loves and share the news of Joseph with him.

It seems John has inherited the spirit of the old prophets. He fears no ones' opinion of what he says. He tells them all to repent and prepare for what is to come. The Romans write him off as a crazy Jew who has been too long in the desert.

I must admit I am immediately attracted to his boldness. He says what he believes while too many fear to speak the truth. John called the Pharisees and Priests vipers and tells them how shallow he sees their faith to be. He actually challenged them in front of the people to do things backing up their supposed faith. He implores them to flee the coming judgment.

No one has spoken to the religious leaders so openly and called them to account for their hypocrisy in recent memory. I think he would be better received if he were cleaner and dressed more traditionally. I got close enough to tell his camel hair tunic still smelled like an old camel.

According to his followers, their number has grown significantly during the last few months. They keep trying to persuade him to enter Jerusalem and preach there, but he will not hear of it. He refuses to abide by customs or conventions the other self-proclaimed prophets have established to increase their popularity. He gives lip service to no one.

Calling for genuine repentance, he claims to be preparing the way for one who is mightier. Most of those who claim to be forerunners are really gathering followers for themselves or picking the pockets of the gullible. John obviously cares little for money or possessions. Whether he is crazy or the real thing, he lives what he says and takes nothing for himself.

John is worth watching. Father and I choose to remain with him for a time to investigate for ourselves. Perhaps his followers can be of use in our work against Rome. Perhaps we can get him to expand his focus to include condemnation of all who oppose the laws of God.

The Baptist In The River

The intensity at the Jordan River increases. In this beautiful wide bend of the river the craggy rocks of the hillsides and the lush green trees of the verdant Jordan valley complement each other to offer a sense of rugged beauty. It brings to mind the essence of John's message as I view the barren hills and the rich green life surrounding the Baptizer's words. The dead practices of the Pharisees and the living words of John are the beginning of a great divergence. The flow of it is just beginning and may sweep us all away.

The crowds grow larger every day and John shows no sign of grasping at the power offered him by the people. The Pharisees obviously disapprove of John but the people like him. There is rumbling about his comments concerning King Herod. Apparently, the King has decided to marry his brother's wife and John does not approve. As the King of Judea, Herod knows the Law forbids him to marry his brother's wife but he has done so. He has flaunted the Law of God whilst sitting on the throne of God's people. As I mentioned, John does not mince words.

To our estimate there are nearly a thousand people camped along the Jordan. Some of them act as if the Messiah is going to just step out of the crowd and lead us all away with him. It is Tuesday and we plan to leave after lunch to reach Cana by the Sabbath.

John walks out into the river later than usual to begin his baptisms. Before anyone can approach, he calls for quiet. He explains who he is in answer to the many who have asked. Pointing to himself, John speaks, *"This is he who was spoken of through the prophet Isaiah: 'A voice of one calling in the wilderness, Prepare the way for the LORD, make straight paths for him.'"*

Shifting his attention from the crowd to the Pharisees standing above him he speaks to them as well. "You brood of vipers! Who warned you to flee from the coming wrath? Produce fruit in keeping with repentance. Do not think you can say to yourselves, *'We have*

Abraham as our father.' I tell you that out of these stones God can raise up children for Abraham. The axe is already at the root of the trees, and every tree that does not produce good fruit will be cut down and thrown into the fire."

John turns his attention to the crowd again, "I baptize you with water so you may change the way you think and act, but after me comes one who is more powerful than I, whose sandals I am not worthy to carry. He will baptize you with the Holy Spirit and fire. His winnowing fork is in his hand, and he will clear his threshing floor, gathering his wheat into the barn and burning up the chaff with unquenchable fire."

As he says this, there is movement next to me. Jesus steps away from the crowd into the Jordan. John sees him coming and shakes his head saying, "I need to be baptized by you, and do you come to me?"

Gently, humbly Jesus answers, "Let it be so now; it is proper for us to do this to fulfill all righteousness." Nodding his understanding, John consents. I watch as the elder cousin without asking for Jesus to confess anything lowers him into the water and raises him again. Immediately Jesus makes his way back to the river bank. As his foot touches the shore there is a rumble in the sky. The air seems split and heaven opens. There is a loud voice and the Spirit of God descends like a dove. It lands on Jesus. Then a voice from heaven says "This is my Son, whom I love; with him I am well pleased."

I can see the change in Jesus instantly. He does not look different but he is transformed. He reflects something intangible. Father offers him a linen cloth to dry himself. I am still awed by what I have seen. A voice from above has just proclaimed my friend Jesus to be the Messiah.

As he passes me, he says, "Come Simon and Judas, we must return to Nazareth, there is much to do and we must gather our help."

We go to the wagon and as we pass through the throng to get to it, others are pointing and whispering. I can hear John calling out loudly for repentance and confession. Jesus had come out of the water with no confession done. Yet still, heaven declared him the Son of the Father. Jesus was recognized by God with no repentance. Again, I dare to think we have found the Messiah.

On the journey back to Nazareth, we go around Jerusalem. We talk of the things in the Law and the Prophets pointing to the Messiah. Jesus answers every one of the questions concerning the Messiah father and I bring up with intelligence and humility. He explains how when he and his family stayed with us in Kerioth, they were escaping Herod. He was the one the soldiers sought to kill in Bethlehem.

When we reach Sychar it is almost dark. Syrus welcomes us and informs us Longinus and Syrah are there. We dine with them and it occurs to me this meeting is the kind of thing the Law pushes us toward. We are eating with a Roman soldier and his Samaritan wife.

I notice Photina is there but the man she is with is not the husband Barnabas who helped with the inn when Nahum died. It is obvious to me she is being forward with the man and I think to address the impropriety. Then I catch a bit of conversation between Longinus and father. Longinus says, "...and further, it is a mistake for us to expect Jews to behave like Romans or Greeks. Portimus friend, Lucious, was telling me how in the Northern provinces they no longer require slaves to give up their gods. Apparently, it makes them more peaceful."

Father grunts in reply, "Our Law is given to us from God." Looking knowingly at Jesus, he continues, "He will not long tolerate his chosen people being abused by other nations. I mean no insult to you, Longinus, but Rome will not survive the arrival of our Messiah."

Longinus grins broadly "Do not repeat that in front of Patrius or there will be trouble. When your Messiah comes, however, I hope you will tell him I have always treated his people well."

"I must say," responds father, "Maxim and his officers, including you, are better than what I consider when I think of Rome. I am sure when our God walks among us, he will know this."

To his credit, the Centurion shows no sign of intolerance or pride at father's words. Jesus looks intently back and forth between the men, taking in the conversation and saying nothing. He sees me listening as well and smiles. We sleep, arise in the morning, and depart for Nazareth. Longinus and Syrah are returning to Jerusalem. The report is that the rest of our families moved on to Nazareth two days ago. We have only been apart two days but I see our families in a very different light. Much is going to change.

The Carpenter King

Father and I arrive in Cana again a full week before the scheduled wedding feast. True to his word, father reminds Jesus that he and any guests he wishes to bring are invited as our personal attendants. The bride and groom are local and do not have many friends to attend. They welcome the idea of filling out the banquet room for them.

The last thing Jesus asks of us before we leave Nazareth is we not spread word of the occurrence at the Jordan until it is time. Without us asking he adds he will tell us when it is time. He journeys with us to Cana saying he has business in Galilee. My family is glad he stays with us over night but the women take over the preparations for the wedding a week away the moment Jesus departs.

In addition to our regular work on the vineyard, in the garden, and among the orchard, we have cleaning and staging to do. Sari and Puah insists that if we do not all sleep in the shop and the shed, we will soil the inside of the house beyond repair. Veena and I bring the younger girls with us so they can rest well and be refreshed each morning for the day's work.

I am admittedly anxious for the change Jesus signifies. I am distracted all week and take every chance to speak of it with father.

He shares my excitement and wonders when we will begin to move Jesus toward the throne.

The morning of the wedding arrives and contrary to Puah's fears, all is ready. Guests begin to arrive mid-morning and among them are Mary and her children. Jesus arrives a bit later with some fishermen from Galilee. He introduces Peter, Andrew, James, and John; two pairs of brothers to his family and then to mine. Puah immediately gathers clean wedding garments for the rugged Galileans. I hear her mutter something about there not being enough of something and she returns to the kitchen.

I take Jesus' friends out to the wine shed to wash and change. They express their approval of having so much wine so near at hand. After washing and dressing we return to the house proper. Darius is there serving as wine steward. He gives us each a cup of wine and explains to me how he has reserved these last three large jars for this wedding. He assures me more will be ready in two weeks and we are shown to our seats to await the couple. Mary greets her Son again and makes intelligent conversation about fishing with the four fishermen. Before long the sweet wine is flowing and we are all enjoying the celebration. There seems to be quite a few more guests than anticipated and we open the tall doors so we can use the lawn for additional seating. It seems all of Cana has turned up to celebrate the resumption of weddings in Cans. The couple arrives; there is a ceremony similar to that which Veena and I shared, and the feast begins properly.

Father is seated next to Mary and I see Darius make his way over to them. The Roman's face is quite serious amidst all of the joy of the wedding. He speaks to father whilst Mary listens intently. Before father can answer Darius, Mary speaks, "See my Son, Jesus over there." She points past me. "Go to him and do as he says."

The Carpenter King

The four fishermen, father, and I all turn to look at Jesus. He quietly says, "Mother, what does this have to do with me? It is not my time."

Mary smiles at her Son with a warm mother's love I have never known and says, "But Son, they are out of wine."

Darius calls over some servants who are here for the wedding. They all go to Jesus and pointing at the door, I hear him say, "Take those jugs by the door and fill them with water."

Father gasps and turns to me, "Is he speaking of the purification jars we use for the dead?"

I am too interested in what is happening to care. The servants take the empty jars and return with them filled with water. They place them in their stands by the door. Then they return to Jesus.

He gently commands, "Take some from the jar and give it to the bride's father."

Darius does this personally. On the first sip I can see the father's eyes brighten. He calls across to his new son-in-law, "Every man serves the good wine first, and when the guests are drunk, then he serves the poorer wine; but you have kept the good wine until now."

Delighted Darius nods to the servants and they begin to pass out the wine. The fishermen, father, and I are dumbfounded. We have just seen Jesus turn water into wine without touching it. I am immediately wondering what else he can do. This is no small thing and I ponder it for the remainder of the wedding. After the feasting is done, Jesus and his friends sleep in the wine shed. I tell Veena what I have seen with the wine. I have had a few cups of it and I sleep very soundly.

In the morning Jesus tells me he would like my father and I to meet him in Bethesda in six weeks. The fishermen will meet us there as well. He explains he has to conclude some work before we can begin our endeavor. I agree, still marveling at this power over water.

The Judas Scroll

We spend the remainder of Spring preparing all that is necessary for father and I to be away from our home for a space. Father hires two men from the village to replace our hands in the labor. Veena and Calah will see to things being done properly.

After all is ready, father and I journey to Bethesda in Galilee. Father has asked Darius to aid Veena and Calah to see to the farm and grove as well as the vineyard. I am sure Veena will see all is done well. Amulius will watch over our family. We do not know how long we will be away. We are walking to the sea to meet Jesus in Bethesda as planned.

We have funds. Father has some coin as does Jesus. He asks me to act as their buyer and seller. It is an easy thing to procure food and sell the few provisions we brought with us when needed. We are not going hungry and we begin to encounter others in need. It is easy to see Jesus does not care for money. It is also simple to conclude we have more than we need.

We arrive in Capernaum and the town is busy. Jesus sends Andrew and John to find us lodging for the night. Jesus continues on toward the market to await our rooms. The well in Capernaum is within earshot of the porch of the town Synagogue. Jesus invites us to sit down. The four of us all sit on the stones forming a large circle around the well. Jesus begins to speak of the difficulties we all face under the rule of Rome and a corrupt priesthood.

The Law teaches us we are to respect the Priests and Pharisees. The Sanhedrin Council in Jerusalem sits and interprets the law to protect us from ourselves. From where I sit, they seem rather to be protecting their purses and the quality of their life style. Jesus speaks of the temple tax used to further squeeze money from the people they charged to watch over. The tax is designed to assure the temple remains in good repair. The temple needs repair but it is the kind done by removing its corrupt caretakers and replacing them with men of the people.

As Jesus speaks, a crowd gathers. Most of them are victims of the heavy taxes in this region. The message is favorable and Jesus balances the social needs of the people with a clear reminder of how they are to be dedicated to the Law and the Father. His balance is so precise no one can accuse him of anything other than speaking the truth of the Law of Moses.

John and Andrew return with lodgings secured for us with a wealthy family who has plenty of room. We will take the Sabbath with them. Jesus concludes his remarks and promises to read in the Synagogue tomorrow. With that, he asks Andrew to lead them to the house. We share the Sabbath meal with the family and find our rest in a comfortable house with all we need.

In the morning we go directly to the Synagogue. Others speak and then Jesus is asked to do the same. It appears the priests have heard of the gathering in the market yesterday. They want to hear what Jesus will say. All goes quiet as he takes the center of the platform. This Synagogue is built in the Greek style with seats rising from the center speaking area.

Father is enraptured by the authority with which Jesus speaks. As he unfolds the heart of the Law, we all are astounded at the wisdom and humility with which he guides us to apply all we do to loving the Father. Then, a noise erupts from our left. A man suddenly thrashes about screaming curses, interrupting Jesus.

People move away from the man as he descends toward Jesus. He speaks spitting out vile epithets, "Go away! What do you want with us, Jesus of Nazareth? Have you come to destroy us? We know who you are—the Holy One of God!"

Jesus, ever calm looks deeply into the man. "Be quiet!" he commands. "Come out of him." The demons in the man have no choice other than to obey. Shrieking hideously, the demons flee and the man crumples to the ground. Having no authority in the presence of the Wine Creator; the Holy One of God, the demons depart. The man is unharmed. Those who were moments ago shrinking away from him rush to his aid. Jesus signals to us and we depart to return to the house. There is nowhere to hide in Capernaum. The people will observe the Sabbath but tomorrow will be different. The people will come. Word will spread. I go to sleep wondering what Jesus will do.

Jesus knows he cannot avoid the crowd. He goes directly to the market instructing me to pay the homeowner for his hospitality. Our host refuses seeing the power Jesus commands. I set the money aside to use for those in need. When I arrive at the well there is already a crowd. Jesus sends James and John to buy us some bread and meat for breakfast. I give them some coins from the bag.

Whilst we wait, Jesus moves around the market speaking as he did yesterday. At one point he stands beside the line of people paying their taxes. I can see it disturbs him to watch the tax collectors increase what others owe to make their own wages. Jesus locking eyes with one of the young Jews mindfully taking the tax, speaks to him, "Follow me," he says. It is all he says. The young man, looking at an older man next to him nods. He rises and walks over to Jesus, who without another word goes back to the well at the center of the town.

It is clear something has passed between this Jew and Jesus. He says, "If I have cheated anyone, I will repay them. I will follow you." As he says this, James and John return with food. Jesus tells us to eat and he begins to walk among the crowd.

At first, we are too focused on eating to see what is happening. There is noise in the crowd wherever he goes. John is the first to see something is unusual going on. Jesus is speaking to people who are sick or afflicted. The murmurs are because he is healing them. The Wine Creator, Demon Banisher, is also a Healer. My breath quickens as I am now certain the Messiah is among us. My heart soars as I realize the time of our enemies is soon to pass.

Later that day father and I speak of what we have seen. We agree this is the Messiah and we are on our way to the destruction of our enemies. We are excited and anxious for him to act as our conquering King. At this point, we know it will take time. We are ready to wait because we see how much people love what Jesus is doing. It is soon known I handle the money for Jesus and some who have been healed leave coins with us out of gratitude. I resolve to use this coin to do good for others. There are so many poor and hungry to consider. Eventually, there will be a revolution to fund.

We remain in Capernaum for over three months. I cannot find the words for the many things Jesus does. Daily he teaches with more authority than I have heard or have heard tell of. Many are healed, rescued, and given new hope. Jesus speaks of his Kingdom. Father and I begin to send word to those we know to be loyal to the Sicarii. Many try to pay us for healing and Jesus always dismisses them. Those who have been healed who give money to support our cause are accepted.

James, Thomas, Thaddeus, Phillip, and Nathanial have joined the ranks of those specifically called by Jesus to follow him. I count twelve of us altogether. Some women have joined us and there are men and women who have left all they have to follow Jesus. I have sent word to Veena explaining father and I will be away for some time. She responds reassuring me all is well in Cana and Darius continues to manage our endeavors faithfully. She adds we are sending a portion of everything to Amulius as payment for the service of his steward.

After six more months around the sea, Jesus has become so famous we cannot go anywhere without a great crowd gathering. His efforts toward the poor, the sick, and the humble are astonishing. At one point he feeds four thousand people using just few loaves of bread and a couple of fish. When winter approaches, we return to Nazareth. After a couple of nights in Nazareth, father and I return to Cana.

Things are so good at home it is as if we need not have returned. Veena is of a different opinion and suggests my lengthy time away demands I spend more time with her. It is the kind of demand I would never refuse. We attend to our daily work spending most of our time working together, talking, and marveling at the things Jesus does. Each time I tell her a story of my travels with him she listens and then asks deep thoughtful questions.

Father and I speak often of what we saw around Galilee and we go to Nazareth on days where Jesus will be teaching in the Synagogue there. Increasingly my work at home is given over to those willing to help. Not everyone embraces what we say about Jesus, but everyone loves the carpenter and his family. I should say, those who know him. Both Nazareth and Cana have those who find fault with him even though he does nothing wrong.

Following a restful winter for father and I in Cana, Jesus has sent word he wishes to depart early for Jerusalem. His fame has not diminished. The twelve of us gather in Nazareth two weeks before Passover. I have noticed how even during our time at home, many come to Nazareth seeking out Jesus. The Romans have noticed as well. There is concern even among our Centurion friends over his growing popularity.

As we start out for Jerusalem, there are almost one hundred people traveling with us. When we reveal we are going through Samaria, many of them choose to travel the route avoiding it. They will meet us in Jerusalem. We stop in Sychar. At father's suggestion we ask for and receive permission for Jesus and the twelve of us to stay in the garden behind the inn. We are told by Syrus he does not have enough to feed us but we are welcome to sleep in the garden. It is clear he is busy.

Jesus insists if we wish to go get food, he will take care of getting water for all of us from the well. It is a short way into the town from the inn and I take the money so we can eat for the evening and for breakfast. We will make Jerusalem in time for dinner tomorrow.

Matthew organizes us into four groups as we go to the market. His intent is I give each of the groups enough money for meat, bread, vegetables, and cheese respectively. I hand out enough money to each trio. Father, Bartholomew, and I seek out the vegetable vendors in Sychar. It is a small market but the vendors have an ample supply of early spring vegetables.

After buying enough to feed us all for dinner and breakfast we move to the cart at the entry of the market to await the others. I can hear father and Bartholomew talking whilst I watch for the others. Father, who has studied the law more deeply than our young friend, is explaining how our failure to resist all intruders has cost us our freedom and our favor with God.

I catch puzzlement in Bartholomew's voice as he asks, "Has not the Master told us to live in peace and to love others?"

"Yes," agrees my father, "we are to treat strangers in the land with kindness and respect. We are also to destroy the enemies of God and be his hand of judgment upon them like Joshua of old. You will see.

As Jesus gains popularity among the people, he will begin to turn his attention toward Rome. They will not see it until it is too late. Amidst their devotion to him we will plant seeds of destruction for Rome. He will destroy them and we will make him King."

I can tell the younger man has more to say but Peter, Andrew, and Thomas return with enough fresh goat to feed us all well Thomas hands over the few coins left from their money and I set it aside in the fund I keep for those within our cause who are in need. We have enough set aside to a few dozen men for a week if needed. The other two groups return with enough food for us to eat well and have some to share. We return to the inn thoughts of a filling dinner filling our minds.

Jesus is in the garden. He has enough water for the evening and has already laid our bedrolls out around the fire pit. Peter and Andrew begin to cook our meal. Syrus comes out just before it is ready with a jug of wine, some flatbread, and some of the seed cakes for which the inn has become famous. With him is Photina carrying some of the fare.

Syrus exchanges greetings and blessings with all of us then says he must return to the inn as it is quite busy. He explains Photina will check on our needs throughout the evening and in the morning. We assure them both we do not wish to burden him when the inn is so overrun.

After they depart, Jesus offers a proper blessing for the food and we talk as we eat about Passover, the growing number of people following us, and plans after Jerusalem. As the night descends, we sleep in the garden with full bellies and hearts full of delight at the time we are at in our lives. I ponder how Jesus is growing in power and wonder when he will make his move. It is too soon, but Passover seems the right time when it is time.

The Carpenter King

That first Passover showed me Jesus could be moved to action. We had arrived and set up our place with the selling carts of our two families. I recall how Jesus and Joseph had both felt concerning the merchants selling in the temple court. When we arrived there was a notable change in the Messiah's demeanor.

He stepped into the market and began to drive out the merchants and money changers. He made a lash of cords and did not hurt anyone but they all fled from the fury of this strong carpenter. He acted in the name of the Father. He demanded they see the Temple as a house of prayer.

I think it was at that moment I began to see Jesus would eventually act and action would free us all. The priests for the most part were outraged. We heard talk of it all through Passover week. It occurred to me he was not consumed by anger but, rather, by zeal for the Father's house. I see the wisdom in his actions. I understand the value in building a following and using its momentum. That first Passover was also one in which I saw how much I missed being with Veena and my family.

Once news spread throughout the region Jesus had challenged the practices in the Temple market, those following him increased daily. Directly after that first Passover we all went to the Jordan and baptized hundreds who were in agreement with Jesus' teachings. Quietly, a few at a time, even some of the Pharisees and Sadducees were believing Jesus to be the Messiah.

The crowds kept growing and at one point, at the Olivet, Jesus addressed the vast crowd for an entire day. He spoke of the Kingdom of God as if it were about to appear. He directed everyone back to faith and love. He spoke of meekness with great power and authority.

I saw Matthew had begun to take notes on what Jesus was doing. I still kept my own writing of these events secret.

We returned north two weeks after Passover. There were things needing care at both our homes. The intent was a short stop in Nazareth and Cana, then we would finish out the summer in Galilee. The plan is to stop in Sychar again for the night.

We arrive in Sychar around noon and Peter suggests getting food in the town market. Jesus says this is good and he goes to Jacob's well to get water for us. It is obvious to all of us he is tired. We repeat the efforts from our last visit to the market and return to collect Jesus.

Jesus is talking with Photina, one of the Samaritan women helping at the inn. She is very excited about something and rushes past us toward town. She has left her water jug behind.

I suggest to Jesus, "We know you are tired. Come eat something and we will draw the water."

Jesus smiles the smile we have come to know he is informing us he is otherwise engaged. "I have food of which you are unaware."

Andrew wonders who would have brought Jesus food so quickly. It is then we see a crowd of people coming toward us from Sychar. Leading them is Photina. She is saying something about living water, all she has done, and most alarmingly, Jesus being the Messiah. This last bit being told to a Samaritan woman does not set well with any of us. As much as we love the inn here and the people, some of us still view them as less than Jews. Obviously, Jesus does not.

The crowd coming from Sychar arrives at the well. Jesus begins to speak to them and they all grow silent. Once again, his words captivate. You can see the people listening, understanding, and many accepting what he says.

I ponder the way we treat the Samaritans. My family is good to those few Samaritans we know but many avoid them altogether. Jesus is not only speaking to them; he is proclaiming his Kingdom just as he does at the synagogues. He has even revealed to them he is Messiah. Whilst he speaks, we wag our tongues over our various opinions of this.

Jesus concludes speaking and the Samaritans ask that he stay with them for a time. We remain in Sychar for two days. Jesus does not do anything miraculous unless you count his words imparting hope, love, and redemption to so many rejected by God's people for so long.

We enjoy the days there sleeping in the Inn's garden, drinking water from Jacob's well, and seeing Jesus' words transform anyone who has a listening heart. After he is finished fulfilling the two days, we journey back to Nazareth and Cana. There we take some time with our families.

Father has to meet with some of his Zealot friends. I provide some coin I have set aside for their provision with word to keep still for now as we see Jesus' influence growing. Father leaves me to care for our home whilst he journeys north for his meeting.

Little enough care is needed as the combined efforts of Veena, my aunts, and Darrius have things well in hand. My aunts, nephews, and nieces all do their part. The garden, vineyard, and grove all prosper under the care they are given.

I spend the time getting and understanding of where we are headed financially and remembering why I love Veena so dearly. After three weeks word arrives from Nazareth that Jesus is ready to set out for Galilee again. He asks we join him in Capernaum the following week. Father has returned from his trip north and I am oddly anxious to be back with the others who follow Jesus.

What lies ahead in Capernaum will cement many things that are to come. The things unfolding are beyond my imagination. We have seen Jesus' power in so many ways. I had never thought we would also wield it.

We are all together again in Capernaum within a week. Jesus continues to teach, heal, counsel, and comfort those who flock to us. We are kept busy with the practical aspects of keeping all we do in order. Over the season we make a full circuit of the sea, returning to Capernaum for a week of rest.

Father and I make a brief visit home. All is well except Darius says he has been having headaches of late. Veena assures me she is keeping an eye on him and not allowing him to work in the heat of the day. During our stay at home, word reaches us that Jesus' cousin has been arrested and imprisoned by Herod. We hasten back to Capernaum but not before father sends word to his Zealot contacts we may be needed in Jerusalem.

Quietly he sends out the sisters with messages to his five Zealot leaders. Not even I know who they are. Just father and the sisters are aware of their identities. As soon as the women are on their way, father and I discuss what we could possibly do to rescue John.

When we are with Jesus again, he seems to have no thoughts on his cousin's imprisonment. It is one of those moments where I first think Jesus needs external motivation to move more quickly. I am sure he is the Messiah but his family is a peaceful one. His brother, James does not get along with him but it is always James who antagonizes Jesus. To his credit, Jesus never takes the baith his brother dangles. Even in this I see there could be a deeper success if Jesus were nudged to engage with James. I have heard the Messiah reduce the priests to silence with simple questions. Surely, he could do the same with his brother.

Even with the news of John, we keep working around Galilee. Jesus seems to not even miss a step. People have heard of his healing and come to be healed. They have heard his words of the Kingdom and long for him to make it a reality. He even refers to David's kingdom and his relationship to it often. Matthew has verified he is a descendant of David through both Joseph and Mary. His parables all talk about how to live in the Kingdom he will establish. Then, today, he seemed to step in the role more deeply.

We were walking through a field on our way to the Synagogue in Bethsaida. The Pharisees from the village had come out with a great crowd to greet us. One would think this an honor but we have learned better. The people are happy to see us but the Pharisees rarely are.

As is often the case, Phillip had his mind on food. He and a few others began plucking grain heads and eating the grain. Immediately the murmurs of the Pharisees reached our ears. One of them asked Jesus, "Why do you allow your followers to do what is unlawful on the Sabbath?"

Jesus stops and looks him directly in the eye. Again, Jesus invokes David, "Have you not heard what David and his men did when they were hungry? They ate the bread in the Tabernacle. Or have you not read Moses where he states that priests do things on the day of worship that are considered work but they are innocent of violating the Law?"

Then, Jesus makes the statement that will set them on edge. After reminding them the Father wants mercy more than sacrifices, he says, "The Lord of the Sabbath has authority over the Sabbath." With a nod to Phillip, he leads us on to the Synagogue.

Once there, quiet tried to hold the worship time. Jesus, however, saw a greater need. Some of the people who had been in the field with us pointed out a man with a paralyzed hand. One of them asked, "Is it allowable then for you to heal this man on the Sabbath?"

Even though Jesus has just proclaimed he is an heir of David, Lord of the Sabbath, they are still testing him. He looks directly at the gathered Pharisees, "If your lamb falls in a ditch on the Sabbath, do you not rescue it? Truly, a human has more value than a lamb."

Shaking his head he turns to the man. In the Synagogue, in front of hundreds of witnesses, Jesus says to the man, "Hold out your hand." He does not touch him. He does not say anything else. The man obeys and the hand becomes just as whole as the other one.

Making a great show of it, the Pharisees storm away from the Synagogue. It was not until later I learned they began plotting a way to kill Jesus. Had I known it then, I may have chosen a different path than the one before us. Before I say more about that, there were some changes that happened after this confrontation. These events directly put us on the path to the events of Monday last.

We should start with the request Jesus made once we were away from Bethsaida. A vast crowd follows us out of town and Jesus stopped in a large barren field to talk to them. He listened to everyone who wished to speak to him. He healed anyone in need of it without question or price. I could tell it tired him but it also fulfilled him. He said to each of them not to tell anyone else what he was doing. They agreed.

The other members of our inner circle were as surprised as I was. There were many who insisted on giving us a few coins for support of Jesus or to pay for his services. Jesus always refused them but the others knew to send them my way. Most of what we received went to help us feed or care for the poor we encountered. I was keeping aside a percentage to fund the Zealots who had also left home and family but without the benefit of the Messiah to see to their provision. Things were building even in the requested silences from Jesus and from me. I did not realize at this time father and I were the hub of the Zealot focus. Then, we received some visitors who reminded us just how violent things were to become going forward.

The Carpenter King

At first, I could not place the men who visited us late in the afternoon. The crowd had been lighter today and we were already preparing dinner. There were six of them. As they approached Jesus, he focused on them in obvious recognition.

Over the last eighteen months, I have learned the nuances of how he greets people he knows. I guess being all knowing does not preclude human tells. I often wonder where the line is between the Son of God and the Son of Mary. That, however, is for the Scribes to debate.

Still, I can see Jesus greets these men with friendly kindness. I can make out their conversation but I do not stop slicing the goat that is part of our meal. It is their conversation that changes things for all of us.

One of them speaks to Jesus, "John sent us to ask you if you are the one who is to come or should seek someone else?"

Jesus' answer removes any doubt of his plan to restore the Kingdom of David and the throne of the LORD in Judea. "Tell John this," he begins, "Blind people receive sight again, lame people walk, those with skin diseases are made clean, deaf people hear, dead people are brought back to life, and poor people hear the good news of the Kingdom of God."

There it is. He invokes the Kingdom again. Even in prison, John is being sent hope. It must be true. Jesus plans to act soon. Then he continues, "Whoever does not lose his faith in me will be blessed."

I am sure it was in that instant I resolved to do whatever was necessary to see the power of Jesus on the throne of Judea. As John's disciples depart, he addresses those still around him. He verifies John is the forerunner and the Messiah has indeed come. He masterfully handles explaining the prophets and how they point to him. Then he turns things to the practical and he speaks like a King who is God.

He warns them he has performed miracles that would have changed Sodom. He shows them they have not needed faith because they have seen his power but they still have not changed how they think and act. With every phrase he sounds more like God and less like man. I imagine he is about to reveal it all but he does not. He calls them again to come to him like little children. He asks them to take on the rule of his yoke because it is easy to bear and light to carry.

It is obvious what the paradox is. They want him to conquer their enemies so they can make him King. He wishes them to accept him as King so he can wipe away their enemies. The matter of priority could not be clearer.

As he finishes speaking, Peter calls us all to supper. We are all buzzing about the impending changes. Jesus, it seems has other ideas. As the quiet of eating captures us, Jesus draws our attention. He begins to tell us what is next and we are all unsure.

"I am sending the twelve of you out in pairs," he begins. "Here is what you will do: Don't go among people who are not Jewish or into any Samaritan city. Instead, go to the lost sheep of the nation of Israel. As you go, spread this message: 'The kingdom of heaven is near.' Cure the sick, bring the dead back to life, cleanse those with skin diseases, and force demons out of people. Do these things without charging, since you received them without paying." He pauses and looks at me as he utters this last. I am so entranced by how close we must be to him revealing the Kingdom that I consider nothing else. I can see him on the throne, our enemies his footstool, and the world at peace.

Jesus continues his instructions, "Don't take any gold, silver, or even copper coins in your pockets. Don't take a traveling bag for the trip, a change of clothes, sandals, or a walking stick. After all, the worker deserves to have his needs met.

When you go into a city or village, look for people who will listen to you. Stay with them until you leave. When you go into a house, greet the family. If it is a family that listens to you, allow your greeting to stand. But if it is not receptive, take back your greeting. If anyone doesn't welcome you or listen to what you say, leave that house or city, and shake its dust off your feet. I can guarantee this truth: Judgment day will be better for Sodom and Gomorrah than for that city.

I am sending you out like sheep among wolves. So be as cunning as snakes but as innocent as doves. Watch out for people who will hand you over to the Jewish courts and whip you in their synagogues. Because of me you will even be brought in front of governors and kings to testify to them and to everyone in the world. When they hand you over to the authorities, don't worry about what to say or how to say it. When the time comes, you will be given what to say. Indeed, you're not the ones who will be speaking. The Spirit of your Father will be speaking through you."

I am overcome. The Son has just said the Father will speak through us. He warns us our own families will hand us over to the priests for judgment. He reminds us that like him, we will be called devils. He asserts all we need do is endure and keep to the faith we have in him. He promises, "Before we have gone through every city in Israel, the Son of Man will come." He explains even though we are to be peaceful, he has come to bring the sword. One would think we were at a Zealot council the way he speaks.

When he finishes, we are all too excited to rest. Father and I choose to go aside from the others. Jesus sees this and joins us. I hand him the money bag and have to ask, "Where will you be when we are away?"

He smiles the same smile he gave me when we met in Jerusalem twelve years ago. It is the familiar smile giving us all faith, courage, and determination to heed his words. "I have other sheep to attend you do not know. Tell the people of Israel the Kingdom of God is at hand. We will meet again before winter in the town of Julias. It will be a joyful reunion with many stories to tell of the Father and his loving care."

After asking us to head south to Kerioth, he suggests we take the Great Sea Road there. It is familiar to us and we are the right people to share the Good News of the Kingdom in the place I grew up. Jesus moves on to the others to direct them and father and I try to sleep. We are anxious to see the power of the Father work through us to set in motion what we have wished for all of our lives.

Sheep Among Wolves

The first morning of a journey always excites me. Father and I say our farewells to the others and head west from Bethsaida. The first stop is back in Cana to tell of our journey to the family. Veena expresses no difficulty with our travel but does insist we stay the night at least.

We do and, in the morning, she has bundles prepared for both of us. I explain we are not allowed provision or money for the journey. We set out early, intending to make our way to Joppa and then turn south. Since we are not to work in Samaria, we will take the southwest road out of Nazareth leading to Antipas. From there the road curves south to Joppa. We often used this route when traveling to Nazareth from the south. It is one of the two trade roads leading to Syria in the north and Egypt in the south. We plan to follow the coast south visiting each town and village along the way.

We will not be able to travel through Samaria before it is time to rest for the night. Father and I both notice we feel little fatigue and a sense of great optimism. We find some ripe figs and pomegranates growing along the road near midday. They refresh us along with sitting in the shade of the pomegranate tree for a bit.

Father reminds me of the time Jesus first taught us about the Kingdom. "Jesus told us not to think about where we will sleep or what we will eat. I suppose when he establishes his Kingdom, we will be busy caring for the places other than Jerusalem. This is to prepare us; this exercise in not knowing where our provision is coming from."

Smiling, I reply, "I am sure that is part of it. We also have to learn how to use the power we are given the way Jesus does. I am anxious to help others almost as much as I am to see our enemies cast down and destroyed. The idea there are Jews who have seen his power and still will not hear his message burdens me."

Father gives me the loving look he has held for me all my life, "We must be his representatives of his motivation in places where he is not. We cannot make those in Galilee understand. We can try to tell others the Kingdom of God is at hand. We can do whatever it takes to see Jesus on the throne of David."

In those words I hear the Zealot and the wounded husband so damaged by Roman soldiers we now call friends. I also hear the love father has for his son, his nation and for Jesus. We return to the road ready to see how the plan unfolds. The *Via Maris* running from Nazareth south is always filled with travelers. There is always opportunity.

With the longer days, we can travel further. We are not tired when we reach the last of the bright light for the day. We see nothing in sight until we crest a small hill. As the road descends its far side, there at the base is a pair of wagons, three tents, and a large fire. We can smell the goat roasting as the wind carries the smoke and aroma upwards to us.

We must appear harmless enough as two women and a man greet us from the fire. They motion for us to stop. The short round man, obviously a Jew, steps toward us, "I am Jabez from Joppa. The sun is setting and you two look like you have nothing."

I let father speak for us, "We are heading south. We have lacked for nothing so far."

Sheep Among Wolves

"You are welcome to dine with us and sleep in one of our tents," offers Jabez. "My brother Hiram and his wife Cassis are preparing supper. It is only right we share with fellow travelers when we can."

"I am Simon and this is my son Judas," replies father. "We are grateful for your kindness and ask God's blessing upon all of you."

We sit with them by the fire and in a short time Cassis is passing out food for us all. With the goat is some roasted grain and flatbread. There is also ample water.

The sun sets and the sky turns dusky as we talk about our vineyards and the wine trade. Cassis rises to tend the cooking pot before it is too dark to see. She stumbles and catches herself on the pot still sitting by the fire. Her cry of pain makes it obvious she has burned her hand.

Her husband and brother move to her side, wiping away the spilled fat still burning her hand. Father looks over at me and nods. I rise as well summoning all Jesus has said to us to mind.

"Please allow me to help," I ask. "What I am about to do is so you know Jesus of Nazareth is the promised Messiah and the Kingdom of Heaven is at hand."

Passing my hand over hers, the burns go away and the hand is made whole. Gasps issue from both men and the woman. We talk long into the darkness about Jesus and his plan to redeem us all and establish his Kingdom.

After a peaceful restful sleep, I awaken to father, Jabez, and Hiram already speaking of the things we have seen Jesus do in our travels with him. Father explains to them they too must let others know the Kingdom is at hand. They too must proclaim the Good News of God's favor.

When Cassia sees I am awake she brings me water, fresh fruit, and some warm bread. Her smile is broad and kind. I join the others around the fire and we dine with a quiet peaceful joy flowing directly from our shared faith in Jesus and his provision.

Jabez offers to give us a ride to Joppa but father and I agree we should walk. We set out whilst the family packs up its camp. They refused our offer to help and when they pass us later in the morning, ask again, if we will ride with them. We refuse but after they move down the road, we pray their gratitude to the Father will not diminish.

We also ask the Father provide for when we arrive in Joppa. We pray the work will have gone ahead of us to entice curious minds and listening ears. Joppa it seems is not as curious and attentive as one would hope.

✦✦✦✦✦✦✦✦

When we arrive in Joppa, a group of priests wait for us at the gate. They are flanked by some Roman Legionnaires as well. One of them, obviously a Pharisee, steps forward. "Some of our merchants have caused a stir regarding two men they met on the road. Are you these men?"

Father answers, "We come to proclaim the Good News of the favorable day of the LORD. Messiah has come to establish his Kingdom, to sit on the throne of David, and to show his power and might to all the children of Israel."

One of the other Priests laughs. The Pharisee who addressed us holds up a hand to silence him. The other Priest's immediate compliance sends a clear message of who is in authority regarding spiritual matters in Joppa. He address us both, "Who is the Messiah of which you speak?"

"He is Jesus of Nazareth," I answer, "and we have seen him heal the sick, multiply food for a gathering of thousands, and speak the Good News of the Kingdom to the poor. He has sent us to..."

"I have heard of this man," interrupts the Priest. "Where is he? Why does he not represent himself in Joppa? He has stirred up much trouble at the Temple."

Father replies, "If by trouble you mean he has called us to change the way we think and act by loving the Father, caring for each other, and accepting his Kingdom rule, you are correct. It seems we all long for freedom from those who oppress us, but are not willing to accept the King who offers it. We are here to proclaim he is ready to restore the throne of David as promised by the prophets."

The Pharisee stiffens, "We do not need instruction in the Messiah from those who have not become learned in the Law and the Prophets. You are not needed here and without proof your message is as suspect as any who have come lately bearing news of the Messiah. Hospitality requires we provide you with a place to rest but your message is not welcome in the Synagogue or the streets of Joppa."

Looking over at the Legionnaires, he continues, "These soldiers will provide you a place for the night. I also believe they have some questions of their own for you."

One of the Romans steps forward and signals for us to follow him. His Hebrew is poor and accented but he makes it clear we will spend the night in the Garrison of Joppa. Father whispers for me not to resist. I know I have a way out for us if I need it.

We are led into the Garrison and conducted to an empty room with a work table and four chairs. The table is littered with letters, scrolls, and reports. The Legionnaire points us to two of the chairs closest to the door. He sits in the one opposite the table and furthest from it. We wait.

As we are waiting, I take in the differences between this Roman and the ones we call our friends in Nazareth and Cana. The Legionnaire does not show the personal discipline those of the Nazareth Garrison show. His armor is scuffed and tarnished. The leather is dry and cracked. It has not been, cleaned, oiled, or polished for some time. The man's face is hard, his scabbard is worn, and even the hilt of his Gladius seems headed toward ruin.

He notices me looking him over and grunts, "What interests you so much about me, Jew?" He almost spits the last word. The intended insult is known to us all.

I smile, pondering how I will show love to this man who clearly hates me. "I know more than a few Romans," I answer, "and I always notice the variations in armor and arms even though they appear identical to the less observant."

His attention is drawn in the direction I wish it to be. "What do you mean you know Romans? Surely a Jew hates us all. Truly, I am an enemy you would destroy at the first opportunity."

"I would not contradict you," I reply. "The Romans I have come to know and call friends are good men who deal with us justly. My father and I will give anyone that chance now we have learned this is possible. We live well with the Romans who protect our village."

"I have never met a civil-tongued Jew before today," he retorts. "Our Garrison Commander will be surprised at this. I hear him approaching now." The Legionnaire stands.

Out of respect, father and I stand as well. A Centurion, almost as old as Maxim enters in clothing as worn and uncared-for as the Legionnaire's. The lack of self-respect is inherited here. The soldier is following the example of his commander. This is not a good sign.

"What drags me away from my routine duties, Legionnaire?" barks the Centurion. "Surely these two Jews are not worth my time and attention."

A flicker of worry rushes through the eyes of the Legionnaire. "These are the two men he Priest, Asa asked us to watch for. Your orders were to bring them to the Garrison if they arrived."

"Yes," yawns the Centurion, "but I did not say to worry me with them. Warn them not to stir up any trouble in Joppa and send them on their way. I do not wish to be caught in a tangle of Jewish religious squabbles."

"I will do as you request," replies the Legionnaire. "I would point out their 'message' includes the overthrow of Roman rule in Judea. Surely, Asa will send a complaint to Herod and Pontius Pilate if you do nothing."

The Centurion, vexed at being dragged into this chooses to make an example of us. "Very well; give them a minor beating and expel them from the city. Post a warning stating any further talk of sedition will result in full floggings."

The Legionnaire calls three of his fellow soldiers and they conduct us back to the city gate. In front of the Priests, the gate guards, and anyone else who wishes to watch he strikes father and I each ten times across the back with a wooden rod. He then orders us back on the road away from Joppa.

As we painfully turn to make our departure, Asa steps forward. "We never send our countrymen away hungry," he says, handing each of us a water skin and a loaf of bread. "Be warm and well fed on your journey."

Father takes the offered food and water. He then stands up strait, obviously in pain from the beating. Very deliberately he kicks the dust from his sandals and speaks, "I recall the blessing I offered you when we arrived. Had you only heard us it would have remained. We leave now and take it with us. It will not go well for you in the Kingdom coming at the will of the Messiah."

There is no venom or anger in father's voice. Rather, there is sadness in pronouncing the words we were given. We turn south toward Jabneel. We stop once we are away from Joppa to inspect each other's wounds from the beating.

Father comments, "It does not hurt as much as it did. Pull my shirt up carefully in case the linen sticks."

Lifting the blood-stained shirt, I expect to find several wounds from the rod. Instead, there is nothing; not a mark. I gasp in surprise and then realize I feel no more pain as well. "Father," I blurt, "check my back quickly. I suspect you will be surprised."

He does and we both take a moment to marvel. In the wisdom he always expresses, father summarizes the moment, "We had to endure the suffering so he could heal us. Even far away he cares for our pain. He does this to remind us he will heal all things when he asserts his rule of the world."

Shaking my head, I marvel even the pain of the beating is a fading memory. We will not make it to Jabneel before dark, but we know we will be safe wherever we rest. We stop just at sunset in a small grove of Juniper trees to enjoy the bread we are provided.

Father prays a blessing over the bread as sincere as any I have heard. He also asks the Spirit of God go before us into Jabneel and soften the hearts of the people there. Whether it is realized or not, we agree we will do this before each city we enter. Our faith will yield hope for us and perhaps reclamation for our people.

Sleep overtakes us quickly by the small fire under the Juniper trees. What stirs me is the neigh of a horse. I awaken quickly but the morning light throws the horse and rider into silhouette. The just rising sun winks off the point of a long spear. "To think I would find friends napping under a tree so far from home amazes me" comes an almost laughing voice from the horse's rider.

Sheep Among Wolves

I shift to see if I can make out who it is. The helmet crest tells me it is a Roman and there are few enough of those who would call me friend. As I shift so do horse and rider to keep me from escaping the masking effect of the sunrise. "The steward at my Garrison always gives me too much food for my travels. Perhaps you two would enjoy sharing some fruit and cheese with a humble soldier."

Father is much better at recognizing voices than I am. I did not notice he had awakened. He answers, "If you can stop playing with my son long enough to join us, we would gladly join you…Longinus."

My awareness matches his dismount and we greet the Centurion Commander with happy hearts. We set back down under the Junipers and Longinus passes out plentiful food and has skin of fresh nectar. The Centurion explains he is journeying to Gaza to meet with one of the Egyptian Centurion Commanders. There have been reports of a sect of Egyptians who have risen up to challenge Roman rule in Egypt. They are meeting to discuss strategy but trying to do so quietly. He does not wish to draw the attention of Herod.

We relate our experience in Joppa and assure Longinus we do not expect him to take any action against the Romans or the Jews there. After this we tell him of our journey and what Jesus has asked us to do. Worry creeps across the face of Longinus. "This new Governor, Pontus Pilate will want to cement his relationship with Judea and with keeping the peace for Rome. He will see any talk of establishing a Kingdom as an excuse to act violently."

We agree, and father adds, "Jesus has not shown any concern for physical threats. We have seen him thwart attempts to do harm to him."

"This is good to hear," says the Centurion. "I have been involved with Joseph's family since before Jesus was born. I cannot say what his importance must be. I can say everything about him has been unusual. Jerusalem will be dangerous for him if he is seen by the rulers as a threat."

"We believe Jesus is the promised Son of God," I reply. "That makes the situation dangerous for them, dear friend. If he chooses to use his power in Jerusalem, nothing will stand against him."

Longinus ponders this for a moment before answering, "I do not know he is the Son of God, no matter which god you may mean. I do know Maxim and Portimus hold him above all men in regard and respect. They believe he is different and so Jesus and his family have my loyalty."

The Centurion shifts the conversation to the road and travel. "I will leave word in Jabneel, Ashdod, Ashkelon, and Gaza ordering you two are to be unmolested. If I am still in Gaza when you arrive, we will dine together more properly."

"That would be good," says my father. "We are glad you found us. You may wish to consider something as you ponder all of this. You are a part of this more importantly than you realize. Your part is not over yet I think."

Longinus smiles, "I am too simple a man to get involved in portents and destinies." Lifting his pack and retrieving his spear, *Fatum*, from the tree where it leans, the Centurion swings up onto his horse with little effort. "I will not put myself at odds with Jesus or any of his followers. Where I can I will make a safe path for you. It is the least I owe you both as dear friends."

Before we can respond, Longinus turns his horse and moves south toward Jabneel. At least we will not be beaten again in the near future. I ponder the burden Longinus carries regarding my mother's death. I whisper a prayer asking when Jesus destroys Rome, this man could somehow be spared.

Jabneel also has guards at its small gates. The welcome, however, is quite different. A Jewish merchant, Samuel is there awaiting us when we arrive. He is filled with mirth as he welcomes the "friends of Longinus."

We are taken directly to his house where servants await to see to our comfort, bathing, and feeding. We are then shown to a courtyard where our host proclaims, "You may speak of Jesus freely here and receive any who wish to see you. The Centurion Commander has asked me to show you every deference and I intend to."

A table behind our seats holds roasted meat, fruit, vegetables, and bread. A male servant stands by the table waiting for us to ask for anything. After just a few moments sitting there, we are joined by a Priest and two other well-dressed Jews. "I am Deneb, the appointed Priest to this small town and its Synagogue. Whilst you are here, it would be my privilege to manage audiences with you. We will also expect you to come to the Synagogue to read for us and speak, if it pleases you."

I am certain I have never been treated with such deference in my life. I am uncertain as to why until people begin to come to us the next day. After a restful sleep in genuine comfort, we dine in the morning with Deneb and two other priests. They inform us they have brought several who need care with them.

We are led to an outer courtyard where Samuel has appointed cots and seats filled with people who are sick, injured, or have deformities. A ripple of fear runs through me at the expectation having just descended upon us. Father puts a hand on my forearm and whispers, "Jesus has not let us down yet. This is what he told us to do. Use your faith son."

I do it. I summon all I have in belief based on what I have already seen. We move among the thirty or so people present praying and healing. The recoveries are all instant and complete. Samuel is astonished and Deneb is still unsure of what he witnesses.

When we are done, I turn to Samuel, "Please feed everyone before they leave. I will speak to them as the food is prepared."

"I will see to their hunger," Samuel responds, "but I also wish to hear your words. I want my servants to hear you as well."

My father responds, "We will meet with your entire household after these have been cared for. Your generosity merits you hearing the Good News we bring without distraction."

Samuel hastens away to gather food for our guests. Father begins to explain who Jesus is and our history with him. Everyone listens as we tell the tale of his miracles, his love, and his message of hope for the restoration of the Kingdom. I note Deneb listens intently. The questions coming from these people as we conclude are all the kind springing from belief.

As food is served to them all, we talk about the other needs of Jabneel. There are poor here and some who could not come to seek healing. Father and I promise to visit them the next day. Those we have served depart reluctantly.

We are not tired from the morning activities but we are burdened for the needs of so many and how simple it is to care for them. Father and I discuss the need for individuals to be cured of their ills and both of us wish we could do it collectively. We understand the necessity of personal encounters with Jesus, even if they are second-hand through his followers.

Samuel assembles his household but Deneb excuses himself to attend to priestly duties. We pass the afternoon telling the household of Jesus and all we have seen of him. We talk about the prophets and the ways in which their words are being completed by Jesus' actions. Samuel responds by promising to continue to help the needs of anyone in Jabneel he can help.

We spend the next two days seeking out those in need in town who could not come to us. Samuel, good to his promise, goes with us providing food and coin for any in need. We do this in the mornings and spend the afternoons at the Synagogue speaking of Jesus and answering questions about him.

Those asking when he will restore the Kingdom all receive the same answer. Jesus had told us, "Before we have gone through every city in Israel, the Son of Man will come." We explain there are five other pairs on the same journey with us throughout Judea. We are all sure it will be in the very near future.

When we feel we have done all we can for Jabneel, we thank Samuel. He gives us provisions for at least a week and offers coin as well. We accept the food but decline the money explaining Jesus has asked us to carry no money with us. Most of the town is at the gate in the early morning when we depart. Deneb is curiously not. When I ask, one of the Legionnaires says he left yesterday evening, traveling north.

Our welcome in Ashdod and in Ashkelon are similar. Longinus has made arrangements for our welcome in both towns and Samuel has given us letters proclaiming we should be welcomed as friends. He has addressed these to merchants he knows in each town.

Ashdod is larger and we are there for ten days before we feel we have cared for everyone we can. Our time in the Synagogue there yields more questions from the Priests and some challenges to our authority. That ends when the overwhelming reports of our work with the sick and injured becomes common news.

Preparing to depart for Gaza, those who hosted us walk to the gate with us. As we say our farewells, a single keening wail rises from a house near the gate. The soldiers do not react but some of the people do. One man who had been listening to us the entire ten days speaks, "The wail is coming from the house of Bartus and Hannah. They were wed just eight months ago."

Father nods and we walk that way. The man who spoke leads us to the door. Stepping into the house he beckons us to follow. Hanna is seated in the bedroom on the bed. Her husband is laying there, his face pale and drawn. Hanna sees us and cries out, "He has died in his sleep. When I woke up, he was just like this."

I feel father's hand on the center of my back, "Go to him," he whispers, "you know what to do. You have seen it."

Doing as father asks, I reassure Hannah. "He is asleep. Let me see if we can awaken him."

"But he is not breathing. He is cold and rigid," she protests.

"Let me see to it. I have a lovely young wife and would like to end your distress as I would for her." As I say this, I stretch my hand out to Bartus. "Wake up Bartus. The LORD is counting on you to care for Hannah."

Instantly, color returns to his face and he takes in a deep breath. I look at Hannah and speak softly, "Get him something to eat."

She falls to her knees on the floor but I quickly pull her back up. "It is not my power that has done this. It is the power given me by Jesus. He is our Messiah and his Kingdom is coming soon. This gift from him is to call you to receive his Kingdom."

Hannah nods and then Bartus speaks, "We will do whatever is required of us."

A crowd has gathered outside and word spreads quickly we have raised the dead. We know it is time to move on but now the entire town seems to be focused on what we have to say. Father asks them to not hinder us but to listen for further word of Jesus of Nazareth. Still in awe, the people let us depart. We too are still amazed at the

Kingdom portents we see being done by God through our willingness. We walk in silence for almost half a day.

By midday we know we will make Gaza before sundown. Father breaks our silence by suggesting we stop to eat. There is a rock outcropping providing some shade and we sit there. The discussion is almost always about Jesus.

"Do you think this will take long," I ask? "It seems with all twelve of us out proclaiming the Kingdom in different areas, we can reach all the cities in a short time."

Father agrees, "It will not take long and he said 'the cities of Israel will not all be reached before the Son of Man comes.' I do not think he meant Ezekiel. That is not one of the returning prophets."

"Perhaps," I offer, "that is one of the names he chooses because of his being the Messiah in human form."

Father shows his deep understanding of the prophet Daniel, "Remember the Son of Man is the one who can approach the throne of the Ancient of Days. He is the one who can represent men before the Father." I nod my understanding as he continues, "Messiah is a conqueror's title. The Son of Man is the servant of the Father. Just as Jesus is our deliverer as Messiah, he is also the servant King."

I ponder how often Jesus is a servant to all of us. It sometimes seems like he is being less than God. Still, humility is something the Father cherishes. If Jesus cannot be humble, he cannot be God. I have a further concern.

"Father," I ask, "how will we know when to strike? We must be needed to overturn Rome. We will have to fight like Joshua, like the Maccabees."

"We will know when to act just as we knew when to follow Jesus," he reassures me. "The things the Father plans will unfold as they should. We will know when to be a part of it. For now, our task is to do as Jesus asked when he sent us out. Now, let us finish our walk to Gaza before we lose the light."

There is a full Centurion on duty at the gate of Gaza. When we arrive there is about an hour of daylight left. The Centurion steps forward as we approach, "Are you Simon of Galilee and Judas ben Simon?"

My father says we are. The Centurion motions us into the city where two Legionnaires await his command. Gesturing to us he speaks to them, "These are guests of the Centurion Commander. See them to the inn where a room is prepared for them. Remain there to see no one bothers them until the Commander or I dismiss you. If your duty should stretch into the next watch, I will send relief."

They salute the Centurion and we are escorted to an inn where our arrival causes a stir. Some of the Jews approach us immediately and the Legionnaires send them away. Father begins to protest but he is politely informed the Commander has made his will clear.

The innkeeper shows us to our room. On his heals is a young woman with a tray of fresh food. We were not only expected but are being provided-for as well. The food is excellent as is the wine. We are told there is a bath here and we are welcome to it.

We choose to forgo the bath and rest in the room. Just after the dinner hour Longinus joins us along with the other Centurion. The Commander greets us with little regard for what the other Roman may think. The reunion is a welcome one. We report his request to be treated well in the other cities was respected and more. This pleases him and then he turns a questioning eye to the Centurion who is with him.

The Roman speaks directly to father, "I broke protocol when I did not introduce myself to my Commander's friends properly. I am Aris, Centurion Leader of Gaza. Your stay here will be one of an honored guest. It was not my intent to insult you."

Father extends grace to the man, "I am sure with your position you have many things on your mind. You did not insult us. We are thankful for the accommodations."

I can see Longinus is thankful we do not hold the breach in protocol over Aris' head. "Well that is enough formality between us. I see you have eaten; how shall we pass the evening?"

"I suppose we could explain further what Jesus is doing," offers father. "I am sure you have heard or even seen the vast sea of followers he gathers. He sent us out to tell Israel to prepare for the arrival of the Son of Man."

Aris is stern but not rude, "Your words will sound like sedition to those who rule over us. We are all warned of this national hope you carry of a deliverer. We have seen many claim to be him and they have all ended badly."

I answer, "We too have seen those who claim to be a Messiah but did not have the power to verify it. We have also seen Jesus heal, provide, forgive, and restore. He is the Messiah and he will bring the Kingdom of Heaven to us. Longinus knows the story of his birth. He can attest Jesus is the Son of God."

Longinus does not like that I have cornered him. He grits his jaw, "I cannot say he is the Son of God. I can say he is like no one I have known. His family is more intertwined in who I am than even yours is, Judas."

I feel the pain of my former hatred rise in me. This Centurion, who is my friend, still carries the spear he used to kill my mother. I believe it was an accident but I also know the wound has never healed for me. That he mentions the history here must mean he is uncertain of how to respond to the events that are unfolding.

Longinus explains the Priests in Jerusalem have already tried to find a way to kill Jesus. They asked the Romans to do it and were refused. "Jesus is popular with the people and does not speak of violence or sedition. My position allows me to reject the requests for his head. I only wish I could have done the same for John."

"What do you mean?" asks father, "which John do you mean and what has happened?'

"I received a dispatch from Jerusalem this morning," sighs the Commander, "Herod beheaded John, the cousin of Jesus and we are warned to look for uprisings in protest of it. We have to protect a king who beheads his own prophets on a whim. Your talk of a Messiah could be dangerous right now."

Father seeks to reassure our friend, "We are here only to help the sick and those in need. We will speak only the Good News of the Kingdom and not foment any sedition. We journey without weapons or even a staff. You know us."

"I perhaps know you better than you know yourselves," smiles Longinus. "No one in Gaza will harm you. See to it you do not make me regret that." There is no malice or threat in his voice. He is obviously worried about us.

We talk of other things for an hour and then the Romans leave us to our rest. They depart and my father's anger boils over. "Herod killed John. I pity what will happen to him when Jesus comes into his own. We must stick to the plan before us, but I am certain this will motivate Jesus to act sooner."

It takes me some time to get to sleep. I vacillate between grief and anger for some time before I settle on peace and forgiveness. Sometimes, forgiveness is an act of obedience before it is an act of love.

Whilst we are in Gaza, news spread throughout Judea that John has been killed. It reaches Gaza on our fourth day there. Quietly, four Legionnaires begin attending our gatherings. Some days, Longinus or Aris are present as well. I smile knowing Romans are hearing the Good News without us having to invite them to do so.

There is no tension or even opposition from the priests. I think they are off balance from the death of John. Still, I feel a deeper urgency for Jesus to act. I feel a growing need for it to all be settled before anyone else dies.

We make our way east from Gaza to the villages leading through what was the territory of Judah and Benjamin before the kingdoms were divided and then destroyed. There are still many faithful Jews in these places and we visit each village to deliver the message Jesus sends.

In each place we find those in need and offer care for them. Once we reach the Salt Sea, we turn south, skirting the shore. Again, we are either received or rejected based on the temperament of the Priests in each town. Some change their minds when we begin healing the sick. Some still reject us and we part as we were told by Jesus.

It takes a full three months to reach Kerioth. Father has sent word ahead to his cousins telling them we are coming. We are welcomed there as warmly as if we had always been there and been away for only a short while. After we settle at the home I in which I grew up, we take dinner with my cousin Kirin and his family. Father had rented them the house when we moved to Cana. Kirin trades in horses and donkeys. He has enlarged the barn to house the animals in bad weather. It is built over the place where our garden used to be. He still tends the olive groves and sends us our portion of it each year. After supper we go to the barn when asked to by Kirin.

There must be thirty men here. They are all unknown to me but some know father and all know Kirin. After introducing my father as Simon of Galilee, my father makes sure all present speak Hebrew. When all have agreed they do, he begins to speak.

"Men of Kerioth," he says, "we have awaited a long time for the news I bring you. I am here to proclaim that which was promised since the time of Adam. We have waited for the Messiah to come. We await the good and favorable day of the LORD. I tell you we have found him and the day is at hand."

A murmur flows throughout the gathering. No one speaks directly to father but they all speak to each other both in agreement and in doubt. Kirin quiets them, "We all know who Simon is. We need to hear him. He is not just bearing tales but has proof."

A swarthy man in the back of the barn barks, "What proof do you offer to prove Messiah has come. God has been silent for centuries. Why should we believe he speaks now?"

Father looks at me. "What would it take for you to believe?" I ask. "What proof is enough?"

The man growls at me as if I were the enemy, "The blood of Romans running in the streets would be a good start. My Sicarii cutting the throats of our enemies would be better. If Messiah has come, have him destroy our enemies and we will crown him king."

Murmurs of agreement roll across these men. I understand now that they are part of father's Zealot network. I offer something that may quell their anger long enough for them to listen. "The Messiah has promised he will reveal himself soon. We have been with him for eighteen months and seen many wonders. Father and I have healed and helped many in his name."

"Healed," shouts another man near the front. Holding up a damaged hand he continues, "This was a gift from a Legionnaire who crushed it with his shield. Make it whole and I will do whatever you ask."

Father does not hesitate. "Stretch out your hand, he says. Jesus wants you to know he has come to heal the whole world. Starting in Kerioth with your hand is a good place to begin."

The man hesitates. I can see on his face he wrestles with doubt and hope. Walking up to father, the man begins to shake. The hesitation born from hope causes the man to stand before father with very little distance between them. The entire room is fixed on the space between the two men.

Father speaks, "So you may know the good and favorable day of the Lord is here, Jesus gives you back your hand."

He extends his own hand touching the man's damaged one. We all see the change. The wrinkled flesh from the broken then poorly knit bones smooths. The sunken part of the forearm rises. The muscles take the proper shape instead of the atrophied one they had.

Father speaks again, "What you have promised you must fulfill. I ask you to proclaim to all who know you and your injury that Messiah is here. He will be in Jerusalem for Passover as he always is."

The man stammers in shock, "I will do all you ask."

Father then tells the entire story of Jesus to these Zealots. They listen as he relates how Jesus and his family have intertwined with our lives even when we were here in Kerioth. He tells of all the wonders he has seen. He relates the promise of the Messiah establishing his Kingdom.

We stay in Kerioth the entire week. Many come for healing. More come for hope. When we depart, is seems the entire city will be in Jerusalem for Passover. Father and I are certain the commemoration of our freedom from Egypt is surely to be our freedom from Rome.

It requires another full month to work our way back to Jerusalem. We are both accepted or rejected depending on the town. We are not beaten again. The people seem willing to hear our message. Any trouble we have is with the Priests. When we arrive in Jerusalem, we meet James and John near the market. They have gotten word Jesus is in the wilderness west of the Sea of Galilee awaiting all of us.

We choose to go through Sychar to get to the sea. It will allow father and I to visit Cana on the way and to see if any of the others are in Nazareth. In Nazareth we collect Juda and Thomas. They are newly arrived there and we are happy to see them. General Maxim, upon hearing we are in Nazareth insists on a full account of our journey. He advises us there is great unrest among the Priests and some of the Romans concerning the collective impact of our journeys. He has used his position to keep Pontius Pilate placated but is unsure how long will last.

We spend three days in Cana with family and I enjoy some solitude with Veena. I was worried my time away would wear on her. She reassures me the business of the Messiah is more important than anything else. When father and I depart for Galilee, we are certain the time of the Kingdom is closer than we imagine. What we cannot imagine is what the next year will bring. We were sheep among wolves in this journey, What we do not expect is what our Shepherd has planned as we gather back to him. It is what changes everything and makes my plan necessary.

Son of Man

The reunion with Jesus and the others in Capernaum is astounding. We all share stories of our journey and the ways in which the Father provided all we need. We have brought provisions from Nazareth to the place where Jesus waits for us. It is just the twelve of us and some of the women.

As we feast and celebrate, I can see a tinge of sadness in Jesus not there before. Still, he gives us his full attention as we share our stories of the road and our visits with the villages throughout Israel. The crowd here recognizes him and there is pressure to address them.

Jesus, however, wants time with just us. He directs us to a boat and we make for the far western shore. We reach it and journey far into an unpopulated area in the hills. Whilst we are resting, Peter asks Jesus about our reward when we are in the Kingdom. The fisherman points out how we have left everything in our lives behind to follow him.

Standing and gathering all of our attention Jesus answers Peter, "I can guarantee this truth: When the Son of Man sits on his glorious throne in the world to come, you, my followers, will also sit on twelve thrones, judging the twelve tribes of Israel. And everyone who gave up homes, brothers or sisters, father, mother, children, or fields because of my name will receive a hundred times more and will inherit eternal life."

We immediately talk amongst ourselves wondering at the possibility of being rulers over the tribes. The evening ends with us all fed and content. In the morning, however, the crowd begins to arrive.

At first, it is a few groups who followed Jesus from the cities by the sea. They wait patiently for him to speak. I can tell he is awaiting something but I am not sure what. Others are speculating as well. Simon and Andrew welcome each group. Jesus moves to the top of the large hillside and takes a seat on a rock outcropping. From this place the field below looks like a large wide bowl.

By late breakfast-time more people have arrived. At midmorning they are coming in droves. Matthew is counting and is already in the thousands. The day is not too hot and there is no wind. It is still morning when Jesus calls down into the field below. Everyone can hear him.

As more people join the group seated on the ground, Jesus begins to teach. The crowd swells as Jesus speaks of the coming Kingdom. He talks of the ways in which we are to live, think, and love if we are part of the approaching Kingdom. I have seen and believed the power Jesus wields is genuine. Now he uses his influence to unite us in our love for the Father.

As the day flows, Jesus continues to speak to those gathered below. There are Jews from every profession. A group of Priests and Scribes stand off to one side. They often chatter among themselves when Jesus says things about how we should behave based on a loving understanding of the Law of Moses. There are even some Roman soldiers among the crowd. They are engaged in listening and paying little attention to anything else.

It is late afternoon when Jesus pauses to drink some water. Andrew takes the opportunity to approach Jesus. He speaks for all of us, "Master, it is evening and none of these people live around here. Really, no one does. We should send them away to find food."

Jesus looks at each of us in turn. It is clear he expects something but none of us seem to get it. The sadness is in his eyes again, " They don't need to go away. You give them something to eat."

He is addressing us. He expects something but none of us seem to follow. I speak, "Should we spend a year's wages to buy them food?"

Jesus looks deep into me and I instantly feel there is another answer I am missing. Jesus looks at the others. There is a sigh then he asks, "What do we have?"

Andrew answers again, "We have five loaves and two fish."

A smile flickers through Jesus' as he says, "That is enough. Have them sit in groups of fifty and we will feed them."

I am not the only one who responds with an incredulous look. To our credit we do as he asks. Then, he takes the loaves and fish, offers a prayer of gratitude, and begins to divided them. As he tears each loaf in half, it becomes two whole ones. Each time he picks up a fish it is two.

We feed everyone with plenty left over. No one really understands what has happened. When we discuss this later, it occurs to me Jesus was wanting us to use the power he had given us to feed the people. He wanted us to act instead of waiting for him to do it. He was not done showing us what we could do in his name.

There is so much food left no one will hunger on their journey home. As the crowd drifts away in groups a small knot of Romans stands off to one side. There are under a hundred people left and Jesus guides us down the hill. The Romans approach and we recognize Amulius at once. He, another Centurion, and the Legionnaires with him approach and I greet them as friends so as to set aside any worry on behalf of the others.

Amulius, wearing his Centurion field armor is grim when he speaks, "When we saw the migration from the villages, we were worried it was an uprising."

"It still may be sedition," offers the other Centurion. It is Patrius. "We have heard much talk of the overthrow of Rome and the establishment of a new King of the Jews. That phrase has long been foul to me."

No one speaks. We are waiting for Jesus to respond. He looks Patrius in the eye and says nothing. I can see the hard Roman grow uncomfortable. It is the Patrius that breaks the tension, "This lot is favored by General Maxim. We had best leave them alone for now. Come Amulius, we have better and less bitter duties to attend."

Amulius looks at Jesus, "Where are you going next?"

The patience and warmth in Jesus' answer is disarming, "We will go to Capernaum and then begin the journey south after that. It will be slow as we will stop often to care for those in need."

Patrius issues a grunt and turns with the Legionnaires to leave. Amulius looks at us all with sadness. He knows he cannot disagree publicly with Patrius because the Centurion is his senior. He also sees clearly what Jesus is about and has faith in what is unfolding. I feel the pressure building and long for Messiah to move.

As we draw near Capernaum, father and I are discussing the feeding of over five thousand people. I discuss with him my thoughts Jesus wished for us to do it and not him. He wanted us to use the power he gave us to care for the needs of the masses. Father agrees it is in line with what Jesus teaches about the Kingdom he is bringing. "We must be ready to act," he says. "It may be part of his plan is to act through us as he did the Judges and the Prophets. We have heard him say John was acting in the spirit of Elijah. We must be ready."

I concur with father. I will look for ways to fulfill the things Jesus says at any opportunity. He is our Messiah and he is counting on us to do his bidding. That is enough for me.

It takes us four days to make our way to the edge of Capernaum from the hills. There is a small group of people walking out to meet us. This has become common. What is uncommon is this group is led by Priests. We have been in Capernaum enough to know Nicodemus. He and Jesus have met "privately" on several occasions. He is one of the small number of Pharisees and Sadducees who seem to believe Jesus is the Messiah.

They approach us quickly and we stop in a field to speak with them. Nicodemus addresses Jesus, "I have come to plead for the life of a servant. Darius, the servant of the Centurion Amulius is gravely ill. He sent word to ask for your help with this servant he dearly loves. He has been good to us. His money helped build the Synagogue here in Capernaum. Amulius knew you were coming and has brought Darius here."

Jesus says nothing but gestures for Nicodemus to lead him on. Father and I discuss the needs of our friend, Darius. We pray as we walk. We also discuss how we will act if we are too late.

Only a few streets away from the Capernaum garrison three Roman soldiers ride up to us. Amulius and Patrius dismount. With some fear in his voice Amulius speaks to Jesus, "'Lord, don't trouble yourself, for I do not deserve to have you come under my roof. That is why I did not even consider myself worthy to come to you. But say the word, and my servant will be healed. For I myself am a man under authority, with soldiers under me. I tell this one, 'Go', and he goes; and that one, 'Come', and he comes. I say to my servant, 'Do this', and he does it."

I see a look of delightful awe break across the face of Jesus. Looking at the Pharisees, then at us, and then at Patrius he says. "I tell you; I have not found such great faith even in Israel. I can guarantee that many will come from all over the world. They will eat with Abraham, Isaac, and Jacob in the kingdom of heaven. The citizens of that kingdom will be thrown outside into the darkness. People will cry and be in extreme pain there."

Turning to Amulius he says, "Go, it will be done for your servant as you believe." As the Romans ride away, he gestures for us to follow. Turning to Peter he says, "Shall we go to your house? I am sure your family longs to see you."

Peter agrees and we make our way south of the Garrison. As we pass it one of the other Pharisees who was with Nicodemus turns aside to enquire about the servant. We will learn later Darius was healed in the very moment Jesus and Amulius were speaking.

Arriving at Peter's house, his wife greets us with both joy and concern. The joy is because her husband is home. The concern is because her mother is sick with a fever and she is not sure how she will care for us all. Jesus goes to her bed and stands near her. She is immediately healed and helps her daughter prepare dinner for us all.

Word spreads Jesus is in Capernaum and after dinner there is a crowd outside of the house of those who are sick and in need of care. A group of Priests are gathered by one window watching. Jesus allows the sick to come in for healing. Whilst he is doing this the door to the rooftop is removed and a litter on ropes begins to descend.

All grows silent as Jesus gives his attention to the man on the litter. Smiling at the faith of the man's friends, he says to the man, "Go your way. Your sins are forgiven."

Immediately Jesus turns to the Priests and Scribes at the window. "What are you thinking? Is it easier to say, 'Your sins are forgiven,' or to say, 'Get up and walk'? I want you to know that the Son of Man has authority on earth to forgive sins."

It seems the Priests cannot bear Jesus standing in his own authority. Healing a Gentile and forgiving sins all in the same day is too much for them. They storm away and I think this is when they became serious about killing him.

Early in the morning, Jesus leads us away quietly. We take the Galatian road skirting the western shore of the sea. The crowd swells around us each time we stop. Hundreds follow us each time we travel. He speaks to them but we also have a following of Priests who oppose him. At Tiberius we take a boat to the southern end of the sea to escape the crowd. From there our destination is the cities and towns leading toward Jerusalem. The winter is turning toward spring and we spend some time in the wilderness between Mount Tabor and Mount Ebal.

We will begin the journey south again at Sychar. Something has changed since we left Galilee. Jesus is speaking with authority still but he speaks more of the redemption of sin than he does of the coming Kingdom. Something is changed but none of the others seem to notice it. Then Jesus begins to talk about death.

There is other odd behavior. Whilst we are in the wilderness, Jesus takes Peter, James, and John up on Mount Tabor. They do not immediately speak of what they did there. Their being singled out does lead to arguments among us concerning who is the most important. We are still speaking of the Kingdom but Jesus is not.

Exiting the wilderness at Sebesta, we find a large crowd, almost a thousand there looking for us. Rather, they are looking for Jesus. The crowd gathers around him on the edge of town and he agrees to speak to them. He explains he is headed for Jerusalem in time for Passover. Then, he begins to single out pairs of people and call them aside. These must believe to have waited the winter to find him.

Sending all but those he has chosen away for the day; Jesus gives them the power he gave us when we were sent throughout Israel. He tells them he is sending them in pairs to all the cities between here and Jerusalem. They are to proclaim the Kingdom is at hand. They are to ask every town to prepare to receive him.

They depart the next morning and Jesus has us remain with him in Sebesta. Whilst there, others come from all over the region. Some seek healing, some release from spirits, and some seek only Jesus. He helps all who come and has us working to aid them as well. Even the stories Jesus tells have turned. His shepherd is now willing to die for the sheep. The Kingdom is not physical but spiritual.

Father and I talk late into the nights about this. The crowds swell by day. We think Jesus is tired, sad, and discouraged by the lack of faith in cities where he has performed great miracles. We agree to push on for him when he is weary and to encourage him to act at every chance.

After three weeks the pairs sent out begin to return. They tell the tales we know well of healing and freeing others from spirits. After all have arrived, Jesus announces we will resume our journey south. He intends to visit each of the towns to which he sent his followers. The first is one with which we are all familiar. We are excited to return to Sychar.

The half day it takes to walk to Sychar extends to almost an entire day because of the large crowd. Jesus chooses to stay outside of town near Jacob's well so as not to overburden the city. Some come out at once seeking his care. They also bring food and draw water for us all. As we are eating dinner, the city leaders come as well. These men make it clear we are not welcome here. When asked why they explain we are taking the Kingdom to Jerusalem instead of it being in Samaria.

I can see this rejection hurts Jesus. He does not argue but simply retreats. In the morning we move on toward the next town. The other small villages enroot to Jerusalem are more welcoming. Jesus cares for the needs of all who come to him and continues to speak of the Son of Man and his Kingdom but it is now always punctuated with talk of death.

Opposition from the Priests grows and Jesus begins to speak more of sheep, shepherds, and the shepherd giving his life for the sheep. I have begun searching for a way to help Jesus see how popular he is and how much can be done if we act now. Three weeks before Passover week, we are near Bethany.

The Priests are seeking a way to arrest Jesus. We leave the large throng of followers and retreat to the place where it all began. We are on the west side of Jordan where John had baptized Jesus. It should be a time of commemorating and celebration. Instead, there is a silence and foreboding like the one before the storm on Galilee. I am no longer certain the Son of Man is in the business of calming storms. Then, a messenger reaches us from Bethany.

The messenger pushes his way through the people gathered around Jesus. He is talking about those who follow out of belief and those who follow for their own purposes. The man walks straight up to Jesus and speaks to him quietly. He is from Bethany, sent by Mary and Martha. He says, "Lord, the one you love is sick."

Jesus reassures the man, "This sickness will not end in death. No, it is for God's glory so God's Son may be glorified through it."

We stay at the Jordan for two more days. Jesus loses many of his followers as he speaks more of death and the cost of remaining faithful. Even though the man is popular for his healing and care of others, he is not delivering the message of disposing of our enemies the people wish to hear. The Priests grow bolder in challenging him even though his responses confound them.

After two days, Jesus calls us to his side. He says, "Let us go back to Judea."

"But Rabbi," says Thaddeus, "a short while ago the Jews there tried to stone you, and yet you are going back?"

Jesus answers, "Are there not twelve hours of daylight? Anyone who walks in the daytime will not stumble, for they see by this world's light. It is when a person walks at night that they stumble, for they have no light."

We are all confused by this but he continues, "Our friend Lazarus has fallen asleep; but I am going there to wake him up."

Peter replies, "Lord, if he sleeps, he will get better.

Jesus puts a finer point on his words, "Lazarus is dead, and for your sake I am glad I was not there, so that you may believe. But let us go to him."

Then Thomas says to us, "Let us also go, that we may die with him."

We hear the noise of the wailing mourners long before we arrive at the home of Mary and Martha. One of them informs us Lazarus has been dead for four days. As he is speaking Martha runs down the road to us.

Lord," Martha says, "if you had been here, my brother would not have died. I also know that even now God will give you whatever you ask."

Jesus says, "Your brother will rise again."

Martha answers, "I know he will rise again in the resurrection at the last day."

Jesus clarifies his position, "I am the resurrection and the life. The one who believes in me will live, even though they die; and whoever lives by believing in me will never die. Do you believe this?"

"Yes, Lord," she replies, "I believe that you are the Messiah, the Son of God, who is to come into the world."

The power of her words captivate me. I realize what he is about to do and remember my time in Gaza. Martha runs back into Bethany and Jesus stands where he is, waiting. In a short space Mary comes down the road trailed by several Sadducees and Pharisees. Many people had come from nearby Jerusalem to mourn Lazarus including these Priests. Mary falls on the ground at Jesus' feet, weeping, "Lord, if you had been here, my brother would not have died."

It is so odd to me to see Priests weeping over the dead. Most of what they do is usually show. Here I see genuine mourning. "Where have you laid him?" Jesus asks.

They all tell him to come and see. Then I see sadness grip Jesus again and I see him weeping as well. I can hear the mourners commenting on how much Jesus must have loved Lazarus. Some speculate he could have saved Lazarus had he been here.

The Priests lead us to a tomb which is a cave with a stone rolled in front of the entrance. Jesus is still weeping and commands, "Roll away the stone."

Martha is there and objects, "It has been four days. Surely he will stink."

Jesus wipes away his tears and responds to Martha, "Did I not tell you that if you believe, you will see the glory of God?"

The men roll away the stone and Jesus speaks again, "Father, I thank you that you have heard me. I knew that you always hear me, but I said this for the benefit of the people standing here, that they may believe that you sent me." When he had said this, he calls out in a loud voice, "Lazarus, come out!"

I think the moment between that command and Lazarus appearing in the doorway of the tomb seemed forever to those who doubted Jesus. Lazarus looked otherworldly in his burial linens with his face covered. The binding sheets made it hard for him to walk. Jesus dispels the shocked inaction by saying simply, "Take off the grave clothes and let him go."

The cacophony that erupts is as loud as the mourning that has now passed. We remain with Mary, Martha, and Lazarus overnight. Then we return to the wilderness until six days before Passover. That Friday we return to Bethany for a feast at Lazarus home.

While we are dining, I admit I am consternated because the Zealots have sent word for money to sustain during the last week. I am uncertain now if Jesus will act. Whilst we are eating Mary approaches Jesus with an alabaster case of nard. She breaks the cask and anoints Jesus' feet with it. Then she dries it with her hair.

Irritated at the overt showing of emotion, I forget myself, "Why wasn't this perfume sold and the money given to the poor? It was worth a year's wages." I am really thinking about the needs of those who stand by to support Jesus when he acts.

Jesus, however, has other things on his mind. "Leave her alone," Jesus replies. "It was intended that she should save this perfume for the day of my burial. You will always have the poor among you, but you will not always have me."

Even though it is the Sabbath, a large crowd has gathered outside and I use their presence to distract the others from my error. We rest for the Sabbath day and I keep my distance from Jesus. It is because of this I learn from one of the Pharisees who believe the Chief Priests have an active search for a reason and place to arrest

Jesus. It is then my plan forms and I realize I must get this account to you, as I seek a way to materialize my idea.

I will give daily accounts of it so my record is the first we have. Jesus told us tonight he intends to enter Jerusalem on a white donkey tomorrow. The thousands reached by those sent out some weeks ago will be in Jerusalem for the Passover. If Jesus makes his move, then we are ready. If he is not ready to make his move, we will motivate him to it. It is time and the time is what will tell. Five days hence, Jesus will be King.

The Entry – Five Days until Passover

Sunday morning is promising even in the earliest light. We are all up and have our breakfast. We know Jesus plans to go to Jerusalem today. He instructs Juda and Bartholomew to go into Bethphage and retrieve a young donkey they will find there. I never ceased to be amazed by the things he knows ahead of time. That he has sent for the symbol of the arriving King thrills me. Perhaps today is the day he makes his move.

The two return within an hour with the foal and his mother. We all prepare to enter Jerusalem. The city has already swollen in population for the week long celebration leading to Passover. The word has gone out as well: Jesus is coming to the city. He is the Messiah and all await his arrival. I know this is true but have no idea just how many will greet him.

We follow as Jesus rides to the city. So much of our history and our hopes hang in the air during this ride. Jesus will act. He will triumph over our enemies and institute the favorable year of the Lord. The King rides to Jerusalem to show his power, declare his station, and take his throne. I believe all of this and feel relieved I will not have to enact my plan.

By the time we begin to descend the Mount of Olives many of the disciples have gathered. Hundreds we have seen over the last two years gather along the roadside. They spread their garments on the road in honor of Jesus. They begin to cry out and to sing, "Blessed is the King who comes in the name of the Lord! Peace in heaven, and glory in the highest heaven."

The Priests are there as well. They are not pleased. The man they desire to kill is riding into the city they think is theirs in triumph and glory. Jesus has raised his hand to no one and yet won the devotion of the masses. The Priests register their displeasure demanding, "Teacher, tell your disciples to be quiet."

I see compassion for those entrusted with the Law in Jesus' eyes. He responds, "I can guarantee that if they are quiet, the stones will cry out."

Those of us who know Jesus instinctually look to the rocks expecting them to actually speak. They do not. As we draw close to the city gate, the crowd teams in the thousands. Jesus is smiling and waving but deep sadness is still in his eyes. My joy is cut short by his next words.

Looking over the thousands welcoming, waving palms, and cheering for him he quietly weeps and speaks, "If you had only known today what would bring you peace! But now it is hidden, so you cannot see it. The time will come when enemy armies will build a wall to surround you and close you in on every side. They will level you to the ground and kill your people. One stone will not be left on top of another, because you didn't recognize the time when God came to help you."

We follow Jesus directly to the Temple. I recall this is where we first met so many years ago. His words have shown me he has given up hope of establishing the Kingdom now. Our last visit here was not one any will forget. Things at the Temple are worse than last year.

The Entry – Five Days Until Passover

The temple terrace resembles a bazaar more than an entryway to the house of God. The Pharisees have a new law for us to supposedly protect us from being defiled by Rome. We can no longer make our offerings in coins other than those minted for the use specifically in the Temple at Passover. Apparently, these coins are more holy than the ones I carry around to buy food and clothing.

The process is a simple one, and quiet an ingenious way to steal from the common man. My silver pieces were made for use in the market place and they are Roman coins. Since God has called us to be a separate people, we should not offer our gifts to God with Roman coins. This means the temple rulers have had to mint shekels solely for use by God. The moneychangers sit outside the temple and, for a nominal fee, will exchange our worldly silver for their kosher temple coppers. The fee of course must be paid in your worldly silver and not in the holy temple coppers. The coppers may then be placed into the offering troughs or used to buy approved spotless doves and lambs for the sacrifice.

All of this seems quite normal until you consider a few things. The temple shekels may only be spent on temple grounds. The Pharisees and Rome in a rare moment of agreement, have said they are worthless elsewhere. The exchange is one for one between the silver coin and the copper one. This seems slightly in the favor of the Pharisees. Since the Roman coins may not be used in the temple, the Pharisees in their usual self-sacrificing way volunteer to soil themselves by keeping the silver. Since the copper coins are given back to the temple or used to buy things only in the temple, the temple never runs out of them and can sell the same copper shekels back to the people each week. I have marked several of the shekels, hoping to get them back and confirm the absurdity of the cycle.

When Jesus arrives at the Temple, it becomes clear the Son of Man has seen enough mistreatment of his Father's house. Again my mind ebbs and flows between hope and despair. We all watch as Jesus makes a scourge of cords and drives the money changers from the Temple. He overturns the tables and those there to exchange coin scramble to pick up the scattered silver and copper.

Neither the Priests nor the Romans dare act against him for fear of the crowd. Once the clamor subsides, he begins to call those who are sick or injured to him. At the Temple, in sight of the Priests and the Romans, Jesus begins healing anyone in need.

Clearly his power and popularity are at their fullest but he will not act. I have a way to force his hand for the good of us all. I must make arrangements soon. As we journey back to Bethany for the night, I realize there is nothing left but this course I have planned. I know if he is cornered, Jesus will act. I believe the power he has will emerge if he is pressed.

Fig Trees and Fear – Three days until Passover

We begin the walk back to Jerusalem early again. It is odd to me that when he sees a fig tree without figs, he curses it. He could have just commanded figs to spring from it. I grow more concerned he has lost his way.

We stop at the Mount of Olives where Jesus teaches about the Kingdom but not in the way he has. There is still love and compassion for all but a growing sadness is there as well. Everyone can hear the disquiet in his words.

There are still thousands cheering Jesus on as he enters the city. He repeats the activities of yesterday, driving the Money Changers from the Temple and teaching there. Still, he has authority but I can see the people growing impatient for him to act. They clamor for what he can do instead of what he is. They wish for the fruit of his power rather than the beauty of his being. He must act or they will turn against him. When we return to Bethany for the night, I notice the fig tree is dead. I pray our hopes have not died as well.

Promises and Payoffs – Two days until Passover

As we return to Jerusalem today, the others see the fig tree is dead. Peter askes Jesus about it and Jesus answers, "Have faith in God! I can guarantee this truth: This is what will be done for someone who doesn't doubt but believes what he says will happen: He can say to this mountain, 'Be uprooted and thrown into the sea,' and it will be done for him. That is why I tell you to have faith that you have already received whatever you pray for, and it will be yours."

Later, as he is teaching at the Temple, he says to us quietly, "As you know, the Passover is two days away and the Son of Man will be handed over to be crucified."

The clarity I needed comes from this. I have always had faith in the Messiah. Even before I knew it was Jesus, I knew he would come and deliver us from our enemies. I knew his Kingdom would become a visible reality. Jesus wants us to use faith.

I believe he will act. I will hand him over to the Priests. The crowd will see it and long for him to use his power to save himself and deliver them. He will seem cornered and I know my faith will bring about his action. Faith has been the requirement with him at every turn. He said he was going to be handed over "to be crucified."

He did not say he would be crucified. He said before that the Son of Man would be revealed. I am convinced all the talk of death is to force the others to quit squabbling over and vying for position.

When we are at the Temple, I slip away and ask to speak with Caiaphas. He and Annas meet me outside of the Temple proper in the court of the Gentiles. I can see they are dubious about my desire to talk.

I begin by choosing to motivate their desire. "Jesus caused severe disruption at the Temple the last two days. I can feel him losing the favor of the people."

Caiaphas answers, "We have discussed how his words and actions endanger us all."

Now I need to seem greedy, "What would you give me were I to hand him over to you?"

Annas looks at one of the lesser priests with them. He says, "The High Priest would allot thirty pieces of silver for your assistance."

"That will suffice," I respond. "I will find you after the feast when I know where we are going. I will hand him over to you so that things may be as they should."

They give me the silver. I already plan to send it to you to finance the needs of the other Zealots. We will all be in the Kingdom by Saturday. I am sure. Now to prepare for the Passover and Gethsemane.

Open Opposition – One Day until Passover

I write this last part in haste so I can get it to you before Passover. Today the Priests were very bold in their opposition to Jesus. They challenge and mock him. He refutes them and explains he is the Son of Man. He makes it clear he is the Messiah and they have seen his wonders.

In part they must be emboldened because they think they will stop Jesus. They cannot outwit him and will learn he cannot be outmatched as well. As our enemies fall before Jesus, the Priests will see the King Jesus is. I hope it is not too late for them.

Everything is arranged for Passover and for the garden. We will spend one more night in Bethany. I am sending this scroll via messenger. I will give you the silver tomorrow when we return to Jerusalem. Defend me, dear friend should things go badly for me. I am only doing what I am sure Jesus wants me to do.

Epilogue –
A Letter to Theophilus

Greetings your Excellency Theophilus,

I am sending this scroll to you out of respect for your treatment of Luke's request for historical data regarding the story of Jesus of Nazareth. I trust you will receive this with the understanding and the patience you have shown in dealing with the strife caused by both Jerusalem and Rome.

Judas was my friend. He entrusted to me the only documents showing his heart and motivation. After I was arrested for murder, I had no way to get to the scroll and pass it on. When the people chose to exchange my life for Jesus', I was too overcome to do anything. By the time I could reach the people who mattered, Judas had already taken his life and no one was interested in listening.

I failed to listen to Judas and his father when they cautioned us to hold back our fervor until Jesus acted. Had I not acted, I would not have been arrested. I do not know if there will be any way to prevent Judas from only being remembered as one who shed innocent blood and handed over our King. Even the resurrection did not clear him. Perhaps this is what Jesus meant when he said it would be better had Judas never been born. He loved Jesus and simply wished for him to do what he came to do; to free his people. None of us saw clearly what Jesus meant by it. Judas acted and has paid the price for innocent blood as required by the law.

I remain now a follower of Jesus Christ, the resurrected LORD, a friend of Judas no matter what others may say, and your servant most excellent Theophilus.

After Word

Thank you for taking this journey with me, Dear Reader. I am sure some of you do not agree with my assessment of Judas. Feel free to write me if you wish to discuss it. As others have said, he is the most hated man in history., It does not change the truth of his being loved by Jesus.

As I wrote this, some obvious questions arose. Here are some thoughts and historical notes to help you think:

Under the Law, Judas is guilty of shedding innocent blood. He goes to the Priests to confess it and they refuse to allow him repentance. Being guilty of this means he must die. If true, Judas is the last to use and need the forgiveness of sin as proscribed by the Law of Moses.

A quality argument can be made for Simon the Zealot and Judas being Father and Son: John 6:70-71 *"Then Jesus replied, 'Have I not chosen you, the Twelve? Yet one of you is a devil!' (He meant Judas, the son of Simon Iscariot, who, though one of the Twelve, was later to betray him.)"*

Other ancient authorities read Judas Iscariot son of Simon; others, Judas, son of Simon from Karyot (Kerioth). Some see Iscariot as a play on words. They were from Kerioth and were Sicarii or Zealots. I chose this path to justify the place of the Zealots in

Jesus followers. One may argue against it but none of us can prove conclusively what is true.

In the same passage the quote is rendered "Yet one of you has a devil." I do not dispute this but I do not believe this bars him from having good motives for his evil act. In truth, we all justify our sin at some juncture. We believe we are doing what is needed and even convince ourselves we are doing it for God.

I would offer one further argument for the redemption of Judas. If we look at Matthew and Luke's accounts of Peter asking about the reward for those who have left everything to follow Jesus, there is an interesting note I have not considered before writing this novel. Here is the text of Matthew 19:27-28:

> 27 Then Peter replied to him, "Look, we've given up everything to follow you. What will we get out of it?"
>
> 28 Jesus said to them, "I can guarantee this truth: When the Son of Man sits on his glorious throne in the world to come, you, my followers, will also sit on twelve thrones, judging the twelve tribes of Israel.

When Jesus responds to Peter, he makes a guarantee to the twelve apostles. He guarantees each of them will "sit on thrones, judging the twelve tribes of Israel." We spend so much time wondering about the promise and the prophecy, we do not consider a fact peculiar to our story. Judas is one of the twelve of whom Jesus speaks. Jesus has promised without qualification Judas will be with him in his throne room.

I believe the rawest form of taking the name of the Lord in vain is using God for our own purposes. Judas' purpose is to destroy his enemies. He does not understand his actions are not in line with the Father's purpose. He loves Jesus zealously but has not embraced the truth of loving his enemies as well.

Ironically, we face the same difficulty if we do not love Judas. At the outset, this was the challenge I offered. You see, Dear Reader, I do love him. I even believe he wished to see Jesus on the throne of David. I think he tried to corner Jesus and manipulate the situation. He also repented. That has to be enough for me. We will not find out until we reach Home. No matter what the answer is, I will love him because Jesus loves him. I will love you whether you agree with me or not. Until next time, I ask the Father to bless you for your time with me and I look forward to our next adventure together.

Wishing you joy in the journey,
Aramis Thorn

Coming in the Future

Thoughts and Questions on Colossians- Spring, 2022

This will be the fourth installment in the Thoughts and Questions devotional series. You may obtain all of these from my publisher.

A Thieves' Tale–November, 2022

Three men share a cell in Jerusalem as the trial of Jesus takes place outside their barred window. Each has encountered Jesus previously. As the Messiah's fate unfolds, they share their stories leaning how each interacts with the fate of the Son of God.

A Cell in Jerusalem

Wounded and beaten, Dismas lays fitfully on the hard floor of the cell. Gestas, his partner, sleeps chained to his right, equally battered, but resigned to his fate. Gestas snores steadily in the rest of the guilty. Two days of running and hiding have exhausted them both. To his right is a man the soldiers called Barabbas. They called him that while chaining Dismas to him. They kicked him to be sure he was still alive. He only groaned and rolled onto his side. He too sleeps as if resigned to a fate beyond his control.

Dismas shifts uncomfortably attempting to relieve the pressure from the lash marks on his back. The dirt from the cell's floor grinds into the open stripes. Once captured, the two received sound beatings from the Romans. The soldiers beat them more fiercely when they realized the identities of their prey. Gestas neither considers nor fears death. Dismas can think of nothing else and terror stalks his thoughts, denying him sleep, pushing him close to madness.

There is uncertainty as to the passage of time. The light barely reaches their cell but the cacophony of outside activity rouses Dismas' sleeping companions. Whatever is happing in the courtyard can wait. Someone is approaching the cell. A servant delivers stale bread and a bucket of muddy water. As they eat the bread and force down the foul water, they begin to converse.

Gestas nods to the stranger, "The Roman's called you Barabbas. Is that your name? Are you from Jerusalem?"

The hard brute grunts a reply, "I am, and I am not. How does it concern you two?"

Dismas realizes his charm is needed to protect Gestas from himself. "Gestas is just being friendly. He does not realize you may not wish your identity known. The Romans know me as Dismas, but my name is Jared. I give you my real name as a show of good faith."

Barabbas grunts, "I have faith in nothing and in no one. Since we are imprisoned together, we may as well share our stories. We are dead men anyway. No one will remember us. At least we can die knowing we were known by each other. Where are you two from and what landed you here?"

Neither Gestas nor Jared needs encouragement to tell their stories. Gestas speaks first. "I am from Joppa. I used to be with the Zealots but they became too interested in politics and not enough in money for my liking. I struck out on my own a year ago when our band was disrupted. Our leader, Simon turned into a religious fanatic. He and his son began to follow some crazy preacher."

Not too long after that, I caught this one trying to cut my purse. He would have succeeded had someone not bumped him. Instead of turning him over to the authorities, we joined forces. His charm and my brains have kept us in good food, fine wine, and adequate gold for a long time.

Things turned sour because of some religious fanatic. We had plans to rob several of the more wealthy widows during the bazaar. We did not know the Governor had ordered more guards because of the large rabble that follows this new religious leader. So many people claim to be our Messiah that I have a friend who takes bets on what will happen to them. The Pharisees seem upset by this one. They tell people to ignore him. This means more people are listening. He has caused quite a stir for a carpenter."

Jared starts visibly, "You did not tell me he was a carpenter. What else do you know about him?"

Barabbas offers, "I heard he was from Nazareth. They say this one heals the sick and raises the dead. He refuses to speak rebellion against Rome or use his power against them. He challenges the corruption of the priests. I have to say I like that."

Gestas continues his story but Jared no longer listens. His thoughts turn to a time and place he has not considered in many years. His whole life's work had been an effort to push the memories of Bethlehem from his mind. Now here in prison with his own death just hours away, the very memories he avoids assault him.

Jared feels a light kick. Gestas has finished his tale and wants his partner to begin. Snapping out of his reverie, the thief stares at the two for a moment. They both see sorrow in his eyes. Gestas never recalls anything but mirth from the man in three years. So startled is he that concern for his partner overtakes his bravado and attitude. "What is wrong Jared? Are you ill? Perhaps they have poisoned the food."

His partner waves the concern aside. "I was thinking of things I have not considered in years. I will tell my story but parts of it will be new even to you, Gestas. You may find the irony to your liking. We seem to have nothing but time, so I will start from the beginning. You see, I know this carpenter. I have known him since he was born."

CPSIA information can be obtained
at www.ICGtesting.com
Printed in the USA
FSHW010928270921
85002FS